Falling From Grace

They reached the line where John Proctor threatens to give Abby a whipping, and shakes her. Father Gabriel was actually shaking her. His hand grasped her shoulder as he spoke the line. Leonie found herself breathing heavily and not wanting him to stop. She gazed up him, seeing John Proctor's anger and desire on his face. His face. Not John Proctor's.

Abruptly he let her go and stood back from her. He looked horror-struck.

"My God Leonie, I'm sorry. I don't know what came over me."

She couldn't let him break away like that. She stepped towards him, standing close to him. She looked up at him, seeing the desire that was still on his face. Ignoring what he had just said, she asked: "What does it mean, 'clutched my back'?" She knew what it meant, and Gabriel knew that she knew what it meant.

He paused, only for a second. Then something overtook him.

"Like this." He grabbed her hips roughly and turned her around. He clutched her against himself, moulding her against his body. She could feel his hardness pressing on her through the fabric of her school skirt and his own clothing.

His breath was on her neck, his lips so close to her skin. "Like this. This is what he did." His voice was husky.

His hands gripped her waist, preventing her from moving away. Leonie could smell his scent, a fresh, male aroma with a trace of incense. She could feel the heat from his body. Anger and hot desire.

She could hardly breathe, she wanted him so badly.

FALLING FROM GRACE

Noël Cades

First Printing, 2018

ISBN: 0-6480874-4-1

ISBN-13: 978-0-6480874-4-1

This book is dedicated to my grandmother

1

Being banished to a boarding school in Britain was the last way that Leonie wanted to spend her senior year.

Back in Boston, all her friends would be enjoying the final months of high school, partying and going to prom. And she would be stuck in a cold, rainy country thousands of miles away, locked up like a nun.

But her grandmother had insisted. Either that or she wouldn't pay for Leonie's college.

St Winifred's School appeared to be in the middle of nowhere. Her grandmother's chauffeur drove her up and the journey felt endless. Leonie looked out of the car windows in increasing dismay as small towns gave way to villages and eventually to nothing but bare, bleak hills and some scattered forest.

Unless there was a boys' school hidden behind the trees, this was going to be the dullest of dull years.

"It's your own fault," a little voice told her. Leonie decided to ignore it. She felt miserable enough without her conscience pricking at her.

The Bentley finally pulled up along a sweeping gravel drive and Leonie looked upon what could surely only be a mental asylum. Grey, grim and gargoyled, it was like something out of a Victorian novel.

Leonie loved English literature at least. That was the one slim redeeming feature of being imprisoned here in this foreign land, that she would get to focus more deeply on that subject than at her high school back in the US.

Jenkins carried out her trunk for her. The school required students to bring their possessions in old fashioned trunks rather than suitcases, imagine that! All around her there were people hauling huge trunks to the front door of the school: girls in the grey St Winifred's uniform and their parents, brothers and younger siblings. Leonie even saw some nuns walking past the end of the building.

She stumbled and tripped while carrying a box that held some extra items that she hadn't managed to stuff into her trunk. The gravel bruised her knee and the contents of the box tumbled everywhere. Mainly books, but most embarrassing of all, her battered old teddy bear Buster. She scrambled to pick everything up just as a male voice, with an English accent, asked if she was okay.

Leonie looked up and into the bluest eyes she had ever seen. The face they were set in - also possibly the most handsome she had ever seen - belonged to a young man. He wore jeans and a grey sweater and held out a couple of the books that she had dropped.

She felt a jolt in her stomach as his gaze bored into hers. For a moment the world stood still.

"I'm okay, thanks," she said.

He raised an eyebrow, clearly unimpressed by her clumsiness. Then his eyes fell on Buster and Leonie wanted to die of shame. Was it her imagination or was there a faint smile on his face that he quickly suppressed? Leonie wished the gravel would swallow her up.

He said nothing, but helped her gather the rest of the scattered things and stood up. Leonie was struck by how tall he was, with such broad shoulders. Powerful arms. Thick, dark hair. A strong jaw and perfect features.

Why oh why had she managed to make such of a klutz of herself in front of him? And why hadn't she stuffed Buster into her trunk rather than risk everyone seeing him?

"Thank you."

"It's no trouble." He didn't smile, but there was a look in his eye that pierced her to the core. She actually felt heat in the pit of her stomach.

She was sure he must feel it too. A connection.

Before she had a chance to talk to him properly, he turned and went on his way. Damn. He must be someone's brother, so he probably wouldn't appear again until the end of term.

Leonie put the books and Buster back into the box, resolving to find out who his sister was and make best-friends-forever with that girl.

He looked way too old to be a high school student himself. He was probably at college, she reasoned. Or university as they called it here.

Still, at least there was one hot guy in this country. She'd imagined British boys would all be pasty from lack of sun, with bad teeth. But this one had model looks. He was the first hopeful thing she had seen all day.

Leonie had done her homework before coming to St Winifred's. She had read all of the Malory Towers girls' boarding school stories by Enid Blyton, where the only American student was a character called Zerelda Brass.

Zerelda was described as dumb, lazy and vain with ambitions of becoming a film star. Like Leonie she also had an English grandmother.

Given that Leonie herself dreamed of becoming an actress there were some horrible similarities. She hoped she wasn't quite so vacuous as Zerelda.

Next she had watched a movie called The Trouble With Angels since it took place in a Catholic boarding school, albeit in Pennsylvania. It wasn't very encouraging either, since Leonie had absolutely no plans of becoming a nun herself which seemed to be the central plot.

Finally she had found a very old movie called Girls' Dormitory. Set in a Swiss finishing school, it turned out to be less about boarding school life than a sultry French student seducing the headmaster. As St Winifred's was staffed by nuns and headed by a Mother Superior, Leonie couldn't see her school career taking that route.

In a bit of a blur with everything being so new, she joined a group of girls crowding around a noticeboard. They were looking at lists to see who had been assigned to each dorm. Leonie was encouraged to hear some colourful expletives from those disappointed with the selections. These Brits didn't hold back when it came to swearing. There were no goshes and darns here.

Finally she reached the front and could look for her dorm. All the bedrooms seemed to be named with Catholic terminology: Rosary, Liturgy, Matins, Ascension, Beatitude. Leonie eventually discovered her own name next to Pentecost.

She was apparently sharing with three other girls: The Honourable Iphigenia Davenport, Mai Li Chen and Lady Harriet Venn. What the hell? Was this school or Aristocrat Academy? Leonie could only imagine how they would look down on her as a yank.

Mai Li sounded okay, but she'd doubtless turn out to be a Chinese princess or something.

With a very heavy heart, Leonie trudged up the wide staircase to the third and top floor, where Pentecost was supposedly located.

Inside her dorm she found a thin, tall girl with small wire-framed spectacles. She was pretty enough, but looked kind of shy. She also stooped a little as if to downplay her height. Then there was a shorter, very pretty dark-haired girl who was clearly Mai Li.

They introduced themselves as "Mai" and "Figgy".

Leonie was confused. "Figgy?"

The tall girl, who had a nervous appearance with wisps of wavy hair escaping her ponytail, blushed. "Iphigenia. It's a bit of a mouthful, I know."

"So she's Figgy. Much simpler," Mai said. "You're obviously Leonie. Feel free to bags the other window bed. Harry's rarely here so she won't care."

"Bags?" Leonie was confused.

"Reserve it. Grab it for yourself."

Pentecost dorm was at the corner of the building, giving it windows on both sides. This meant three beds enjoyed being next to windows, with the fourth by the wall and the door. They were simple, iron framed beds with grey woollen blankets and Leonie couldn't help thinking of the movie Annie.

Hoping that Mai was right about Harry - presumably Lady Harriet - not minding, Leonie put the box she was carrying onto the bed. She'd have to go back for her trunk, and probably have to beg someone else to help her carry it up the stairs.

As if reading her mind, Figgy asked: "Need any help with your trunk?"

"That would be super kind, thanks."

"You're American, aren't you?" Mai said. "What made you come here?"

"My grandmother. She's British." Leonie hoped this would be enough explanation. She really didn't want to get into any specifics.

Fortunately Mai didn't question her any further. She looked at her watch. "There'll be tea in the dining hall now but it's casual today, we can skip it if we like. Then nothing but unpacking until supper at seven."

Leonie, who was feeling hungry, said she should probably find out where the dining hall was.

"I'll take you after we've got your trunk," Figgy offered. "It's usually a good spread on the first day."

"It's so any parents dropping by don't realise that they'll starve us from tomorrow onwards," Mai said.

Leonie hoped she was joking. Given the dorm looked like a film set from Annie, she had a horrible feeling that cold mush might be on the menu.

Over tea Mai grilled her about high school in America. Leonie was amazed how much actual tea these British girls drunk, she had thought the stereotype was a joke. But it was more than true.

"I envy you so much. No uniforms and all those hot guys and parties," Mai said.

"Hot guys?"

"Yes, like on TV. Driving around in open top cars and wearing designer clothes."

Somewhere along the line Mai had got the impression that the whole of the US was an episode of Beverly Hills 90210.

"It's really pretty dull, at least where I'm from," Leonie said. She found she was already starting to pick up their idiom and
12

avoid words like "darn", though she wasn't sure why. "Like small town, no beach, no rockstars."

"What about cheerleaders? Were you a cheerleader?"

Leonie laughed. "In Junior High."

"In those outfits with the little skirts and the pompoms?" It was clearly some kind of dream for Mai.

"We had cheerleading uniforms, yes. But truly it wasn't that exciting."

Mai wasn't deterred. "But LA though, that must be amazing right? Hollywood stars everywhere you go."

Leonie had to explain that she'd never been to LA, let alone Hollywood. Mai's mouth fell open.

"Doesn't everyone go there? That's like being in England and never visiting London."

Leonie tried to redeem herself by mentioning she had been to Washington DC and New York several times.

Mai buttered a piece of bread. "New York's cool, I guess. Like Friends or Sex and the City. We don't get to watch that here though, it's not considered suitable."

"They have TV here? At school I mean?" Leonie asked.

"Of course. We're stuck here for months on end, there's not much else to do. Unless you like chess or knitting or you have a lacrosse stick welded to your hand like Harry. So what subjects are you doing?"

This hadn't been determined yet, as Leonie was arriving half way through A-levels. She said that she hoped to do Maths - she remembered to use the UK English term and not say "Math" - as well as English and History of Art.

"Maths is awful but the other two are okay. We all do English too. Why those subjects?"

"I guess they seemed the most similar in the US and UK," Leonie said. "Shakespeare is Shakespeare and trigonometry is trigonometry, wherever you go."

Figgy nodded. "And History of Art is universal too. I'm taking that."

"So what do you want to do when you graduate?" Mai asked. "Will you go to an American college and join a sorority?"

Leonie suspected that Mai's notion of US college was the opening scene of Legally Blonde.

"I actually want to be an actress," Leonie confessed. She always felt as though this needed to come with a disclaimer. "But not Hollywood. I mean theatre acting, like Shakespeare."

"You should use your time here to learn a British accent then," Mai said.

Figgy was concerned that Leonie might have taken offence at this. "Actually it's believed that the American accent is closer to the Elizabethan accent than how we speak now."

Mai shrugged. "Good luck finding a casting agent who wants Ophelia saying aluminum and acclimate. Anyway you couldn't be as bad as Gwyneth Paltrow. When she plays English roles she sounds like she has a broomstick up her backside."

Leonie laughed. She looked along the table at the other girls, wondering which one of them would be Lady Harriet Venn. "Is Lady Harriet - our other roommate - here?" she asked.

Mai started choking on her sandwich and her sandwich and Figgy had to slap her on the back, causing people to notice. One of them was a girl with wavy dark hair and a kind of pretty-but-bitchy look going on. She seemed to regard Mai more with contempt than concern, staring over and clearly giving her the evil eye.

Pouring a glass of water for Mai, Leonie asked her if she was okay.

14

By now recovered, Mai grinned. "Fine. It's just that no one ever calls her that. You'll see why. I just found it really funny, particularly with your accent."

"Harry's very down to earth," Figgy said. "She'll probably be at some lacrosse team thing. They're all so mad keen having not played all holiday that they start straight away."

Leonie had never played lacrosse and wasn't entirely sure what it was. "So what do you do for fun around here? Is there a boys' school nearby?"

"Nowhere near. I can promise you that there isn't a single cute guy in a fifty mile radius," Mai said, stirring sugar into yet another cup of tea.

"I saw one earlier. I guess he was someone's brother?" Leonie asked. But the others had no idea who the mystery blue-eyed guy might be.

Leonie kept replaying the way his eyes had met her over and over again. And then the terrible moment when he'd seen her teddy bear. Even if she did find out who his sister was, she'd probably blown it. Who would be interested in a girl who still needed a big furry teddy bear guarding her bed?

2

On the first morning there was a long assembly which involved hymns interspersed by various announcements. These were held in the school hall after morning mass, which was compulsory. For Leonie everything was a new experience so that at least gave it some interest value.

The headmistress was a tall stern nun by the name of Mother Benedict who taught Latin to the sixth form. Her hair was hidden behind her wimple but Leonie suspected it was a steely grey. She felt some relief that since she wasn't doing Latin, their paths wouldn't cross too frequently. Mother Benedict, called Reverend Mother by the students, looked very formidable.

"This year we're pleased to welcome some new faces to the teaching staff. As you know, we bade farewell to Sister Marguerite last term, as she left us to embark upon a mission in Peru. I'm happy to let you know that she writes to say that she is well, and the Lord is issuing many blessings upon the community she is working in. She left us with a sad gap in Modern Languages, and replacing her will be Sister Assunta, who is newly arrived from Padua," Mother Benedict announced.

Sister Assunta, a small and very Italian looking nun, stepped up from her seat and gave a pleasant nod to the assembled girls.

Mother Benedict continued. "Father Aloysius, who assisted Father Stephen in his duties last term, has left us to earn his Doctorate in Divinity. Replacing him will be Father Gabriel."

Father Gabriel stood up and Leonie felt a jolt in her stomach.

It was him.

There was the cute guy with blue eyes.

And he was way more than cute, more like drop dead film star gorgeous. From the suppressed murmurs around her as the other students saw him for the first time, she wasn't the only one to think so.

What a waste! That totally gorgeous guy locked away in a black robe, committed to celibacy. Why did he have to go and wear jeans yesterday? If she'd realised who he was - what he was - she wouldn't have developed an insta-crush and had wicked dreams of him all last night.

Well, Leonie tried to think so. Looking at him now in his priest's garb he seemed more remote but even more attractive. He'd be eye candy, anyway.

"What did Father Aloysius teach?" she whispered to Figgy.

"He took some A-level English classes. It's such a shame he's left, he was really brilliant," Figgy told her.

A shame? Not if Father Gorgeous was about to take his place.

Leonie tried to give herself a strict talking to. Getting a crush on a teacher was foolish enough, but on a priest was a really dumb idea.

If only his eyes weren't so blue. And those lips. They had that kind of firm but sensuous look that you just knew would make him an amazing kisser. That intense look in his eyes, pushing her up against a wall, starting gentle and then devouring her. She could just imagine his hands all over her body…

Although he was some distance away for a second he flicked his eyes in her direction, and Leonie got paranoid that he could read her thoughts and felt her cheeks flame.

She sighed, causing Mai to shoot her a sharp glance, and finally the organist struck up some kind of music that everyone gradually exited to. It was time for classes to begin.

The schedule included quite a few study periods. Leonie had such a period first up, followed by Maths. English was later that afternoon, followed by History of Art.

Harry, whom Leonie had finally met, was also doing maths. It was true that Lady Harriet Venn looked nothing like Leonie had imagined an English Lady to look. She had formed an image of someone who was a cross between Princess Diana and Grace Kelly, draping herself about and looking languid and beautiful while she chattered about her princely beaus.

Instead, Harry was short and stocky with a sensible brown bob of hair. But Leonie liked her on sight. She had merry eyes and a frequent, hearty laugh.

"Glad to have someone in the dorm doing maths at last. The others were no good at all for swapping homework notes," she told Leonie.

Leonie just hoped her mathematics ability would be up to the task. She didn't want the others thinking she was some dumb American. Which if anyone looked at her grades last year, was exactly what they would think. But she knew deep down that was her fault for cutting so much school and other stuff.

The other stuff that she was praying she could keep secret.

Harry was off do something related to lacrosse yet again, so as Leonie didn't have anything to study yet in her first free period, she headed outside. It was probably forbidden as they were supposed to be in the study hall or the library. But she hoped they'd cut her some slack on the first day. She wanted to get some breathing space. Amid all the bustle and the crowds of girls and the kindness of her dorm mates, she was feeling strangely lonely.

The last place Gabriel had planned on ending up was some school in the middle of nowhere teaching a load of toffee-nosed, over privileged rich girls. It was absolutely the last place he wanted to be.

When he'd taken holy orders he had envisaged working among the needy, in a poor inner city area where kids were desperate for anyone who could open a door for them. Children who had no future except drug addiction and deprivation. It would be worthwhile work. He could use his vocation to make a difference.

Instead he'd been sent to St Winifred's School for Whingers, at least as he saw it. These students had no damn idea how lucky they were or what real life was like for most of the world.

"This is not what I had in mind for my service," he had complained to Canon Francis, head of the seminary.

"The Lord frequently has other plans in mind for us," Canon Francis told him.

It was not an answer Gabriel wanted to hear.

But his life was no longer his own. It belonged to the church and to God, so he gritted his teeth, prayed for patience, and packed his bags to head into the wilderness.

Even a boys' school would have been better. He had his own reasons for being wary of females.

Gabriel was feeling some faint anger as he walked around the side of the school that morning. He hadn't had a class to teach first period so he had used the opportunity to catch some autumn sunshine following the assembly. The sky was flawlessly blue, the leaves turning copper on the trees. It was a day when you could feel the full glory of the Creator in his creation.

It was remote here, but at least it was beautiful. Lines of Gerard Manly Hopkins came into his mind, one of his favourite poets.

And the azurous hung hills are his world-wielding shoulder
Majestic—as a stallion stalwart, very-violet-sweet!—

He must get back to work on his thesis. The one consolation of this place would be some peace and quiet to absorb himself in it again, at least outside school hours.

As Gabriel approached the building he saw a girl sitting on a low wall that extended from some stone steps. He recognised her instantly, it was the one who had dropped all her books in front of him. American, he remembered. He had also remembered her eyes: an unusual green and gold colour.

Eyes that as he drew nearer, he noticed were misty looking. Had she got herself in trouble already? He couldn't think of another reason why she was outside class by herself, crying.

This was where his duties of Pastoral Care came in. "Are you alright?" he asked her.

Leonie raised her head and a shaft of sunlight lit her amber hair like fire.

Gabriel was momentarily taken aback. For a second she looked like the golden statue of an angel he had once seen and he was transfixed. But she was just a flesh and blood girl, he reminded himself. He tried not to let his thoughts linger on that flesh and blood.

"I'm fine, thanks," she said.

He could see now that it was a different kind of grief in her eyes than repentance from being sent out of class. Homesick, he guessed. St Winifred's was far enough away from most English civilisation, let alone the US.

"If I can help?" He didn't know why he offered. It would probably be more appropriate for him to get one of the Sisters.

"Just missing my family, you know?" Leonie said. Then she thought that he probably didn't know since priests and monks and nuns left their families for God, didn't they?

But he seemed sympathetic. "I understand. Your home is pretty far away?"

Leonie liked his accent. It was very… English. Not the kind of Hugh Grant foppishness you got in movies, but solemn and clear.

"Boston, Massachusetts."

"Witches?"

Now she smiled. Gabriel found himself unexpectedly glad he had achieved this.

"Not so many these days, I hope anyway," she said. "We've modernised since the days of The Crucible."

"If you're taking English it's one of the texts on the syllabus this year. You'll be at an advantage, having lived there," he told her.

This was great news. Naturally Leonie had studied The Crucible before and seen it half a dozen times at theatres in Boston. She was a little surprised they would be studying it at a Catholic boarding school, and said so.

"It's on the A-level syllabus," Gabriel told her. "It's set by the exam board, not the school." He cast his mind back to his own A-levels. Macbeth and Tess of the D'Urbervilles, he remembered.

He knew he should get back to his classroom but he couldn't resist asking: "What brings you to an English school?"

"My grandmother is English," Leonie said. She didn't tell him why her grandmother had insisted she attend boarding school. She was hoping no one would find out.

"How do you find it over here?" He must get back, but something drew him to her.

Leonie wasn't sure yet. "I only arrived two days ago, so I'm still figuring things out."

Gabriel was surprised. "This is your first year? But you're in the final year, right?"

"Yes. I finished high school in the US, but my grandmother wanted me to try an English school," Leonie explained.

There was some mystery here, Gabriel was sure of it. But it wasn't his place to ask. Still, it added to this girl's intrigue.

She met his eyes and they gazed at one another for a moment.

Then they were interrupted by a loud clanging from the bell. Recess. Or break time, as they called it here. "I have to go," Gabriel told Leonie. He felt a strange reluctance to leave her and told himself it was because she had been lonely and distressed.

"I guess I'll see you in class." She smiled, and for a second the sunlight made her an angel again.

Gabriel felt a stirring inside that he hadn't felt for years. He had thought it was long buried. But even angels could be witches below the surface, he reminded himself. He would need to be very careful.

3

All four of the Pentecost dorm residents were taking English. Across the classroom Leonie also recognised the girl with wavy dark hair who had been at their dining table. Next to her sat a plump girl with freckles and curly ginger hair - Leonie mentally named her "Annie" - and the other side was a thin blonde girl with a pointy face.

There was a tense feeling of excitement in the room as everyone waited for the new English teacher to arrive. Most had arrived early, probably because they wanted a chance to check him out, Leonie thought.

She got the sense that the girl opposite was glaring at her and Mai. "Who's that?" she whispered.

Mai rolled her eyes. "That is the bane of my life," she said, under her breath. "Suki Laverne. Total bitch with a capital B. I'll tell you more later."

Just then the much-awaited man entered the room, and there was a rustle and scrape of chairs as everyone sat up straighter.

He looked absolutely devastating. He also looked pissed off. He was completely unsmiling as he carried in a pile of books and put them on the desk of the girl nearest the door. "Pass these around." The desks were arranged in a horseshoe shape, and Suki and her friends were on the opposite side to the Pentecost girls.

The books were new copies of The Crucible. Leonie had been surprised that the school supplied all the text books, you didn't have to bring your own. Which was helpful as it meant they all had the same edition.

Father Gabriel had turned to the board and was writing "The Crucible" in fast, sharply elegant letters. Leonie found that even his writing style seemed sexy, then mentally kicked herself for being so foolish.

Even in his black cassock you could see how tall and muscular he was. It might not have the definition that jeans and a shirt did, but he had a really powerful figure, Leonie noted. She wished the St Winifred's uniform wasn't so awful. All grey and woollen and a horribly unflattering length to the knee. Perhaps she should have emulated the Zerelda Brass character and had hers tailored by a stylist.

She felt the flat heavy wool of the St Winifred's school skirt over her thighs. No, there was nothing you could do with this garment to make it anything but awful. You couldn't even get away with shortening it: skirts had to touch the ground when you knelt down or you got into huge trouble.

Leonie thought Figgy had been joking about this when she had told her, but it turned out she was deadly serious. "You get all these negative House points and if you get a certain number, you get suspended," Figgy had said.

Getting suspended would be an escape from this prison, but Leonie feared the wrath of her grandmother.

There was just one other reason for staying here. Leonie cast her eyes up and saw Father Gabriel rapidly move his away. Had he been looking at her? She was probably imagining it.

"I expect most of you will have heard of The Crucible," Father Gabriel began. "But for those that haven't, it was written by American playwright Arthur Miller."

Suki stuck her hand out. "He was married to Marilyn Monroe, wasn't he?" She looked smug with herself for knowing this.

Mai made a tiny vomiting noise in her throat and Leonie had to try not to giggle.

"Yes, he was, later on. The Crucible was published in 1953, based on Miller's research into the Salem Witch Trials. What I think we'll do is get stuck in and deal with the history later. Since we have a Boston native among us - " his gaze fell on Leonie, causing the entire class to look at her " - why don't you read the part of Abigail? Then we'll need four more for the other roles in the first scene." Gabriel selected several girls, casting Suki as Reverend Parris, which made her pout.

"I'd rather take a female role," she said.

"It's just to read around the classroom, I'm not casting a West End production," Gabriel told her.

Suki looked furious.

"She's desperate to be an actress," Mai whispered to Leonie. "She'll absolutely hate you if she finds out it's your ambition too."

Gabriel called for quiet. "We'll have someone read stage directions, why don't you give that a go?" he asked Figgy, who looked nervous at the suggestion.

The read-around began. It was easy for Leonie as she had read the opening scene a dozen or more times before.

While they were reading, Gabriel berated himself for singling out the American girl. What had possessed him? She was probably having a hard enough time fitting in anyway. He shouldn't be showing any of them special attention.

But when he heard Leonie's voice speaking the lines of Abigail, something in him was gripped. He noticed other girls in the class looking at her as well.

It was partly her accent, though it wasn't quite the same as how she usually spoke. There was a different note to it which he couldn't place. A strange, timeless note. She was telling her uncle, the Reverend Parris, that there were rumours of witchcraft about, and the way she said the line was absolutely arresting.

Witchcraft indeed. Gabriel found himself transfixed.

Suki broke the spell. "I can't do it with her doing that weird accent. It's putting me off."

Leonie went bright red. "I'm sorry, we got taught to how do it with a historic accent. I guess I slipped back into it."

"There's no need to apologise," Gabriel said. "You read it very well. Miss Laverne, isn't it?" he asked Suki, checking his register. "Regardless of how other people read, we will keep going. As I've said, this is not a performance. So just worry about your own lines."

Suki looked venomous. Her evil eye was now fully fixed on Leonie.

The reading continued and Leonie tried to use a more contemporary accent. It was hard though, something inside her seemed to take over. She felt as though another girl, from a long ago time, was speaking through her. She knew that Miller's dialogue was often as close as possible to the vernacular of the time, and that he had used actual court transcripts in writing the play.

They took a break half way through the scene and Gabriel led a discussion of the themes before setting them a homework assignment. He deliberately avoided catching Leonie's eye. He had a feeling it was going to be a challenging class, with the ambitious dark-haired Laverne girl piping up all the time. She had also read impressively well, as much as she had irritated him.

It wouldn't be boring at least, teaching them.

There was a whirl of chatter and analysis following the English class when Gabriel finally dismissed them.

"Isn't he amazing?"

"He's the best teacher we've ever had!"

"And completely gorgeous. I don't know how I'll stop getting distracted just looking at him!"

"He's a priest, remember? Totally off limits."

Leonie listened to the rush of voices going past and couldn't help but agree with them. Father Gabriel was amazing: both to look at and to listen to. She had seen him looking at her a couple of times and it made her feel tingly.

She knew it was only because he looked at whoever was reading the lines, he had doubtless spent as much time looking at Suki and Figgy and the other girls, but she still couldn't get his deep blue eyes out of her mind.

And those lips…

Why oh why was he a priest? And why was she stuck here as a student?

Life could be a pretty cruel joke sometimes. It was like waking up to a Christmas stocking full of amazing gifts that someone had stitched and superglued shut.

"You're quiet," Mai said to her. Mai was never quiet.

"Just thinking about the class," Leonie told her.

"Thinking about Father Hot, more like. I know I am. And I bet Figgy is too. Not Harry though, she wouldn't notice him if he stripped naked and danced the fandango. Unless he was carrying a lacrosse stick." Harry had already rushed off to something lacrosse related and wasn't walking back with them.

Father Gabriel naked… Leonie really had to stop herself from imagining such a thing. She could tell from the strength of his jaw and neck how well muscled he would be underneath…

"I was not thinking of our priest like that!" Figgy protested. "Do have some decorum, Mai."

Mai grinned. "It's all decorum here, that's the problem. We have no chance to have anything else."

27

At that moment Suki passed them, her two friends on either side of her: the ginger and the blonde. Suki shot them a horrible look and whispered something to her friends.

"I'm afraid because of us you're going to be on her hit list," Mai said. "And she can't stand the fact that Father Hot gave you the part she wanted."

"And you did read it amazingly well," Figgy added.

Leonie really had hoped not to make enemies, let alone in her first week. Still, what was the worst the girl could do?

The problem was that they had no other distractions here, other than bitching and plotting against one another. It was kind of like a crucible, Leonie thought.

Did absolutely nothing fun ever happen around the place? "Do you ever get outside of school? Excursions or whatever?" Leonie asked.

"Yes, but they manage to make it even more boring outside of school than in. Museums, churches, ruins…"

Figgy interrupted her. "Some of the sites around here are very interesting. And there are some very beautiful old churches. Sister Rosalind tries to arrange visits to art galleries when she can."

Thinking back to her hometown, and the way she usually spent weekends, Leonie wondered whether she'd not so much ended up in a different country as a different era. Maybe her plane had flown through a time warp over the Atlantic.

No boys, no parties, and the best chance of fun was a trip to a museum.

So Leonie was stuck here. With no boys except one who was a priest, which she told herself was the reason she kept thinking about him. She needed something to distract herself, but what?

"Some of the sixth formers in a previous year managed to steal some communion wine and get drunk," Figgy said. She had dropped her voice to a hushed tone. "Mother Benedict discovered them and they all got suspended."

Figgy clearly found it a really shocking tale. Leonie dreaded to think how Figgy would react if she knew of the kinds of things that Leonie had got up to.

4

Gabriel, still irked by the teaching role that had been thrust upon him, had done the minimum preparation possible for his A-level class. He'd got most of the information about The Crucible from the foreword to the textbook, which he had barely skimmed, and from his own scant knowledge of the play.

Now, following the class, he found himself intrigued to learn more about it. It wasn't a text he had studied himself at school or university. But the girls had responded to it really well, coming up with intelligent questions and interesting ideas. He owed them more than to be half-hearted in his teaching.

There was another reason though. That girl, that voice.

He couldn't get her out of his mind.

Leonie Wilson. She and the other girl, the annoying one, both had a clear talent for acting.

He was still thinking about the reading as he walked through the courtyard, where he was joined by Sister Joan, the Head of English. A pleasant but no-nonsense woman in her late fifties, she had keen grey eyes and was astute enough to know that a young, handsome teacher would have caused a ripple of interest among the girls. Regardless of his status as a man of the cloth.

"How did you find your first class, Father Gabriel?" she asked.

Gabriel wasn't sure how best to respond. "Different than I had expected," he told her honestly.

"Indeed. I trust the girls behaved? They can be unruly with new staff members."

They hadn't been at all unruly. "They seemed very engaged with the text," he said.

Sister Joan frowned. "You're reading The Crucible with them, aren't you?" she asked.

"Yes." Not the most suitable text for a convent school, Gabriel thought.

"You know that the sixth form are supposed to put on a play? We encourage it, to give the girls a feel for the theatrical dimension to the texts they're studying. Usually we do whatever Shakespeare is on the syllabus, but I wonder if this term we might try something more contemporary? How would you feel about co-producing The Crucible for the sixth form performance?"

Gabriel had a sudden flash vision of Leonie on stage, wildly flinging accusations of witchcraft around. "Co-produce?" he asked, trying to quell the disturbingly appealing image.

"Sister Rosalind, who teaches History of Art, also has background in Theatre Studies, although it's not a subject we currently offer here. Her skills come in very useful for our school productions, but it's challenging work to do alone. If you have sufficient time to assist her, I am sure she would be very glad," Sister Joan said.

Gabriel wasn't sure that he wanted to give up any of his free time as he had planned to use it to work on his thesis. But he sensed the Head of English's request wasn't something that could be declined.

"I'd be happy to discuss it with her," he told Sister Joan.

The older nun smiled. "That's settled then. You can arrange a rehearsal schedule with her and begin casting next week."

What had he got himself into? If this was God's plan for his career, it was a strange one. Gabriel had thought that the remoteness and quiet of the place might at least be his recompense for having to teach a load of over-privileged girls. Now it seemed he was to sacrifice his leisure hours as well.

Yet when he thought of listening to the American girl, of seeing the emotions on her face as she read the lines, conjuring up the spirit of the character, he found himself less averse to the prospect.

They might make something of the production, he thought. He had been introduced to Sister Rosalind earlier and remembered her as a pleasant and intelligent woman. If he were forced to work with the opposite sex, rather than have the male seclusion he sought, she would at least be bearable as a colleague.

He knew many of the girls had been looking at him as they weren't supposed to look at a teacher, let alone a priest. But that was to be expected. They were young women, it was natural they would seek male attention. Gabriel cast his thoughts back to a particular woman and his eyes narrowed from the anger and betrayal he still felt. She had certainly been happy enough to seek such attention in more than one place.

Despite his vows, despite his commitment to what he believed was his calling, he couldn't help wish that a certain girl had been among the ones eyeing him up. Because he had to admit to himself that he had been fighting the urge to gaze at her.

Gabriel had planned to rotate the parts for the next scene but he couldn't resist hearing Leonie read Abigail again.

Now, as he sat in his chair suffering the most unpriestly physical reaction ever, and hoping it would subside by the end of class, he regretted his decision.

Leonie was reciting lines where she begged the married man she loved, her former employer John Proctor, to renew his affection. She accused him of "clutching her back" behind his home, and sweating like a stallion.

Gabriel was sweating and he feared greatly that he would end up dreaming about it.

He needed a cold shower.

As Leonie and Mai, who had been given the role of John Proctor, continued to read their lines, he was having to concentrate on his breathing.

Now Leonie was saying how she knew John Proctor, using the word to mean carnal knowledge, and how she could not sleep for dreaming about him.

With some difficulty, Gabriel managed to bring his thoughts back to the themes and structure of the scene, and get the girls discussing it in groups. To try and distract his mind from his body he recited some lines of poetry to himself in his head. Only to be interrupted by one of the girls asking him a question.

"Do you think that some of them really were doing witchcraft, Father?"

The questioner was an earnest-faced girl. Gabriel had forgotten her name. It was Jane or Mary or something. "Twenty years after it all happened, they were all exonerated and families got compensation. I think it's recognised that it was all a kind of mob hysteria," he told her.

"But do you think it's really possible? Witchcraft, I mean? Might some of them really have been conjuring spirits?"

Gabriel shifted in his seat. "I think that's more of a Hallowe'en perception of it all."

"But spirits are real, aren't they?" another girl asked. "What about exorcisms? The Catholic church still does exorcisms, doesn't it?"

"Yes, but..."

"Have you ever done an exorcism, Father? Or attended one?"

Before Gabriel could explain that he hadn't, there was a rush of questions.

"Is it true that it gets very cold when the spirit is confronted?" "Do you still use a bell, book and candle?" "I heard that gravestones can crack in two, has that happened to you?" "What's it like when a person is exorcised, do they froth at the mouth and cry out all the names of Satan?"

This last question came from the little Hong Kong girl, Mai. Gabriel was quite certain she was winding him up. He had caught a glint in her eye more than a few times, and seen her whispering to her neighbour. She didn't appear to take anything seriously.

"This is getting off track from our study of the play." His voice held a commanding tone which silenced them. "If you have questions about… other matters, I am sure Father Stephen can address them." He avoided saying exorcisms. He imagined the last thing that Stephen wanted was to hold a seminar on demons and satanic entities. It was a thorny enough issue for the Church.

He managed to bring them back to the text and got each group to relay what their thoughts were. As ever, he was impressed by many of the answers. There were some keen minds.

Unfortunately when he got around to the group with the earnest-faced girl, they were back onto the subject of witchcraft again. "We were wondering whether it was real, you see, because if they really did do and see all these things, then maybe Abigail was justified in her accusations."

Leonie put up her hand. "There's a theory it was ergot poisoning," she said.

"Ergot?" The earnest-faced girl had never heard of it.

"It's a grain fungus. It makes you hallucinate, like LSD," Leonie said. "You get fits and convulsions, which they may have mistaken for demonic possession. It's just one theory anyway."

Gabriel was grateful to her for rescuing him and cast her an appreciative glance. He needed to do more background study of this play. All the more so since he had agreed to help Sister Rosalind put on a production of it. She had suggested that he direct and she produce, and he had agreed. Gabriel had done some theatre in his own school and university days so it was a familiar enough arena.

Which reminded him, he needed to tell the girls. There was going to be a notice posted on the main board in the next day or so, but he may as well tell them now.

"On the subject of this play, I have a short announcement. The Head of English has suggested we use the text for this term's play, instead of the Shakespeare."

There was a loud murmur of interest at this.

Gabriel continued. "We'll be holding a casting on Saturday for those who would like to take part. It won't make a difference to your coursework grades, this is purely for interest. So those of you with other commitments - " he cast a glance at Harry, whom he now knew was heavily taken up with her duties as school lacrosse captain " - needn't worry if you can't take part. Those that can, keep an eye on the noticeboard."

I have to play Abigail.

It was all Leonie could think. It was all-consuming. It was a role she had always wanted, and now that they were studying the text, she couldn't bear for anyone else to be given it.

I have to win that role.

She knew instinctively that Suki was going to want it too, and that only one of them could succeed. Leonie glanced across at her dark haired rival, and saw the glint of challenge in her eyes.

If she, Leonie, did win it, Suki was going to make her life a living hell.

But it would still be worth it.

5

Half the school had shown up to the auditions for the play, even though only the sixth formers - and those taking English - were eligible to take part. The hall was packed out and the atmosphere was intense.

Sister Rosalind was bewildered by the interest. "I can't think what the sudden interest is for. We usually do Shakespeare. Perhaps that's put girls off in the past?"

Gabriel had a fair idea why so many had turned out. It certainly wasn't due to a preference for American playwrights over English ones. He kept his expression guarded and avoided catching any one girl's eye. The last thing he wanted was to be accused of favouritism.

He suspected the casting would create a lot of conflict among them. He just wanted it over with, so they could start rehearsals. The idea of producing a play was already starting to intrigue him. He had been involved with a student theatre group in his university days, though he had long since given it up in favour of his religious pursuits.

"If the rest of you are here to watch, you can sit quietly in the seats at the back," he ordered them. "Those sixth formers wishing to audition should be in the front two rows."

Mai and Figgy, who had come along only to give Leonie moral support, tried to head for the back of the room but Leonie stopped them. "It will be so much cooler if you guys get parts too."

Figgy looked nervous. "I really can't act. Speaking on stage absolutely terrifies me."

"They may need help backstage though. Please. It will be so much more fun if you're involved."

Figgy reluctantly agreed, and Mai said she would have a go as well.

Sister Rosalind and Gabriel had chosen a short scene from the first act to use for the audition. The girls were put in groups and each group read the same section.

It was a big mix. Some stumbled over the lines, others were monotonous. There were a few natural actors, and then there were Suki and Leonie.

Suki's group went first, with Suki naturally choosing to read Abigail. Watching her, Leonie felt a stab of doubt. Suki was very good. She managed to put a sultry malice in the lines, playing Abigail as a devious, slippery character.

Finally it was Leonie's turn. She stepped on stage and the world slipped away. Even with Figgy reading Samuel Parris in a nervous whisper and Mai managing to perform the Reverend Hale as a clear pastiche of Mother Benedict, Leonie was thrown back three hundred years. She didn't even have to consciously try to act, she simply was Abigail.

Leonie-Abigail was imploring them to believe that she had never sold herself. That she was a good girl and a proper girl. Her appearance on the surface was of earnest entreaty. But below this facade lurked the sly gleam of the lie. She was bewitching and chilling and Gabriel caught his breath watching her.

He looked down at his script, not wanting to show any bias to Sister Rosalind. He saw the nun's eyebrows raised but didn't want to jinx things. After all, why should he care which girl played which part? But he did care. He wanted to see the American girl reading Miller's lines on stage.

"Thank you everyone. Father Gabriel and I will be discussing the cast, and a list will be posted up tomorrow morning. Just remember, those of you who don't obtain speaking parts will still be very much in demand for all the other roles involved in a production. I hope we can all have a very happy time of it." Sister Rosalind dismissed them, and went on her way.

As she was walking out, Leonie couldn't resist casting a glance at Father Gabriel. He looked back at her and she felt a connection between them. When he quickly looked away she was even more sure of it.

Please let me get this role, she thought. It meant so much to her. It was her chance to prove whether she could perform well enough to choose acting as a career.

Leonie knew how hard it was to succeed, even if you had some talent. The competition was insane: there were hundreds of professional actresses for every role. Thousands, even. You couldn't just be good, you had to be exceptional. And she knew that she had a long way to go.

That night, Leonie dreamt of Father Gabriel. She was standing in the dock of a courtroom and he was presiding over her trial, wearing his priest robes.

He looked stern and forbidding. "You know you are guilty," he was saying, and his blue eyes bored into her very soul.

In her dream, Leonie was pleading with him, but whether for her innocence or for his mercy she wasn't sure.

"Prove it then. Now!" he commanded her.

Then they were in some back room of the court, just the two of them. It was all panelled entirely with wood. There were no windows nor door.

"Prove it," Father Gabriel was saying. His voice was close by her ear. She was pressed against the wall and his body was up against hers. "Prove it to me."

I don't know how to prove it, Leonie was thinking. How can I prove it?

He could read her thoughts. "Like this?" he said, one hand reaching up her skirt. Pressing against her in an intimate place, his fingers swirling around.

"No, I didn't do it!" she was crying out.

His other hand was on her breast. His breath was hot on her neck, and she could feel the hardness of his lean muscular body against hers. Her body was throbbing, wanting him closer, wanting his force and his command.

His fingers curled around her breast, teasing it and crushing it. "I know you did it, Leonie. I know. Prove it to me. Prove it."

His lips were closer, closer, nearly touching hers. She ached for him…

Suddenly the light went on and Leonie woke up, startled, to see Mai sitting up in her bed looking over at her.

Mai was frowning. "Are you okay? You've been thrashing around and shouting in your sleep."

Leonie was mortified. Her confused dreams were still rushing through her head. Had she said anything out loud?

"You kept crying 'I didn't do it! I didn't do it!' Have you murdered someone?" Mai asked.

The question was enough to make Leonie laugh and break away from the dream images. "Hell no. I was dreaming about The Crucible. I think it kind of got to me."

"Maybe the spirit of Abigail is possessing you. We should get Father Hot to perform an exorcism. Anyway, so long as you're okay. Sweet dreams." Mai turned the light off again and settled herself back down. Neither of the others had woken.

Leonie snuggled back down herself. Had the dream continued, she suspected Father Gabriel would have been performing far more than an exorcism on her.

The next morning the cast list went up. Leonie felt so sick with nerves that she couldn't even eat breakfast.

There was already a crowd gathered when she reached the noticeboard. Her heart sank to see Suki Laverne turning away, her head held high, a look of triumph glinting in her eyes as she cast a sneering glance at Leonie.

The sun went out of the sky and the day turned grey. Leonie felt leaden.

Miserable, she went to view the list to see if she had at least been given something. She waited until the rest of the crowd had dispersed and she was the last one there.

She scanned the names, starting from the top.

There - right there - at the very top…

Abigail Williams - Leonie Wilson.

What?

What the hell had Suki's expression been for? Leonie guessed that she must have misinterpreted it. Or Suki was pretending not to care and putting on a show of defiance.

Leonie looked further down the list. Suki had been given the role of Elizabeth Proctor, which was still a pretty major part. Mai had been cast as Susanna Walcott and Figgy hadn't made the list. She would be relieved rather than disappointed by that, Leonie thought.

But she, Leonie, was going to be Abigail. She did a little mental fist bump then turned to see Father Gabriel passing by. Thank God she hadn't fist bumped for real.

He paused when he saw her. "You've seen the list, then?"

"I can't thank you enough. You and Sister Rosalind," she added quickly.

Gabriel smiled. He smiled so rarely that it did something weird to Leonie's stomach. "You have nothing to thank us for. You won the role by giving the best audition. I hope you'll do us all proud."

"I will. I'll try to."

They stood there for several seconds, unable to stop looking at one another. Leonie felt transfixed. It had gone past the point of an acceptable pause.

Gabriel managed to get a grip of himself. "I'll see you in class."

6

Leonie was finding it hard to concentrate. She was supposed to be writing her weekly letter home, something all the students were required to do.

"I'm sure they open them and read them," Mai said. "So don't bother telling them about the starvation and the beatings and the daily torture sessions."

"Mai!" Figgy protested. "It's really not that bad."

"If you don't call Hess's law and Born-Haber cycles a form of severe torture, then I don't know what is," Mai said. She had been wrestling with her chemistry homework for the past hour. Leonie and Figgy had enjoyed a much easier time of it writing about Caravaggio's use of light for a History of Art assignment. They shared notes, and the hardest thing was making their two essays different enough.

Leonie had earlier blitzed through her Maths with thanks to Harry, who seemed to have the mind of a genius when it came to trigonometry.

Now Leonie was writing her letter but all she could think of were a pair of piercing blue eyes and that sudden smile.

"Dear Mom and Dad,

"I've settled in here and have some great roommates. Classes are going okay. I got a role in the school play. Hoping you're all well and missing you, Leonie."

That was all she could manage. What else was there to say?

Mai was peering over her shoulder. "'The greatest roommates ever' I think you mean. And what's with 'a role in the school play'? You got the starring role. You should be shouting about it. Won't they be proud?"

Leonie figured it was time to confide in them. "They're not happy about my plans to do theatre. They want me to get a law degree or an MBA or whatever."

"Is that why they've sent you here?" Figgy asked.

"Kind of." It wasn't, but Leonie didn't want to get into all that now. "My mom thinks it's too risky a career. Too uncertain."

Harry put her pen down. "She's right. It is. But that doesn't mean it's not worthwhile trying. Someone has to succeed at it."

Harry didn't speak often so when she did, it kind of meant more.

"I guess. It makes me doubt myself though. And US college isn't like what you have here, it's so much more expensive. If they won't help pay for it I'll have to get into huge debt, and then paying that off on a waitress's salary... you can guess how easy that would be."

Figgy, who had been tidying her drawer, turned to Leonie. "Why don't you study in the UK then? You could go to RADA or somewhere."

Leonie had never considered this. "You'd have to be British though, wouldn't you?"

Figgy shrugged. "I don't see why. Everywhere takes international students."

Mai had an evil smile. "Your only problem might be sharing a room with Suki Laverne. RADA is her dream." She and Figgy left as they had to pick up something from the Biology classroom.

Leonie folded her letter. She felt dejected but she couldn't put her finger on why. She was still getting the intense dreams at night and wasn't sleeping well.

"Are you okay?" Harry asked her, her brown eyes looking concerned. Leonie still found it weird that Harry was a Lady, she always seemed so down to earth.

"I guess. Just things on my mind," Leonie told her.

"When I need to clear my head I go to Confession," Harry said.

Leonie was surprised. "Are you super religious, then?"

Harry laughed. "Not at all. It's just peaceful in there, and someone is listening who can't breathe a word. The Sacramental Seal has its advantages. They can't break it even if you confess to murder. Sometimes I've confessed things I haven't done, just for fun."

Her eyes were twinkling wickedly. Leonie was shocked, she might expect this from Mai, but not Lady Harriet: school lacrosse captain and a prefect as well. "Isn't that going to get you struck by lightning?"

"Not so far. I figure it's entertainment for them. I don't confess to actual murder. I once confessed that I stole Mother Benedict's bra and tied it to a tree. Later that day I saw poor Father Stephen poking around the grounds looking up at all the trees, obviously hoping to find it before it became a scandal."

Despite all the bad things she had done in her life, Leonie couldn't imagine lying in a confessional. But still, going to confession was an idea. She hadn't been since she was really young. It might give her some peace of mind.

These things are sent to test us.

Gabriel tried to be rational about it. It wasn't as though becoming ordained automatically got rid of all physical urges. He still had emotions, he still felt. He imagined Father Stephen did too.

But it was about valuing Heaven more than Earth. About loving God more than pleasure.

He remembered some of the wise words spoken to him during his training. "Even unintended violation of chastity requires opportunity, privacy, and secrecy. It is a wise priest who denies himself these."

There was little privacy or secrecy in a girls' school, so he had those covered.

Until now it had seemed so easy. He had been so angry about Joanne, so ardently committed to his new vocation. He hadn't looked or wanted to look at a girl in five years.

Even now, he barely noticed any of them. Just that one girl. Was it because she was different? Because she was foreign, and seemed somehow isolated?

The image of her came before him when he tried to sleep, when he tried to pray, when he tried to read his bible.

If it were just a sexual thing, a physical impulse, it would have been easier to deal with. But Gabriel found that he actually liked her. He was interested and amused by the things she said in class. Trying to ignore her made it worse. Once or twice he had done so, and he had sensed she was hurt by it.

Denying her attention also singled her out. He couldn't just cold shoulder her or people would wonder what had happened. That might be even more dangerous.

There was debate in the church as to whether a priest might relieve himself privately. The conservative line was that such a thing was never appropriate. But some of his more pragmatic mentors had suggested to him and the other ordinands that if the smaller lapse helped prevent the greater lapse, God might not eternally condemn them for it.

Lying in his bed that night, Gabriel considered trying it. But the moment he touched himself the image of the girl flooded into his mind. He wouldn't be able to face her tomorrow if he used her image for that, and he was unable to conjure up any other image.

So he rolled over and tried to recite lines of poetry in his head, bible verses, anything. It seemed hours before he found solace in sleep.

Gabriel and Father Stephen lived in the small presbytery attached to the chapel, which was separate from the main school building. They usually had lunch in the school dining hall, due to teaching duties, but ate breakfast and supper separately from the sisters and the students.

Father Stephen typically rose before Gabriel and had breakfast underway, with Gabriel reciprocating for the evening meal.

That morning Gabriel needed his coffee very strong and very black. He drank two cups of it before even turning his attention to eggs and toast.

"A restless night?" Father Stephen asked.

"Somewhat," Gabriel admitted.

Father Stephen cast a closer glance at him. "You are troubled, Gabriel?"

Gabriel couldn't lie to the old man. Stephen was far too astute for that. "Struggles which I am sure we all have," he said.

Father Stephen spread marmalade over his toast. "Of the faith or of the flesh?" he inquired.

"Both, I suppose."

The older priest smiled. "Consider it a blessing. A reminder of one's humanity and how we are no different from our flock, though we may separate ourselves from other men. The journey is not supposed to be easy."

Gabriel was certainly discovering that. "Did you ever doubt? That you had made the right choice?"

"Many a time. I am only human. I saw, my heart lusted and loved like any young man. I met a young woman once who made me seriously question the path I had chosen. But eventually I saw that my need for union with the church was greater than my need for an earthly union."

Gabriel was intrigued. "What happened to her?"

"In time she married, had a family, and lived happily ever after. I doubt she was even aware of my feelings for her, or at least the depth of them. Perhaps she wouldn't have returned them if she had known. It was all for the best."

Father Stephen certainly looked as though he was at peace with his life, munching his toast and contemplating the day's duties. He consulted his diary, a small black leather book. "Now I have a meeting with Mother Benedict later this morning. It's a time when I usually provide confession, so if you wouldn't mind filling in, it would be much appreciated," he told Gabriel.

"By all means. Do you usually have many attending?" Gabriel asked.

"One or two. I feel it's important, though, given the enclosed atmosphere of the school, to offer the chance for private confession. The girls are far from their family members whom they might otherwise confide in." Father Stephen stood up and picked up his plate and Gabriel's. "You may of course find yourself totally alone for the hour."

Gabriel hoped so. The peace of the chapel and the silence of the dark confessional might help clear his head.

7

"Forgive me, Father, for I have sinned. I have had… impure thoughts."

Gabriel froze when he heard the voice the other side of the grille. From what Father Stephen had said, he wasn't even expecting someone to enter the other side. Let alone her.

He couldn't speak. Although this was a confession between her and God, with him as the mere intercessor, he felt that he somehow violated her privacy by listening.

It was all in his own head, of course. If he hadn't had such dangerous and inappropriate thoughts towards her, there would be no issue. She would just be any other girl. As it was, this felt like reading her diary.

Unable to speak, he let her continue.

"It's been ages since my last confession. Like, years maybe." Leonie paused, expecting a response or prompt from the other side of the box, but there was only silence. "So I guess there's way too many sins to list. But it's the recent ones that are troubling me. Thoughts that I've been having about someone."

Again she paused. Gabriel knew he was supposed to question her but he couldn't face asking her about some boyfriend. While it was absolutely none of his business what she did, the mere thought of it wrenched his gut.

"Anyway, I keep having these inappropriate thoughts and dreams even, and I just wanted it all to stop. So I thought that if I confessed it, then maybe that would help." Leonie felt an urge to confess it all, but she could hardly let Father Stephen know she had a massive crush on his colleague. The problem with her accent was that he was going to know it was her, and that would be super embarrassing next time she saw him.

She continued. "I think of him all the time, it's really distracting. I just want to be with him so much. I imagine us doing things together, sinful things, and once my mind starts running away with it all I can't stop."

Gabriel could hardly breathe. For the first time he felt the constraints of his vows like a straitjacket, and how he was cut off from the world. Out there, some guy who was free to do what he liked, had Leonie's adoration. While he, Gabriel, had made irrevocable vows to reject worldly things such as romantic and sexual emotions.

After everything with Joanne it had seemed like a relief. Now for some reason, the Lord had decided to torment him. Or perhaps test his faith. Maybe this confession was to remind him that Leonie was destined for another path than he was. He, Gabriel, had chosen his lot.

Yet his body and his heart stirred as her voice continued. That sweet, slightly husky accent so different from the brisk English tones of all the other girls. "The problem is, you see, that he's off limits, which is why it's so wrong," Leonie was saying. "I don't mean that he's married or anything." She said this hurriedly, not wanting Father Stephen to think she was a total harlot. "Just that he's..." the phrase "forbidden fruit" was in her head, and she couldn't bring herself to say that either. "He's committed to someone else." Someone else being God.

Again silence. Was she in this booth alone? Or had Father Stephen fallen asleep? Or worse, had he had a heart attack? Or even worse, was he struck dumb with horror at her confession?

Leonie felt a momentary pang of panic. Yet as much as she desired to get out of the place, she had a weird impulse to stay. There was something strangely intimate about the confession booth, this proximity to the person the other side, only a grille between them. For she was certain that Father Stephen was there. She had that human sixth sense that she wasn't alone.

She wasn't sure if it was appropriate to open the confession box to check on his wellbeing.

"Anyway, so I guess I just needed to get that off my chest," she said quickly. "So I should pray about it, right?"

Gabriel was in agony. How could he have the right to absolve her when he was guilty of the same sin towards her? She longed for some unknown boyfriend, he longed for her.

He closed his eyes, wishing she would leave, and longing for her to stay. Just to hear her voice.

"I'll be going then," Leonie said. She exited the confessional as quietly as possible, feeling confused and uncomfortable. Was that something they did in England, maybe? Just let you speak and hear the voice of God in your own heart or something? That was probably it. She hoped so.

Leonie left the chapel in a hurry, still feeling strangely disturbed. She had heard Father Stephen breathing so he couldn't be dead. Perhaps he had been asleep. If her confession had been so dull as to bore a priest to sleep, maybe there wasn't so much sin to worry about.

She crossed the courtyard to the main school entrance, and stopped in her tracks.

There, coming towards her, was Father Stephen. Then who…?

"Good morning, Father," she greeted him.

"Good morning, my child." Father Stephen saw the puzzlement on her face. "Were you looking for me?"

"Only I thought, to have gone to confession…" she tailed off.

50

"Father Gabriel has been taking confession his morning." He beamed at her and checked his watch. "There is still time now. Indeed there is time at any hour of the day. Whenever you desire to confess, or simply have questions or wish to talk to one of us, the house of the Lord is always open."

Leonie's heart was turning over her stomach in horror. "No, it's okay, I'm fine. Thank you."

She fled.

Mortified, agonised, hideously embarrassed.

Father Gabriel was in there? She had just confessed her sinful crush to Father Gabriel?

Oh God, what had she said? She tried to recall the words she had used. He would surely have guessed it was him. Who else could it be, in this otherwise all-female community?

Madly she wondered if she should paste Father Stephen's photo to the front of her notebook, so Father Gabriel might think her crush was on his colleague. But it was absurd, Father Stephen was in his sixties or seventies.

Oh God, oh God, oh God. What could she do? How could she face him again?

And she had English next period!

It was obvious Father Gabriel knew. He was totally blanking her. He was avoiding even looking at her.

Leonie felt absolutely miserable.

Even when she gave the correct answer to a question, his response was curt and his eyes barely flicked over her before moving to someone else.

"What real life parallels inspired Miller when he was writing The Crucible?"

Nobody put up their hand and most faces looked blank. So Leonie raised hers, and as no one else did, Gabriel reluctantly chose her to answer.

"The rise of McCarthyism, and the witch hunt for Communists in the US."

"Very good." Gabriel's face registered no emotion as he said this, if anything there was faint irritation in his tone. He immediately turned to the board again, chalking up "Political parallels - McCarthyism".

Leonie wished she hadn't even bothered to respond.

Even Mai noticed the English teacher's attitude. "What's up with Father Hot? He seems to be in a really bad mood today."

Gabriel wasn't only short with Leonie, he was severe throughout the class and did not smile once. This at least was something of a relief, as it deflected attention from Leonie. It was still noticeable that he wasn't nice to her though.

She couldn't wait for the lesson to end, and grabbed her things as quickly as possible so she could escape.

But as Suki passed by with her two cronies, she smirked at Leonie and muttered: "I guess someone's no longer the teacher's pet."

Leonie ignored her but Mai gave Suki a sharp shove with her elbow, nearly sending her flying and causing her to drop the folders she was carrying.

Suki glared. "Watch where the hell you're going."

"Oh, I'm so sorry!" Mai said, faking remorse. "Did you trip over that great fat foot that's always in your mouth?" Then she grabbed Leonie and pulled her in the other direction. "Let's get out of here."

"I suppose everyone has a bad day sometimes," Figgy said, as they walked to the dining hall for lunch. "Perhaps he had some bad news from home. Or a headache." She was a kind girl and preferred to take a sympathetic approach.

"He's sexually frustrated," Mai said. "All priests are. Celibacy is completely unnatural."

"It's quite noble though, don't you think?" Figgy asked.

"No. I think it's idiotic," Mai said. "What's the point of having urges if you're supposed to spend your entire life resisting them? What good does that do, anyway? You could spend all that effort on something worthwhile."

Harry agreed. "Other denominations manage very well with married clergy. It's completely unnatural to force a person to suppress that side of life. How can they understand what it's like for their parishioners if they've never had a good shag?"

Leonie's mouth dropped open at Harry saying this. They were so blunt, these British girls. It sounded even more abrupt with Harry's upper class English accent.

She wondered if Father Stephen or Father Gabriel had ever had a "shag" of any kind, good or otherwise. "Do you think they try it out first before they take their vows?" she asked.

"They're fools if they don't," Harry replied. "They should make it a requirement before committing to celibacy. Imagine giving up chocolate before you'd ever tried it. You'd go quite mad, watching other people eat it, and torturing yourself wondering what it might be like."

This turned into a conversation about whether it would be worse to give up chocolate or sex, but Leonie tuned out. She kept wondering about Father Gabriel and if he had ever had a girlfriend before. He was so model good-looking that she could hardly imagine he hadn't. At her high school every single girl would have wanted to date him, if he had been a fellow student.

But he wasn't a student. He was a teacher and a priest, and totally off-limits.

8

Still stressed out about the whole confessional thing and Father Gabriel's curtness towards her, Leonie had to face him at the first rehearsal.

"I hope Father Hot is in a better mood this afternoon," Mai said.

They were working on Act One so only certain members of the cast had been called. Leonie and Mai were in the very first scene together. Mai only had a few lines but hadn't bothered to learn them yet.

"Are we all here?" Father Gabriel made a brief check of the cast members needed and the students assembled before him. "Good. The first scene hasn't been blocked out yet, but we'll use the stage anyway. Don't worry about positioning for now. Just focus on the script. For now we'll just have everyone enter from stage right, though this may change next time."

Stepping onto a stage and smelling the dust and must of the curtains and those unique odours of the theatre always sent a thrill through Leonie. It usually electrified her and helped her with her performance, but today she was simply too stressed.

They began the scene, with the Reverend Parris praying, and then the slave woman Tituba entering. Next came Abigail, ushering in Susannah.

Leonie thought it was a shame that Mai hadn't been given a larger role as she was very animated. But she tended to play up and mimic people. She even managed to make Susanna seem absurd by saying "Aye, sir!" in a comical way, causing some girls to giggle. Father Gabriel's cool glance soon quelled their mirth.

For Leonie it was the opposite. She didn't feel animated at all. She could barely get the lines out and it got worse and worse.

They were practising the early scene where Abigail tries to lure John Proctor back to her, and he refuses. The words were literally sticking in her throat. She was so conscious of Father Gabriel's presence.

Worse, he was the one taking the rehearsal as Sister Rosalind had duties elsewhere. Since Gabriel was directing he was going to be most hands on in the rehearsals anyway.

Leonie tried to speak the line telling John Proctor that she sensed his heat, and that it had drawn her to her window.

But she knew she sounded flat and that her lack of expression was making it difficult for the student playing John Proctor. This was a tall girl with short dark hair called Mercy Braithwaite. It should have been easier playing the scene with another girl, since there was no question of real life sexual tension between the two actors. At least Leonie assumed there wasn't. She guessed it was possible that Mercy might be gay. If she was it didn't bother her either way.

But every line she had to say, Leonie just felt as though Father Gabriel's eyes were boring into her with increasing disapproval.

She tried again to put some emotion in, telling John Proctor that she had seen him burning with loneliness and looking up at her.

But could she say these lines with Father Gabriel watching her? She was stumbling over them, rushing them out with no expression at all.

Mercy was doing such a great job too. There was real conviction in her voice when she spoke of "cutting off her hand" and ordering Abigail to "wipe it out of mind".

Abigail's reply, to taunt John Proctor for being a strong man but having a sickly wife, should have been full of passion and venom. She was goading John Proctor to react to her. But Leonie knew she was getting worse and worse. How she got to the end of the scene she never knew. As the rehearsal was called to a close, she shot an apologetic glance at Mercy. "I'm sorry, I just couldn't get the lines right today."

Mercy shrugged and smiled. "It's okay, it happens to all of us." She was a prefect like Harry and also did History of Art. Leonie liked her, which was why she felt so bad about letting her down. "It's only the first rehearsal, no one even remembers the lines yet."

Except Leonie did. She knew them by heart, burned into her soul even before she got the part.

"I'm sorry anyway."

"Don't worry. It will be great next time. Once we don't have to make an effort to remember each word." Mercy smiled brightly again at Leonie to try and cheer her up, and went on her way.

Leonie went to pick up her pile of folders which she had left on a chair. Mai had already left as Susannah was only needed at the very start. So she had been allowed to slip off early along with a couple of others.

As Leonie was about to leave, Father Gabriel called her back. "Leonie Wilson, if you could stay behind."

Her heart sank. He was going to give the part to someone else, she just knew it. Probably goddamn Suki, waiting in the wings.

When the others had left, Father Gabriel turned his attention on Leonie. "What the hell was that?" He looked angry. He was so devastatingly attractive even when he was angry. Like a furious, dark-haired, blue-eyed saint.

"I'm sorry, I just couldn't get it all together today," Leonie said. It was normally so easy, that was the frustrating thing. Usually Abigail just came over her and through her, and she didn't even have to consciously try.

"That's not good enough. A production depends on every member of the cast playing their part to the best of the ability. We'll go through it again now. I'll read John Proctor. I need to know that you can at least manage the role, since you convinced us at rehearsals that you could."

He was grim, unsmiling. Leonie swallowed, felling even worse than before. Father Gabriel as John Proctor was both a fantasy and a dread. "On stage?"

"Here will do."

She briefly closed her eyes, then began.

She asked John Proctor, now played by Father Gabriel, to give her a soft word.

But he told her no. It was done with.

Gabriel's tone as John Proctor was stern, but there was a caress in his words as well.

Suddenly Abigail Williams was flowing through her veins again. The long-ago witch girl took over. She - Abby and Leonie - longed for John Proctor, she was desperate for him.

She begged him not to be wintry and cold towards her. She told him she couldn't sleep because she dreamt about him.

The stage directions called for weeping here but Leonie didn't even notice them, yet her eyes were moist. She hadn't slept recently, and it was because of him. He haunted her dreams.

Father Gabriel, as John, confessed that he did think of her "softly" from time to time.

Leonie felt the forbidden yearning. The married, pious farmer and the young girl half his age whom he had conceived a deadly passion for. The desire between both of them: Abby's pleading seduction and Proctor's resolve to fight against it.

They reached the line where John Proctor threatens to give Abby a whipping, and shakes her. Father Gabriel was actually shaking her. His hand grasped her shoulder as he spoke the line. Leonie found herself breathing heavily and not wanting him to stop. She gazed up him, seeing John Proctor's anger and desire on his face. His face. Not John Proctor's.

Abruptly he let her go and stood back from her. He looked horror-struck.

"My God Leonie, I'm sorry. I don't know what came over me."

She couldn't let him break away like that. She stepped towards him, standing close to him. She looked up at him, seeing the desire that was still on his face. Ignoring what he had just said, she asked: "What does it mean, 'clutched my back'?" She knew what it meant, and Gabriel knew that she knew what it meant.

He paused, only for a second. Then something overtook him.

"Like this." He grabbed her hips roughly and turned her around. He clutched her against himself, moulding her against his body. She could feel his hardness pressing on her through the fabric of her school skirt and his own clothing.

His breath was on her neck, his lips so close to her skin. "Like this. This is what he did." His voice was husky.

His hands gripped her waist, preventing her from moving away. Leonie could smell his scent, a fresh, male aroma with a trace of incense. She could feel the heat from his body. Anger and hot desire.

She could hardly breathe, she wanted him so badly.

He held her, so close. She was terrified to turn and break the spell.

"Like this, he clutched her back." Gabriel pulled her even more firmly against him.

Leonie was struggling to control her own breathing. She stood there, with him grasping her. Her breath caught in her throat in a small cry. He gripped her more tightly.

How she wanted his arms around her. How she wanted him pressing her to him. Never let go, hold me, take me…

But then he released her. She turned around to him, questioning.

"I dream of you, but I wake."

It wasn't the right line. It was the inverse of what Abigail was supposed to say.

Leonie's own voice was a whisper. She gazed at him, and he at her. For what seemed like ages they stood there.

Gabriel closed his eyes. Breathed out. A muscle clenched in his jaw.

Then he turned abruptly and strode out.

9

Gabriel was in torment. What the hell had he done?

Hell, quite literally.

He was thankful it was the end of the day and he had no more classes. At a time like this the church should have been a refuge and place of expiation. But Gabriel felt too much in violation of his religion to go there.

He was angry. Angry with himself, angry with his vows, angry with the world. He knew that what he had done partly stemmed from this.

For he had felt anger towards his unknown rival. The unknown boy that Leonie had confessed to having feelings for.

Rival! As if it could be termed such. He was in no position to rival anyone: he was a priest, celibate, long removed from that arena.

Leonie had asked him a question, a simple question. Surely she had meant nothing by it? It was just a line from the play.

And he had responded by grabbing her, pulling her against him. Hurting her. Had he hurt her? He had held her so hard he feared he may have bruised her.

Yet the feel of her, the scent of her hair. The soft warmth of her as he had crushed her to him. He had wanted more of her, a longer time with her. To be even closer to her.

Gabriel had never before understood why a man might try to force himself on a woman. Even though this was still a thing he could never do, since he had enough self-restraint for that, he now understood the urge.

That driving, all-consuming desire to possess. To make his.

Barely knowing what to do, he headed into the woods behind the school. To take a walk, to get away. Though he suspected it would take more than forty days in the wilderness for him to get over this. To get it out of his system.

Holding her had only made it worse. Now his desire to be with her raged more than ever.

As he walked through the wood, absorbing its damp and wild aromas, its stillness and peace, his mind calmed. His anger gradually dissipated to regret and sorrow.

The shame did not leave him, nor the guilt. But he felt weary.

He knew that he should resign and probably go into seclusion. Get as far away from this place and the girl as possible.

But even as he thought it, he knew he was too weak. As much as it was torment to be around her, as much as seeing her every day would be a torture, he couldn't tear himself away.

Leonie was left standing in the empty hall. She hardly knew what had just happened to her. What had overcome them? What had made her say those terrible lines to him, a priest?

She felt sick with shame and guilt. A priest, a holy man! A man who had made sacred vows and she had tempted him to break them.

She wanted to run away. She wanted to apologise. Maybe she could just leave the school and go back to her grandmother. Make up some excuse. Write him a letter?

She couldn't cope with the oppressive feeling of the hall anymore. It felt enclosed, a place of sin and darkness.

She went outside and sat on one of the stone benches, her head in her hands. It felt as though the weight of the sky was upon her.

She was so tired.

Yet when she remembered how his hands had felt on her: even more demanding than her dream, how real his heat had been, how strong his arms, she felt a shiver of exhilaration.

A tiny, deep buried, wicked part of her wanted more.

She also wanted him. When he had called her back, been angry with her about her poor performance, there had also been concern in his eyes. He cared whether she succeeded or not. He wanted her to succeed. And not just for his sake in vindicating his decision to cast her, or for the sake of a great production.

For her.

He had seemed to like her in the initial classes and at the auditions, before he had gone strange and cold.

Maybe her confession had made him think that she was a slut? Maybe that was why he had been tempted by her?

Or was it the play? Those wild words of Abigail, her forbidden lust for her married lover echoing through time?

Proctor's lust for her, that had led to his death.

Leonie shivered. A few hundred years ago, she might well have been put to death for what she had done. Even now there were countries when merely to have been caught alone with a man might result in being stoned or imprisoned.

It was a dangerous fire she was playing with. She must do what she could to quench it.

It was inevitable that they would both meet before the next class. It couldn't go on, unresolved. Later the next day, which was a Saturday, Leonie made her way to the chapel. She felt drawn there.

She didn't even have to hope that Father Stephen would be out of the way. She just sensed, deep within herself, that Father Gabriel would be there alone.

She entered, feeling the cool darkness and the faded aroma of incense surround her. Candles burned in the prayer stand. You could donate fifty pence - it was the weird-shaped British coin with seven sides - and light a candle for someone.

Leonie did so now. She took the small tea light and held its wick to an already-lit candle that was near its end. A small flame caught and flared as the wax melted and fed it.

She placed it on the stand. She said a silent prayer for herself, and Gabriel. That they would both manage to overcome this.

She knew he was behind her even as she turned. He was keeping his distance this time.

He looked at her, his gaze solemn but not unkind.

"Leonie."

"Father." How absurd to call him such a title. He was only a few years older than her, and she doubted he felt fatherly towards her, given what had happened.

"The other day..." he ran his hands through his hair. "I can only say how incredibly sorry I am. For treating you as I did."

"It was my fault. I shouldn't have said what I did. I'm sorry."

He ran his hands through his hair. "It wasn't you, Leonie. It was" - struggling for words, he fell back on the old axiom - "these things are sent to test us. And I failed, very badly. I failed you and my vows. I can only seek your forgiveness." And the forgiveness of a higher power, Gabriel thought.

"There's nothing to forgive." She tried to find an out for him, for them both. "I think it was just the play, getting to us. It's so intense, what Miller wrote. All those passions and emotions and tragedy, never really resolved."

She was so beautiful and so gracious, Gabriel thought. After what he had done, it was incredible that she was the one telling him it was alright, trying to make him feel better.

"That still doesn't begin to excuse my conduct," he said.

But Leonie dismissed this. "I wonder if Miller was haunted by it too? You know that he made up the affair between Abigail and John? At least there's no documentation of it. I guess it was partly for the dramatic value that he put those scenes in. But he wrote that he thought there was something between the two of them, Abigail and John. All those people she named, including Elizabeth Proctor, yet she refused even to the end to name him. Miller wondered why."

She worried that she was rambling, but Father Gabriel seemed interested. "Do you think there was something? From what you've studied?" he asked.

"I don't know. Miller changed the ages, they were more like eleven and sixty, so it seems unlikely. That's quite an age gap, isn't it? But those were different times, she had lost her parents. Maybe she resented Elizabeth for casting her out because she wanted him as a father figure?" Leonie said.

Just as you should be to me, she thought. Though she wanted Father Gabriel in a very different way.

"You should be taking the class given all you know, not me," Gabriel said. He managed a slight smile. The tension was still there between them but it was manageable for now.

It was strange, this sudden role reversal. Leonie the teacher, he the student. Maybe that was the answer to this. Maybe they needed to channel this energy into literature, a safe passion they both shared.

He cast a glance to the confessional, remembering his time with her there. Leonie followed his gaze.

"I don't think confession is really for me," she said. She looked him directly in the eye and he understood what she was saying. She wasn't going to confess any of it to Father Stephen, and for that Gabriel was profoundly grateful.

While a priest could never disclose anything he heard from penitents, he might still work to remedy what he knew by other means. It would also put Stephen in a terrible position if he knew.

10

Sister Joan ran the school's poetry appreciation club, which met on Sunday afternoons. It was one of a number of activities designed to occupy the students on weekends as there wasn't much else to do.

Harry was busy with lacrosse and Mai, who played the bassoon, had chamber group.

With nothing else to do, Leonie and Figgy had been browbeaten into joining the club by Sister Joan. "It will be useful complementary background for your A-level syllabus," she had told her sixth form class.

It was one of those things that wasn't technically compulsory but was still pretty impossible to get out of. Leonie and Figgy had turned up reluctantly the first week, wishing they could have just hung out in their dorm and read books.

It hadn't been as bad as Leonie had feared. Sister Joan had chosen some of the British war poets, and Leonie had found the verses beautiful and moving.

This week though there was a change. Sister Joan had to pay a visit to someone that weekend, and asked Father Gabriel if he could fill in for her.

Since he was free at that time, he was unable to refuse. "Certainly. What poets are they studying?"

"I've been doing some of the war poets with them, but you should choose whatever you like. It's good for them to be exposed to a wider range of literature," Sister Joan told him.

Since he was working on his Gerard Manly Hopkins thesis, Gabriel decided to double up and introduce the students to his favourite poet. Hopkins hadn't been on the A-level syllabus for years, if ever. He doubted if many of them would have even heard of him.

It was a warm and sunny late September day, with the leaves already beginning to turn red and gold on the trees around St Winifred's grounds. It was too beautiful a day to remain indoors, and there wouldn't be many left like this as winter approached.

Gabriel decided to hold the poetry club outside. There was a murmur of excitement when he announced this, for Sister Joan always confined them to a classroom. He noticed Leonie and Figgy looking interested at the news.

For the past week he had managed to keep Leonie at arm's length. He hadn't acted coldly towards her but they had both chosen to keep their distance. It had been incredibly hard for Gabriel. Watching her and hearing her in class and rehearsals remained a form of torture for him. He would have to grit his teeth and bear her proximity at poetry club too.

He led the group outside to sit on the grass by a grove of trees. The students sat in a rough semi-circle before him, and he began his introduction.

"Today I thought I would introduce you to a poet who isn't as well-known as other poets you may have studied. But he's a favourite of mine, and I'm currently working on a thesis about him." He had their attention. None of them had known he was working on an academic project. "Gerard Manly Hopkins was born in 1944 and was a convert to Catholicism. He studied Classics at Oxford, and it was during this time that he was received into the Catholic church. Shortly after graduating he decided to become a Jesuit priest, which as you may know is a particularly austere and restrictive life."

Gabriel paused, looking at the faces before him. Most were still politely attentive, including Leonie's. "That may make him sound rather a dry stick. But the poetry he wrote was anything but. It features vivid, passionate language and imagery relating to the natural world, and has been compared to other poets such as Keats."

Gabriel leant back and pointed up at the trees behind them. "Anyone know what those trees are?"

"Larch," someone suggested.

"No, larches are conifers," another girl said.

"Silver birch? They've got white trunks."

"Close," Gabriel told her, "but not quite. The trunks are similar, but these are aspens, a kind of poplar. One of Hopkins' most famous poems is about a line of aspens that were felled during his time in Oxford." He read them the poem:

My aspens dear, whose airy cages quelled,
Quelled or quenched in leaves the leaping sun

Leonie noticed how resonant his voice was when he read. She simply loved listening to him. She had never heard of Hopkins before, though she so far liked what Gabriel was reciting to them. It was also wonderful to actually be outside, looking at the very kind of trees that were being described.

They had a short discussion of the poem afterward, though Leonie didn't contribute anything. She was still trying not to interact with him too much, to give him space. Guilt from tempting him still weighed her down, she still blamed herself for what had happened.

Gabriel read them another poem, Pied Beauty.

Glory be to God for dappled things —
For skies of couple-colour as a brinded cow;

His face was lit up when he read out the lines, and it made Leonie's heart ache. She wasn't sure why.

"As you can hear, Hopkins is keenly aware of the Creator in his works. It's an important dimension for him. He spent some years trying to suppress his desire to write poetry, believing it was incompatible with his life as a priest," Gabriel told them.

Suppress his desire… Leonie couldn't help but catch Gabriel's eye when he spoke this phrase. She quickly looked back down at the grass, which she had been twisting in her fingers.

"So did he give up forever?" one girl asked.

"Fortunately not. He eventually came to believe that they didn't conflict, and that his love of nature could be an extension of his faith. Even when he wasn't writing poetry he kept a detailed prose journal of his observations on the natural world. Then in 1875 he wrote what's considered to be his masterpiece, a poem to commemorate five nuns who died in a shipwreck. The Wreck of the Deutschland is too long for me to read the whole thing, but here's the first verse."

When Gabriel began reading, something ignited in Leonie. It was Gabriel's voice, his passion in reading the lines, and the sheer force and beauty of the lines. She was transfixed. Thou hast bound bones & veins in me, fastened me flesh, And after it almost unmade…

Gabriel began a brief explanation of some of Hopkins' poetical techniques such as the "sprung rhythm" that he had defined and his concepts of inscape and instress.

But Leonie burned to hear him read the poetry again. She didn't dare ask, but she longed for it. She also wanted to read more of the poems herself. She had the sense that Father Gabriel had deliberately avoided reading the Deutschland poem for reasons other than its length. After all, surely he could have read them a couple more verses?

Knowing she was continuing to play with fire, but justifying it to herself as part of her English literature education, she lingered behind afterwards. Most people were keen to rush off to tea though a couple stayed back to ask him more questions. Leonie silently willed them to hurry up and go.

Eventually they did, and she was left with him there. Figgy was waiting for her a short distance away so Leonie couldn't take long.

"I wondered if you had any copies of his poems that I could read?" she asked him. "I wanted to read the rest of it. That last poem."

Gabriel looked at her directly. "You want to read the rest of The Wreck of the Deutschland?" he asked her.

"I want to read the rest of The Wreck of the Deutschland," she repeated, her voice softer.

Something unspoken exchanged between them.

Gabriel held out the volume he had been reading from. "You can take this," he said.

"I can't take your copy."

He laughed. "I've got several different editions. Take it."

Leonie took the book, her fingers brushing his as she did so. Her stomach flipped.

She hugged it to her chest, along with her other folders. "I'll look after it, I promise. I'll get it back to you soon."

Gabriel smiled, his eyes intent on her. "Keep it as long as you need."

She thanked him and walked to join Figgy. As they walked back, Figgy commented on the book.

"That's really nice of him to lend it to you. Father Gabriel really seems to like you, doesn't he?"

Leonie felt her heart stop. "What do you mean?"

"I don't know. Just that he tends to look at you, and he seems interested whenever you answer in class," Figgy said.

Leonie had thought the opposite. First he had seemed to blank her following the confession, then there had been that terrible incident, then he had been distant but polite. "I'm sure he's like that with everyone," she said.

"Maybe. It seems different with you though. He's a priest, of course, so I'm sure it wouldn't be more than a friendly interest. But even priests must have friends, people they like more than others. He definitely dislikes Suki."

That wasn't hard, and Leonie said so.

Figgy laughed. "She's not the most likeable of people, is she? And she's frightfully angry about you getting the role of Abigail over her." Her face became serious. "You probably should watch out. She can be very vindictive when she wants to be. If she ever sees a chance to make trouble for you, she'll take it."

Leonie thanked her for the warning. Right now she had no plans to get into trouble of any kind, so she couldn't imagine Suki gaining any leverage over her. Even if she had wanted to misbehave, there weren't exactly many opportunities at St Winifred's, were there?

11

Gabriel had deliberately not read out any more of the poem because he couldn't trust himself to keep his voice steady in front of Leonie. The second verse in particular mirrored much of the emotion of his own ordination to the priesthood. The struggle he had gone through, and the hours of solitude and agonised doubt.

Doubt that had only resurfaced since he had started teaching at this school.

Thou knowest the walls, altar and hour and night

He remembered the isolation he had felt. The sense of aloneness that no one could answer his questions or assuage his fears.

"It is up to you and your God," Canon Francis had told him. "It is a path that every man must walk alone, a fork in the road where each ordinand must decide his own direction."

One way lay the earthly world with its human love and pleasures.

The other way lay the purity of a spiritual life and the sacrifice of worldly things.

Gabriel had chosen what he believed to be the higher path. Disillusioned with love, he thought he could make more of a difference through forgoing it.

It wasn't as though he had no experience with women. Quite the opposite. Before Joanne he had played the field, dating plenty of different girls in high school and his first years of university.

He had really thought he was prepared to give all that up.

He didn't expect to be tempted - to the point of regretting his vows - by another girl. Yet alone one several years younger than him who was supposed to be his student.

After Vespers, which did nothing to ease the turmoil in his soul, Gabriel returned to the presbytery and started to prepare supper. He was cooking sausages that night. As he cut up some broccoli and potatoes, the domesticity of it reminded him of his time with Joanne. They had lived together - "in sin", as it was termed - from early in their engagement.

He had, he thought, been quite content with their life together. It hadn't bothered him that Joanne didn't share certain passions of his, literature for one. They had got on well enough. Their sex life had been okay, and he hadn't felt much more than a twinge of Catholic guilt over the fact they weren't yet married.

He had certainly never felt that overpowering, almost unconquerable desire for her that he had felt for Leonie when they acted The Crucible scene together. That need to crush the girl against him. To almost hurt her, if only to impress upon her how much she was affecting him. And in his dreams too, if he were completely honest. Gabriel controlled himself well enough in the daytime but at night the images of her came back, unbidden.

He had attributed the intensity of it to his celibate state. Pent up sexual energy that in time his body would learn to process more easily, without affecting his mind. Leonie had just happened to be the target for that suppressed energy. It could have been anyone, he reasoned. His libido was just choosing a random girl.

Now though, Gabriel wondered. The problem was that he found himself longing to spend time with her. Not just with anyone, but with her. If it were mere loneliness then he could have conversed with Father Stephen quite companionably. If he missed women's company, his colleagues among the sisterhood could have provided chaste conversation.

But he couldn't get that girl out of his mind. Her rose gold hair, the unusual, amber-green eyes. The way she smiled, and the emotion in her eyes as he had read Hopkins' poems to the students.

If the real Abigail had been just a fraction as bewitching, no wonder she had managed to seduce a devout man and lead an entire community into destruction.

Some boy out there, the one Leonie liked, was the luckiest guy in the world. Gabriel hoped the two of them wouldn't screw it up like he and Joanne had.

Actually that wasn't true. The thought of her with anyone else made him feel quite violent, though he had no right to feel so.

He turned down the heat under the fry pan, and went to set the table for the meal.

Leonie read the rest of the poems and fell in love with them. She had never read anything like them before.

I did say yes
O at lightning and lashed rod;
Thou heardst me truer than tongue confess
Thy terror, O Christ, O God;

Was that what Father Gabriel had gone through? The choice that he had made when he became a priest, as Hopkins had? It made her wonder what had led to his conversion. Leonie couldn't imagine being so set on a godly life herself. To actually give up the chance of ever being with someone and spending your life with them.

Irreligious as it might seem, she just didn't think God would be a big enough compensation for that.

And the midriff astrain with leaning of, laced with fire of stress.

She couldn't help but think of Father Gabriel's midriff when she read this line. Something had certainly been astrain there.

Was she wicked? Was she some kind of evil temptress?

She just wanted him so much. Even if she could just kiss him once, feel those firm, perfectly moulded lips on hers, it would be enough. She could even become a nun and die happy.

Then she remembered that nuns had to share all their possessions including clothes, and the thought of ending up wearing Mother Benedict's bra one week truly did not appeal. How did they manage that kind of thing? Perhaps they got a special dispensation for intimate apparel.

Perhaps they didn't wear any...

Leonie wondered for a moment what Father Gabriel might do if she wore no underwear to English class, and bent over to pick up a book. Then she felt horrified with herself for even contemplating it. She was turning into one of those wicked women in the Bible. Delilah. Jezebel. Sapphira.

Maybe she should go up on the roof and take a bath like Bathsheba, and hope that Father Gabriel might pass by...

This thought, which wasn't serious, made her laugh aloud.

"What's so funny?" Mai said. She had come into the dorm after finishing some late homework.

"Nothing. Just dumb thoughts," Leonie told her.

Mai sat on her bed which was adjacent. "What's that?" she asked, seeing the volume of poetry.

"Just some stuff from poetry club." Leonie tried to play it down.

But Mai snatched up the book and opened it. She flicked through then peered inside the front cover. "G Brydon. Who is that?"

Leonie hadn't even noticed the name written in the book, she had opened it straight on the verses. Was that his surname then? Strange to think she hadn't even found it out before, nor even thought to find out. She avoided saying anything, but Mai had already figured it out.

"It's not Father Gabriel, is it? 'Gabriel Brydon'. How come you've got his book?"

Leonie mumbled something about borrowing the poems to read more of them, but Mai was determined to dig for scandal.

"What's he doing lending you poetry books? Are they love poems?"

"No, they're more religious," Leonie told her. Mai flicked through and seeing this was so, lost interest. She flopped back on her bed, which as usual was a complete mess. Matron, the nun who supervised the dorms, was constantly berating her about it.

Harry arrived, back from a lacrosse match.

"Score?" Mai asked her.

"Fourteen-nine to St Winifred's," Harry said.

Mai congratulated her. "You are lucky, getting to escape this place. Even if it is only a coach ride to Agnes College and back. Agnes girls are absolute slags," she told Leonie, rolling onto her side. "Their school is in the middle of a town so they can sneak out if they want to. And they do, and they have terrible reputations. They're so lucky." She sank back down on her bed again.

"You'd like to have a terrible reputation?" Leonie asked.

"I'd like the opportunity to get one."

Harry, packing away some clothes, laughed. "You'll have to seduce the new priest then."

"Fat chance. He only has eyes for Leonie," Mai said. "He's lending her books of love poetry."

Leonie felt her face go bright red. "They're religious poems, and it was me who asked for them."

Harry and Mai exchanged an irritatingly knowing glance. "He still lent you his copy though," Mai said. "He could have told you to look in the school library."

"Only because it was convenient as he'd just been taking the poetry club. What if it had been Father Stephen? You wouldn't say that if it were he who lent it to me," Leonie pointed out.

"Ah, but it wasn't Father Stephen, was it? It was Father Hot," Mai said and gave Leonie an evil grin.

Leonie was pretty sure that Mai wasn't serious. She was just messing about. But she felt some relief that the others thought it was okay to joke about. It might mean they would be less outraged if they ever found out about the clutching thing.

Which they wouldn't. Because it was over and it was never going to happen again. He was a priest, she was his pupil. They were both going to contain themselves from now on.

So Leonie tried to convince herself, anyway.

12

St Winifred's "gym knickers" were the grossest thing Leonie had ever seen. They were huge, grey underpants-style things that you had to wear under your sports uniform. She couldn't even imagine her staid English grandmother wearing them. They came up as far as the navel.

Even more bizarre, given the long length required of school skirts, the skirt worn for sport was absurdly short. It was pleated, grey - like everything else - and even shorter than the cheerleading skirt she had worn in junior high.

It barely covered her American fanny or her English fanny - since arriving here she'd learnt there was a pretty significant difference between the two. Worse, you had to wear it rain or shine, winter or summer. And it was winter most of the year here.

It was drizzling rain when she trudged out to the netball courts with Figgy and Mai. Girls who didn't play lacrosse had to play netball, which was supervised by Sister Barbara. Sport was compulsory. Leonie had only played basketball before so she had to learn the rules from scratch. You couldn't dribble the ball which was hard to get used to. She bounced it a couple of times without thinking, which got her the whistle and a sneer from Suki Laverne.

"Yankee Doodle ain't so dandy when it comes to the rules," Suki said with a really bad attempt at an American accent.

Leonie ignored her. Suki was annoyingly skilled at netball. She had one of the shooter positions and was the top scorer for her team. Leonie had been given a position where you just had to run and catch and throw, and you couldn't score goals. She was trying her best for her side's sake, but she found it dull and restrictive.

Mai, although she didn't have the advantage of height that Figgy did, was very agile and nimble. Figgy was supposed to be scoring goals and made a valiant effort, but the other team won.

"Half of me wants to get onto the school team," Mai said as they sat by the side of the court afterwards, "and half of me can't be bothered. If you get on the team then you at least get excursions to play away matches. But then you get forced into endless practice sessions."

There were too many girls to all play at once on the two courts, so the teams had to swap in and out. While waiting they sat on some benches at the top of the slope above the courts, conveniently located under a tree with thick foliage that kept the rain off.

"It would also mean being stuck on a coach with Suki for hours," Figgy pointed out.

"Do you only play against other girls' schools?" Leonie asked. "Or are some of them held at co-ed schools?"

"If they were held at co-ed schools, I would be the captain of every sport team going by now," Mai said.

Figgy asked Leonie if she had played on any teams back in the US.

"No. I did some gym, but I was more of a drama nerd," Leonie said.

"But you were a cheerleader, weren't you?" Mai asked.

"Only in Junior High. Like when I was in eighth grade."

Mai was still fascinated by this. "Can you remember the moves? Can you teach me some?"

Leonie laughed. "Barely."

"Go on, show me!"

Mai was really persistent though Leonie tried to refuse. In the end she gave in. "It's probably not what you're thinking. We did pretty simple stunts."

"Stunts? You mean like human pyramids? The whole team all on each other's shoulders?"

Leonie was sorry to disappoint Mai. "Just really basic stuff. Like thigh stands."

Mai demanded that she demonstrate, and eventually Leonie gave in.

"Okay. But I'll need both of you. We really need four people, because there's supposed to be a spotter." Mai and Figgy looked confused so Leonie had to explain how it worked. Eventually they managed to lift Mai up as the flyer, with her hands on their shoulders.

"This is harder than it looks," Mai said. She half jumped, half tumbled down.

"You're supposed to raise your arms up in a V," Leonie told her. "Then for the other stunts the flyer - that's the person on top - does different positions." She demonstrated a lib or Statue of Liberty pose and got the others to copy her. Figgy managed it better that Mai. It turned out she had done several years of ballet as a young girl.

Getting more confident and stretched out, Leonie attempted to show them a scorpion. For this she had to stand on one foot while pulling her other foot back and upwards. She stood on the bench to do it. When she reached the full extension her sports skirt had fallen forward and the awful grey gym knickers were entirely exposed.

"I'm guessing you need a special type of costume to do that," Mai said.

Leonie grinned and turned her head... only to see Father Gabriel passing by the sports fields and getting a full eyeful of grey underwear.

Mortified, she wobbled as she exited the pose to pull her skirt down, and ended up falling off the bench with a cry.

Mai and Figgy rushed to her aid, full of concern.

"I'm fine, I'm fine," Leonie protested. Except she wasn't, she had twisted her ankle.

In all the confusion she realised that Father Gabriel was helping her up as well. Despite the pain of her foot, his touch burned her.

"You landed heavily on that ankle. Can you walk on it?" he asked.

"Yes, I'm fine." Leonie tried to stand on both her feet to prove it, then collapsed against him.

"We'll have to get you to the school nurse," he said. "It may be broken." He then instructed the others. "Iphigenia, if you could support Leonie on the left, I'll take the right. Mai, could you please let Sister Barbara know what's happened."

Leonie's head was swimming. Overwhelmed by embarrassment, pain and the proximity of Father Gabriel, she could hardly think straight as he and Figgy helped her hobble back to school. She could smell the cologne or aftershave balm he used, it was very subtle, but enough to remind her of that earlier occasion.

They took Leonie up to the sanatorium and got her to lie down on a bed. Father Gabriel then sent Figgy to find Matron. There were no other girls ill at present, so all six beds in the room were empty.

Gabriel gave Leonie's foot a cursory examination while they waited. "I've only done basic first aid but I suspect it's not broken. Can you still feel your toes?"

Leonie could. "I'm sure it's just a sprain. I was able to put a little weight on it."

"That's good." He lowered his voice. "I'm sorry I made you walk. I could have carried you, but I wasn't sure... given what happened. I didn't want to cross any boundaries."

"It's okay." It wasn't okay, Leonie would have given anything to have been fully in his arms. "I'm super heavy. I would probably have broken your back," she joked.

Gabriel looked at her, his eyes serious. There was something in his gaze that she couldn't read. "I doubt that. I imagine it would be pretty easy to take you in my arms."

Then he realised what he had said, just as Leonie felt her stomach dissolve. He straightened. "I mean bear your weight. Anyway, Matron should be here soon and can decide whether you need an x-ray."

Leonie really hoped it wouldn't come to that. The whole thing was so embarrassing. Particularly as it was her own idiocy and showing off that had landed her in this situation. She wasn't really looking forward to having to explain it all to Matron. "I fell off a bench" sounded remarkably stupid.

As if reading her mind, Gabriel asked: "What were you doing on that bench?"

"A scorpion." She didn't elaborate and he frowned.

"A scorpion? It looked very precarious."

Leonie explained. "It's a cheerleading position. I was trying to demonstrate to the others."

"You used to be a cheerleader?" he asked.

"Ages ago."

It really was an image Gabriel could have done without. He had enough difficulty banishing images of Leonie from his head without picturing her in cheerleading gear. The glimpse he had already got of her derrière was disturbing enough.

He was both relieved and disappointed when Matron appeared with a worried-looking Figgy in tow. Matron was a brisk-looking, stout nun as well as a qualified nurse.

"Let's take a look, shall we?" Matron pulled down Leonie's sock and pressed her ankle in a couple of places, causing her to flinch. "I don't think it's broken. But we'll put some ice on it and see where we are in an hour or so."

She turned to Father Gabriel and Figgy. "You can both be getting along, she'll be fine here. Thank you for your help."

Leonie thanked them too.

Gabriel smiled at her. "It had better not be broken, because I need you for my Abigail."

He was only saying it to make her feel better, Leonie knew, but the "my Abigail" phrase made her heart leap. She smiled back at him, unaware of the effect it had on the priest.

As he walked out, Gabriel was still trying to get the image of Leonie cheerleading out of his mind. He also found he was struck by a new sense of possessiveness when he was around her. When he had said "my Abigail" he had meant quite literally his. Which was absurd.

He headed for the chapel. A couple of hours of quiet contemplation and prayer might clear his head. If only it might also quell the physical urges of his body.

13

It was a beautiful Autumn afternoon and Leonie had it all to herself.

Thanks to her ankle she had been excused sport for the rest of the week. While the younger students had to be in supervised study, the sixth formers were free to do as they liked.

So Leonie took the book of poetry that Father Gabriel had lent her, and wandered into the woods at the side of the school. She passed the grove of poplars at the edge, where the poetry club had been held, and went further in.

It was a beautiful wood. Not a thick, dark pine forest but an airy cathedral of beech, carpeted with bluebells in the spring. There were paintings of it in the school art room. Now the leaves were a glorious gold and bronze dome overhead, with the sunlight filtering through. It was dazzling, and the perfect place to lie down and read poems.

Which is what Leonie did. She found a mossy spot flecked with sun and wriggled down until her head was in a comfortable position on the leaves. Then she gazed upwards for a while, looking at the patterns of the leaves against the blue sky. Finally she read some verses of The Wreck of the Deutschland, trying to memorise the ones she liked.

She had been there a short time when she heard someone come up beside her. She knew without looking who it was.

"Leonie. How is your ankle?"

Gabriel regularly walked through the woods during his free time but he had never encountered anyone in this place before. The girls tended to venture into the woods on weekends when he was busier with chapel duties.

There she lay, like a wood nymph, her hair spreading over the leaves.

He had thought of her constantly since taking her to the sick bay. English lessons had been an ordeal. Fortunately - or not fortunately, since he knew he preferred the torment of her presence to the absence of her - she hadn't been needed for the scenes they had rehearsed that week.

She didn't answer him, and he saw that she had his book clasped to her chest.

Knowing he was making a grave mistake, he sat down beside her. She remained on her back, looking upwards, and then she spoke.

I am soft sift
In an hourglass—at the wall
Fast, but mined with a motion, a drift

Gabriel felt a physical ache as Leonie recited the lines. If he kept looking at her he feared he would do something foolish. So - which was probably even more foolish - he laid down with his head next to hers, but his body the other way.

He spoke the next lines. He knew them by heart

And it crowds and it combs to the fall;
I steady as a water in a well, to a poise, to a pane,

They were both silent. Leonie could hardly breathe. She couldn't believe how close to him she was. Her head was practically touching his. She had never felt this intimate with someone else and yet they weren't even having physical contact.

"Read the next verse," she asked him. Gabriel obliged.

I kiss my hand
To the stars, lovely-asunder
Starlight, wafting him out of it; and
Glow, glory in thunder;
Kiss my hand to the dappled-with-damson west:

After the first five lines he stopped and they lay there together in silence once again.

Eventually Leonie spoke. "Do you think Hopkins ever fell in love?"

"He did. But it wasn't, it was…"

"It was with a man, right?" Leonie had already guessed this.

"It was. But the man Hopkins loved died very young. He drowned when he was nineteen. And he loved someone else, though Hopkins likely didn't know this."

Leonie took a while to absorb this. "And then Hopkins entered the priesthood. It's so sad." She didn't specify whether she thought Hopkins taking orders was sad, or the fact the man he loved had died.

Gabriel thought of Joanne and couldn't miss the parallels to his own life. She had loved another and left him, and he had subsequently taken orders. Was it the wrong reason? Should he have waited longer?

But how could it not be the right path? To be closer to God, to follow a life of service and sacrifice?

Even if that sacrifice meant never getting to do what he wanted to do. Which was to roll onto his side and bring his lips down upon the girl lying next to him. But he kept his head fixed and steady, looking upwards.

"How did you know he loved a man?" he asked Leonie, suddenly curious.

"I'm not sure. I guess there's nothing about women in there, except for the nuns. And they're not eroticised. Then there are a couple of poems where - you know - the imagery is kind of..."

"Homoerotic?" Gabriel suggested.

"Something like that. Only subtly, but then I haven't studied all of them as closely as you have," she said.

"The more I study them, the more I feel I don't know about him. Or rather, the more I feel there is to know," Gabriel said.

Leonie brushed off a leaf that had drifted down onto her hair. "He's easy to fall in love with though, isn't he? His poetry, I mean. Like Keats."

Gabriel laughed. "You fell in love with Keats?"

"Everyone does, don't they? You hit the emo stage and go around reciting about being love with Death and calling his soft name and so on."

It wasn't a phase Gabriel had personally been through but he took her word for it. "I hope you don't feel that way now."

"Not at all. Not now. There's too much to live for."

From the way she said it he understood there had been a time when she hadn't felt that way, but he didn't question her about it. He couldn't stop remembering Joanne. Not only was any twinge of emotion for her long gone, but he was starting to feel incredulity. He could never have imagined lying in a wood with her, taking about poets and poetry. She would have been bored after a moment, complaining about the discomfort of lying on the ground, wanting to get up and leave.

Gabriel remembered a disastrous time when they had been on a beach and Joanne had freaked out about sand getting everywhere. People did make jokes about "sand getting in the crevices" but they hadn't even been in a state of undress. Much as he had hoped to get that way at the time.

No, Joanne hadn't been much of a lover of the outdoors. But then he hadn't appreciated nature as much as he did now, past the wild days of college and quietly immersed in his work and his private study.

Leonie was just centimetres from him. If he tilted his head one way he could lean it against hers. He longed to do so. He could smell her hair, the shampoo she used, and it had made him ragingly hard.

In another life, he could have lain with her like this every night and every morning. Every day, as they were now.

Thinking about this reminded him how unwise and inappropriate it was for him to be lying there beside her. But he just couldn't bring himself to leave her just yet.

"What poets did you study in your former school?" he asked her.

"The usual ones. The Romantics. Some Shakespeare. TS Eliot. Lots of Emily Dickinson. She was from Massachusetts."

Gabriel confessed to some ignorance of Dickinson. "I'm afraid I've read very little of her work."

"She wrote nearly two thousand poems. I doubt many people have read all of them," Leonie said. She loved hearing Gabriel's voice. She couldn't see him, in this position, but he was so near to her.

She wondered if he had ever been in love, as Hopkins had. She didn't dare ask.

She rolled onto her side so she was looking at his profile, effectively upside down as he was lying the other way. He had such perfect features: he looked sculpted, like a statue. Had he chosen a different career he could easily have been a model or an actor.

Sensing her looking at him, Gabriel turned onto his side as well. Their faces were inches apart. Thank God his body wasn't facing hers as well, because that might have been temptation too much.

Their eyes were at the same level, and he looked into hers. An expression passed across her face, she looked momentarily sad. He asked her what it was.

"I was thinking of that actress who became a nun. She was so beautiful, she had that glittering career, and she gave it all up to go into a convent."

Gabriel wasn't sure what actress she was talking about. "That's not your plan, is it? Is that how you imagine your life?" The thought of Leonie shutting herself away from the world felt viscerally wrong, though a part of him could hardly bear to think of her falling in love with other men. Like the one she had confessed to being in love with.

"God no! I'm not beautiful or anything. And as for the career, who knows? But I can't imagine reaching those heights, let alone giving it up if I did."

He wanted to touch her so badly he had to curl his fingers into his palms, pressing his nails into his skin to try and distract himself. "You are beautiful, Leonie."

He spoke with such sincerity, not saying it as a platitude or joke, that she felt unable to respond. She didn't agree with him, for she wasn't vain. Normally she would have laughed it off. "Thank you, but I don't think I'll be winning Miss Universe any time soon..." But the words stuck in her throat as she saw the expression in his eyes.

Abruptly he turned from her and sat up. "I have to go, I have duties in chapel." He saw the surprise and disappointment in her eyes at his sudden change of attitude and it was more than he could bear. "I'll see you in rehearsal?"

"I'll be there," Leonie said.

Gabriel didn't have duties in chapel, except to his God and his own soul. He had to get her out of his system. This was getting dangerous.

14

Leonie spent the rest of the day in a mixture of bliss and turmoil. To have spent all that time with Father Gabriel was just amazing.

But it also made things harder. The more she was with him, the closer he was, the more she wanted him.

He can never be yours, she reminded herself. He doesn't see you that way, he's a priest.

And yet…

She knew she needed to curb her imagination, because it was being fuelled by her heart into all sorts of wild fantasies. She was so sure that he had been close to kissing her. But really, a priest? There was a huge difference between him deciding to do something like that, and the physical thing after rehearsal.

That had just been a bodily urge. He hadn't been thinking straight and nor had she.

But why would he lie down with her then? Why talk to her about all those things, and call her beautiful? Or was that just a part of his priestly duty, his pastoral care? Taking an interest in her and trying to lift her spirits.

Leonie wished she had someone to confide in but she was sure her roommates would be appalled. If she had to talk to any of them, oddly she thought that Harry would be the easiest. Although she spent more time with Mai and Figgy, there was something about Harry that suggested she cared less for convention. Even though she was an aristocrat. Or maybe because she was? Perhaps if you reached the top of the social sphere in England you could do as you pleased, without regard to what anyone else thought.

It was a liberating notion.

By chance she bumped into Harry later, walking back from lacrosse with a couple of her team mates. They had to visit Mother Benedict about something, so after greeting Leonie they departed. Leonie was left alone with Harry.

"How goes it?" Harry said. "Ankle any better?"

"It's been okay for days," Leonie said. "I would have been fine for netball today, but Matron gave me a note."

Harry nodded. "It's better not to take any chances with those kind of injuries. Otherwise you could be out for weeks."

Being off netball for weeks sounded just fine to Leonie. If it meant more woodland sessions with Father Gabriel. She sighed, thinking about it.

"You alright?" Harry asked.

"Just the usual. I'm good, really," Leonie said.

"Homesick? Heartsick?"

Leonie grinned. "Probably a bit of both."

"Pining for some hot guy back in the states? Will you get to fly back for the half term holiday?"

Unfortunately not. Leonie was spending the vacation with her grandmother. The semester - or Autumn term, as they called it here - was so long that it was split in half with a week-long vacation.

"No, but maybe at Christmas."

"You'll see him in December, then. It's not so long off. Does he write?" Harry asked.

"Not exactly. He's not…we're not…"

Now Harry grinned. "Unrequited love?"

"Forbidden love."

Harry raised her eyebrows. "Now I'm intrigued. What it is it, a married man? Your stepbrother? A bad boy in a bikie gang? The US president?"

Leonie burst out laughing at this. "Not quite that. But someone I can't have, ever."

"Never say never. Life's too short. If you want something badly enough, just go for it."

Leonie considered this. "If it was you in my position. Let's say a married man, though it's not exactly that. Would you do anything?"

Harry tossed her lacrosse stick up, twirling it and catching it while she thought. "If his wife was a bitch, and I thought he might feel the same, then yes. On the other hand, if he totally adored her and she was an angel, I'd probably just remove myself. Go overseas for a few months and drown my sorrows."

Being a priest, Gabriel's wife was effectively God or the Virgin Mary or something, Leonie thought. Hardly a bitch. And she was sure Gabriel adored his Creator.

And yet…

Harry looked at her seriously. "Life really is too short. You can't spend eighty years being miserable and self-sacrificing, if there's the slightest gleam of hope. Even if you get rejected. Even if it doesn't last. You have to know. Regret is far more bitter, and a terrible waste."

Her tone lightened again. "I hope I haven't just gone and encouraged you to split up your sister's marriage, or something. I think I probably would hold off if it was a brother-in-law, unless they divorced first. Fortunately I don't have any sisters, and my cousin married a man who looks like a horse."

"I don't have any married sisters either, so we're safe there," Leonie said.

"Good. If it's something like a guy who's older, or a college professor, or even someone engaged, I wouldn't hesitate."

Father Gabriel was older than her, Leonie considered. She wasn't exactly sure how old he was, but it didn't seem like an insurmountable gap. It wasn't Hugh Hefner level anyway. As a teacher he was more or less in the same category as a college professor, at least in terms of that taboo. It was the engaged thing she was stuck on. He was engaged to the church. Wedded to it.

Did priests ever leave the priesthood? Were they even allowed to?

Leonie could absolutely not ask Harry about this, as it would totally give her away. Given there were only two priests at school, and it was hardly likely she'd have a crush on Father Stephen.

They had reached the school and were climbing the stairs to Pentecost dorm. "Sometimes these things are better out than in," Harry said. "Get it out and it takes the pressure off. It might even help you get over it, if it's not meant to be." She smiled wickedly. "Or you might end up with the most frightfully complicated mess. Only you can decide that."

A few days later, having agonised over what to do, Leonie had decided to take action. Her feelings for Father Gabriel were consuming far too much of her time. They were distracting her from her schoolwork. She ended up daydreaming at random moments and missing what people said.

If she told him, perhaps it would get it out of her system. She imagined him being embarrassed but sympathetic. He would gently tell her that it wasn't possible, ever, but that he was flattered. He would tell her that it was normal, and that women often conceived unrequited passions for their priest. She would feel silly, and they would hopefully be able to laugh about it and move on.

It would be the hardest thing she had ever done but life was nothing if you weren't brave. Right now it was festering and bubbling and getting harder to suppress. Once it was all out in the open it would be cleansed and start to fade.

After all he must know. He had heard her confession. She couldn't remember exactly what she had said, but surely it had been obvious.

Leonie sat on the wall by the school steps gathering her thoughts and mustering her courage. Then she saw Father Stephen walking out from the chapel towards the school. If Father Gabriel was in the chapel, and she couldn't think where else he would be, it was now or never.

Entering the vestry, she found him stacking up a pile of prayer books. He was startled to see her. "Leonie. Is everything alright?"

She swallowed. She went up to him, so she was about a metre away. It wasn't the kind of thing she wanted to say across a room. "The other day in the wood. I thought that maybe you… nearly kissed me." It hadn't been what she planned to start with, it just came out.

"What?" Gabriel felt cold shock run through him.

"And I wanted you to kiss me."

"Leonie, I'm a priest!" He indicated his vestments.

She bit her lip. "I know. But I still wanted… I thought that you wanted…" She trailed off.

Gabriel rubbed his eyes. He half hoped that this was a dream. Or a nightmare. But when he looked up again she was still there. The most alluring and dangerous thing he had ever seen, because of what she represented.

Leonie was sure he had felt it too. The tension. The wanting.

"Could we just kiss, once?" At that moment she felt it was the only way she could get it out of her system. To break that tension. She thought she might die if she didn't just once in her lifetime feel his lips on hers.

The fear and the desire in Gabriel were fusing into a kind of rage. Rage at himself for his weakness. Rage at his circumstances. Rage at this girl for toying with him. For using him as something to fill in the time with until she saw her boyfriend again.

"What the hell do you think you are playing at?"

He lent closer to her, fury on his face. His features rigid like steel.

And then it overcame him. He gripped her by her shoulders, pressed his mouth on hers. Hungry, hard. Forcing her to open to him, exploring her, tasting her.

Five years of drought and desert and she was an oasis.

He broke off. "Is this what you wanted?" He was glaring at her, his eyes narrowed with lust and anger.

"No, I..." Before she could finish responding his lips were on hers again. He pushed her hard against the wall, crushing her against him. His mouth moved over her cheek, her jaw, her neck. He forced her legs apart with his knee and rammed it up between them. He felt her gasp as he did so.

Leonie was in a terrifying kind of heaven. Every cell and fibre of her body wanted him. She ached for his touch. She wanted him to crush her, hold her, devour her. Yet his wild rage scared her. That she could have unleashed this in him.

She felt his right hand slip between them, moving over her breast. Moulding it so firmly that it was almost uncomfortable. His thumb brushing over her, making her tauten through her school uniform. She shuddered, and the cry in her throat was stifled before it began as his mouth found hers again.

Her arms were around him, feeling the muscles of his back through his clothing. Never had she wanted someone so much.

Then he turned her around. Pushed her so she was bent over one of the desks. His hand went under her skirt and she felt him try to tug her underwear down. She knew what he wanted, and she wanted it too, but not like this. Not the first time. Her first time.

"Stop!" She wrestled to get away from him. He stepped back from her. "I can't... I haven't done his before," she told him.

She looked terrified. Gabriel was appalled. He had practically tried to force himself on a girl who was not only inexperienced but his student. He could say nothing to defend himself. The desire and the rage ebbed out of him as quickly as it had flared up. He couldn't speak, he was so horror-struck by what he had done.

They stared at one another, Leonie pale and stricken, her hair and clothes dishevelled and her lips bruised from his kisses. Gabriel finally broke the silence.

"I don't know what to say to you. Or even where to start."

Leonie couldn't even speak. She had expected him to be even more furious when she stopped him, but instead his face was sorrowful.

"I'm sorry," she managed.

"You're sorry?" He was incredulous. "Leonie, it's not you that needs to apologise." He needed time. He couldn't even think straight.

Before either of them could speak again they heard someone enter the chapel. They both froze. Then Leonie managed to recover herself and slipped out of the vestry door, and fled.

15

Remorse. It throbbed through Gabriel like a punch in the gut with every heartbeat. The guilt was so heavy he could barely breathe.

His head was trying to deal with a complex mix of emotions. Sorrow and regret for his breach of vows and his duty to his God should have been foremost. But it was not.

Instead, his greatest agony was having hurt and frightened someone who had become dear to him. Someone he liked as well as desired.

Gabriel buried his head in his hands. To hope for Leonie's forgiveness was too much to ask.

Only then did he confront his greatest sin: his violation of his sacred duty. He had thought he would always be strong enough to uphold it. He had committed to it. With all his physical and mental strength and courage he had sought to observe those vows.

And now this.

On top of this he faced another spiritual quandary. Having committed a grave sin he was obliged to seek penance. As a priest, how could he consecrate the Eucharist, administer and receive Holy Communion, without absolution?

Yet he shrank from confessing before Father Stephen. Perhaps he could make an excursion and find another church? Confess instead to some anonymous priest.

He knew it was cowardice and hated himself for it.

He deserved to have Leonie report him to Mother Benedict. By rights he should be sacked and sent on his way. Kicked out of the priesthood.

Yet he sensed she wouldn't do this.

The worst thing of all was that he missed her. He still wanted her. He should be feeling the greatest sorrow for his faith and his conduct. But he felt it for her absence.

Father Stephen noticed that his younger colleague was suffering some crisis of faith. Gabriel was throwing himself into his duties with a unusual zeal. He spent nearly all his spare time in the chapel, working or praying. He no longer laughed but was serious at all hours of the day.

Gabriel had even taken to marking schoolwork in the vestry office rather than at the presbytery. Father Stephen missed his company in the evenings, when he would read while Gabriel worked. Gabriel no longer even watched television: he spent every spare moment in chapel.

It was not unexpected: many priests wrestled with aspects of their religion at any time of life. Just as all believers did. It was only human to doubt and question, before the reaffirmation came.

"You're working very late nights in the office," Father Stephen observed. It was his little joke to refer to the chapel as their office.

"I find it easier to focus there," Gabriel said. His tone was polite but closed. He offered no further explanation nor comment.

Aware that Gabriel did not yet wish to confide in him, Father Stephen discreetly put a few books in his way. They were volumes he had found helpful himself, on spiritual direction, faith and doubt, and the struggle of the clergy. He didn't know if Gabriel would read them but they were there if he needed them.

He would have suggested that Gabriel take a break and enter a spiritual retreat for some time, but there were two obstacles here. The first was that the younger man had not confided anything to him, nor asked for leave. The second was Gabriel's teaching work: it would seriously disrupt the students if he took extended time off.

Father Stephen wondered if he should discuss the matter with Mother Benedict but decided against it. If there were any problems with Gabriel in class, the headmistress would be sure to approach him with her concerns. Since she had not, Stephen would continue to give Gabriel time and pray for him.

Father Gabriel must hate and despise her. She had flung herself at him, tempted him to nearly break his vows, and then she had pushed him away.

There was a name for what she had done and it wasn't a nice one.

What were you thinking? Leonie berated herself. He was a priest. He deserved more respect. He had shown her friendship and she had ruined everything.

She was frustrated with herself for panicking. Because she did want him more than anything. She would have lost her virginity to him, willingly. The pace had just been a little fast, the location insecure. Her mind had been more hesitant than her body.

What was she going to do? Leonie thought of faking sickness for a week just to try and avoid him. But she doubted her ability to pull the wool over Matron's eyes. She had heard enough tales of Matron seeing straight through talcum powder-whitened faces and fake stomach pains to know that it would take more than acting ability to convince her.

She could run away. But to where? It would cause the row of all rows if she showed up at her grandmother's, and totally wreck all her college plans.

The one person she wanted was Gabriel. His kindness and his intelligence. His strength.

And she had lost him forever.

Leonie struggled to hide her mood from the others. Her best "bright face" wasn't enough to hide her turmoil.

"Something's up with you," Mai said.

"Malaise," Leonie told her.

Mai looked at her searchingly. "Do you get depression? Like PMT or something?"

"Sort of. Sorry if I'm being a drag, it will pass soon."

The only time Leonie felt free of it all was during rehearsals, where she flung herself into the role of Abigail like never before. It was the only way she could unleash emotion. Her performance became brilliant but frightening. She seemed to be actually possessed, as Abigail had merely feigned to be.

Somehow Leonie managed to get through the next week. She dreaded English lessons as much as she longed to see Father Gabriel. She didn't put up her hand when he asked the class questions even when she knew the answers. She avoided catching his eye.

When he turned to write something on the board she allowed herself to gaze at him. The back of his head was so perfectly shaped: the way his hair tapered to his neck. His shoulders were broad and proportioned and she remembered the strength of his arms.

I'm sorry. She silently willed the words towards him, wishing she could communicate with him. Wishing he might forgive her.

He never showed anger or disgust towards her. He was simply polite but grave.

It hurt.

It didn't help that Suki Laverne was being more and more of a bitch. Leonie wasn't sure why, but the other girl always seemed to be on her back. Maybe it was because Leonie was doing well in rehearsals. Leonie knew this because she herself felt that she was performing better, but also because others had told her.

Even Father Gabriel, though he was trying not to interact with her, had commented on her progress. His praise was cool and detached but this only made it more meaningful.

After rehearsal Leonie, Mai and Figgy were making a late evening cocoa in the Upper Sixth form refectory. This was a room that girls in the final year had the privilege of using, to relax in and make hot drinks. It had battered old arm chairs, tables where you could do homework and shelves with various old novels. They were all respectable works such as Jane Austen and Charles Dickens. The nuns confiscated any modern novels that they considered unsuitable, which was most of them.

Mai was discussing the last rehearsal. "With the rest of us it's like Father Gabriel knows we need lots of encouragement, as most of us are hopeless. With you he takes it for granted that you can do it."

"I wish," Leonie said.

"You must know how good you are," Mai said, heaping chocolate powder into her mug. "Just so long as you don't forget us when you're famous. Make sure you invite us to lots of celebrity parties."

Figgy, who had volunteered to be prompt, had noticed Suki's antipathy to Leonie. "She looks absolute daggers at you and she's always muttering with her friends. Do be careful of her."

"I'm not sure what I can do. It's not like I go out of my way to speak to her," Leonie said.

"At least Mercy has your back. Suki was trying to slag you off to her, but Mercy wouldn't listen to it," Mai told her.

Leonie was glad of this, since she liked Mercy.

"I don't know why she's still so jealous," Figgy said. "The role of Elizabeth is about the same size as Abigail. I think she even has more lines."

"But it's a duller part," Mai said. "Abigail is clearly the star. She gets all the sexy bits too."

Leonie had flashbacks to Father Gabriel voicing John Proctor's lines. Trying to fend off Abigail's advances. The parallels to her own situation were shamefully clear.

Mai was hunting through a jar of cookies. Or biscuits, as she called them. "Some greedy cow has eaten all the nice ones. All the custard creams are gone. There are only boring old digestives left, and they're all broken."

"I've got some chocolate hob nobs left in my tuck box," Figgy offered. "I can get them if you want?"

"It's alright, these will do." Mai crunched a digestive. "You know, while Mercy is great, it would be cooler if we had actual men playing the male roles. Imagine Father Stephen as Danforth, he'd be quite chilling, wouldn't he? And of course Father Gabriel as John Proctor. Just think of him saying those lines to you, Leonie."

Leonie didn't need to imagine this. She had heard the real thing.

Mai continued to crunch on her cookie. "I swear that man has a thing for you. If he wasn't a priest, you'd have to watch out."

"I thought so before," Figgy agreed, dunking a piece of biscuit in her mug. "Now I'm not sure. He seems more formal than he was."

"That's because he's trying to suppress his feelings. It's like The Thornbirds," Mai said. She was half-joking and it was all Leonie could do not to react.

She was very thankful that Harry wasn't there. After their conversation the other day, Harry might have started to put two and two together. "I haven't seen The Thornbirds," Leonie said.

"You should. It's pretty miserable though, they all die. But the main girl gets to sleep with the sexy priest, so that part's good. And he gets her pregnant," Mai told her. "There used to be a copy of the original novel around here, but Mother Benedict stole it. I'm quite sure she read it before burning it. I imagine it inspiring her to give Father Stephen steamy looks and try to get him alone. Imagine if they had a baby. She'd probably do a Virgin Mary and claim it was actually God who impregnated her."

Figgy couldn't help laughing even though she tried to disapprove. "You'll get struck with a bolt of lightning one day, Mai."

Leonie managed to fake a laugh as well but the whole subject was torment to her. If she hadn't panicked and stopped him, such a thing might have happened to her. And there was no way her acting skills were up to the task of passing Father Gabriel's baby off as a divine conception.

16

The following weekend there was a school excursion to an ancient holy well. It was up in the hills behind St Winifred's, beside a ruined cottage.

Leonie was looking forward to going as it would be a break in routine. It would also be a relief to get out of the confines of the school and clear her head. At least she wouldn't have to worry about bumping into Father Gabriel around every corner, and suffering what she interpreted as his cold disdain.

The others weren't so excited about the trip.

"We go at least once a year," Mai said. "It's this endless trek to a load of rubble, and Mother Benedict or whatever nun is with us says a prayer. Then we eat sandwiches and walk back home."

It sounded just the kind of thing that Leonie had read about in English adventure stories. There would always be something like robbers hoarding stolen gold up a chimney. Or a wounded German spy lurking about the place, with a bunch of plucky picnickers solving the mystery and saving the day.

She mentioned this to the others, who laughed at her. "It's just fields for miles. The cottage is half fallen down. We're not even allowed to go inside it any more as it's unsafe," Figgy said.

Harry wasn't coming because she had a lacrosse match. "Though I don't know if we'll get to play as I'm sure it's going to rain. Heavily too," she said. "You'll all get soaked if it starts when you're at the well.

The weather forecast was dry with light drizzle at most. Sister Barbara, who was leading the outing, insisted they would be fine.

"We'll wear raincoats just in case, and be back well before dark," she told them.

Leonie packed her sandwiches and a water bottle into a small bag, as well as her camera. "Can't you drink from the well?" she asked.

"Years ago they used to. But then some farmer told them there were sheep droppings in it, or was it sheep carcasses? Anyway we don't anymore," Figgy said.

They set off shortly after lunch time. The well was only a couple of miles away and it took no longer than an hour to hike there. The grass was thick and it was more tiring trudging through it than over a regular road surface. Sister Barbara appeared to have the sprightliness of a mountain goat and was constantly calling for any stragglers to keep up. "In my schooldays I walked twice this distance to school and back, morning and afternoon. It's good exercise for you."

As they climbed the view became quite spectacular. Rolling green hills, the valley, pockets of woodland. It reminded Leonie of the countryside around Massachusetts yet it was different. She couldn't put her finger on why. It smelt different, that was certain.

They paused for a break half way up and looked back.

"The sky is a bit glowering," Mai said. "I wish Harry hadn't said what she said. She's always right about the weather. It's uncanny."

The three of them looked up at the sky. It was still clear but there was a grey cloud on the distant horizon.

"The air feels heavy. But I don't know if that's just me, struggling up this slope," Leonie said, taking a few photographs of the view.

They continued on their way. By the time they reached the holy site there was already a slight drizzle in the air and definitely more wind.

Sister Barbara was determined to be resilient. "We've come all this way, girls, I'm sure light rain won't be a problem. We all have our raincoats."

She led the prayers and then they sat around in the drizzle and ate their sandwiches. It wasn't a very joyful picnic.

Following this everyone went to take a look at the well. There wasn't much to see. Some mossy stone slabs surrounding a hole coming out of the hillside. "Where are the dead sheep?" Leonie asked. The water looked clear enough.

"It might have been one of those microbes you can get in water. I know they've always told us not to drink it," Mai said.

"We could boil it and make tea. If we had a fire," Leonie suggested. She was dying for a hot drink. The sky had darkened to a leaden grey and it was uncomfortably cold and windy.

The ruined cottage nearby was even less impressive. Ivy grew through the broken rafters of the roof, and one wall was tumbled down. It was more like a cave than a cottage.

"Don't go inside, girls, it's not safe," Sister Benedict told them.

Leonie took some photos of it, as well as of Mai, Figgy and herself. They were all looking bedraggled from the damp.

"Sister, it's starting to get really wet," someone said

The nun cast a glance at the sky. "It does appear to be falling a little heavier. We'd better start back immediately."

They packed up the remains of the chilly picnic and set off back to the school. Leonie was glad to be on the move again, if only because the exercise kept her warmer than sitting about.

They had nearly reached St Winifred's when Leonie suddenly realised she hadn't got her camera with her. She asked Mai and Figgy if they had it or had seen it, but they hadn't. Then Leonie remembered: she had put it on a stone slab while shoving her water bottle back in her bag. How could she have been so careless? It was an expensive one too, a birthday present from her aunt and uncle. It would be wrecked if it was left out there all night, even if no one stole it.

"I'll have to go back for it," she said.

"You can't possibly. The weather's absolutely foul," Figgy said.

"It's just rain and I'm already wet. If I get it now I've got a chance to dry it out. It might still be okay."

Mai offered to go back with her but Leonie refused. "There's no point you getting into trouble. I'll be fine. I'll go really fast. There's over an hour of or of daylight left, and I'll see the lights of the school even if it's growing dark by the time I'm back."

Her friends were very reluctant to let her venture back by herself but Leonie was adamant. She slipped off and ran back up the hillside before Sister Barbara could see and call her back.

Leonie had gone about half way when the sky cracked with thunder and torrential rain began to plummet down. She realised her mistake. She had merely been wet-haired before but now, despite her raincoat, she was getting soaked to the skin. Should she turn back? She figured she was past half way, she may as well get her camera.

Over the next twenty minutes the winds whipped up even worse and Leonie was caught in a full blown storm. She could barely see, the gale and the rains were lashing her face and blinding her. What the hell had she done?

She reached the site and was relieved to see her camera, though it was dripping wet. She picked it up and turned to go.

108

But the storm was in full force. Leonie realised there was no way she was going to make it to St Winifred's until it abated. Since the only place offering shelter was the ruined cottage, she took the risk of going inside.

Leonie was shivering and miserable and knew that she would be in huge trouble. If she didn't die of hypothermia first. She sat down on a stone slab at the back of the cottage and waited for the skies to calm.

Sister Barbara did a headcount as she hurried the girls into the warmth and dry of the school. Leonie's absence was noticed almost immediately.

"Who is missing? Where is Leonie Wilson?" she asked them.

There was an uneasy look among the students. Figgy and Mai had to confess. They were both getting very worried about Leonie due to the worsening weather. "She forgot her camera at the well. She was worried about it getting damaged by the rain."

Sister Barbara was exasperated. "She went back for a camera? Alone, in this terrible weather?"

"It was only just raining when she started. She thought that she could get back while it was still light," Figgy said.

The storm was battering the window panes, causing the evening to be prematurely dark. To think of anyone out there on this wild night was troubling. Sister Barbara went immediately to Mother Benedict. Her footsteps echoed down the stone floor of the corridor as she strode purposefully to the headmistress's study.

She knocked and entered before waiting for a reply. There she found Mother Benedict, in conference with the two priests. They were discussing the order of service to commemorate St Winifred's Day, and some other ecclesiastical matters.

"Reverend Mother, may I have a word with you? In private," Sister Barbara asked. She judged it best not to inform the two priests just yet about the missing girl.

"Of course." Mother Benedict rose, seeing the urgency on the nun's face. "You will excuse me." She stepped outside into the corridor where Sister Barbara told her what had happened.

"I can't imagine what she was thinking. I expect she wasn't thinking at all," Sister Barbara said.

The headmistress's face grew grave. "Foolish girl. I suppose the storm was not forecast, but one would think with the rain... Still, what's done is done. We must send out a search party. I am not sure that we ought not to call the police."

"I had thought of that, Mother, but by the time they are here..."

"Indeed. There is no time to be lost." She went back into the office to inform the two priests. "Sister Barbara brings troubling news. One of the girls on the excursion to the holy well has not returned. She went back for a lost camera, shortly before the storm broke out."

Without even being told the name, Gabriel felt a cold fear creep through him. "Which girl?" he asked.

"Leonie Wilson. The American student."

Leonie. If anything happened to her... Gabriel tried to put the thought out of his mind. "I'll go and find her."

Mother Benedict frowned. "We had thought, of course, to put together a search party, and to call the police."

Gabriel interrupted her. "There isn't time for all that. With the very greatest respect, I have the best chance of getting there quickly among all of us. There's no need for several people to get drenched in the storm." He turned to Sister Barbara. "It's not far, is it? I should be able to make it in forty minutes or less?"

"Not much more, at a good pace," Sister Barbara agreed.

"Great. If you can fetch me a torch, some waterproofs and a couple of flares, I'll head out straight away. I'll send one flare if I find her. Two if I don't, or we need the emergency services. Give me an hour."

"What about a Thermos of hot tea?" Mother Benedict suggested.

Every minute it took to boil a kettle would be a minute that Leonie was alone out there, but Gabriel nodded. "I'll grab my coat." He hastened to the presbytery, threw on a waterproof jacket and swapped his regular shoes for hiking boots. Mother Benedict met him back at the front door holding some emergency supplies, including a storm lantern.

"God go with you, Father. We shall all pray for you," she told him. She repeated the basic directions to the well.

Gabriel thanked her and strode off. His one thought was that with every one of his heartbeats, Leonie was lost somewhere, cold and alone.

He hiked and ran up the hillside. He felt as though someone were guiding him. He hadn't visited the well himself yet: it was one of those things he kept putting off. Despite never having travelled this way, his feet found the path.

The storm was at its blackest, the wind howling. His jacket thankfully kept most of the water off him. But it still got under the hood and drenched his face and the front of his hair. The rain was blinding.

Storm flakes were scroll-leaved flowers, lily showers—sweet heaven was astrew in them

Hopkins' verse rang through Gabriel's head. The prospect of Leonie ending up as a sacrifice to the storm was unthinkable.

He forged ahead. In his haste he hadn't really considered the consequences of what would happen if he didn't find her.

Temperatures weren't yet falling to zero at night. But hypothermia was still possible, particularly with the rain. He said a silent prayer. He could not lose her.

17

Leonie knew that she would have to spend the night in the ruined cottage. It was already dark, the howling sky as black as pitch. Even if it ceased she doubted there would be sufficient moonlight and stars to get back safely to the school. The hill would be treacherously slippery.

You were supposed to stuff crumpled newspaper down your clothes to insulate yourself against the cold in an emergency like this, but she didn't have anything like that with her. She sat and shivered and hugged herself. The wind blew sharply through the broken roof and the window had no glass in it. Outside was a black void.

She tried not to despair. She tried to remember the brave nuns in The Wreck of the Deutschland, and their courage as they went down with the ship. This made her feel even worse, and tears came to her eyes.

After what seemed like ages, like a miracle, she saw a tiny pinpoint of light through the empty window. It appeared to be jumping around, or swinging. Her first wild thought was that it was something magical like a fairy. Then she managed to come to her senses and realised it was some kind of torch.

Someone was coming! Her heart leapt even as new fears came. What if it was a murderer? Or worse, what if it was Mother Benedict come to berate her for being such an idiot? Leonie almost wanted not to be found if that was the case.

Then she heard her named called. "Leonie? Leonie?"

She knew the voice.

It was him.

Leonie instantly felt safe. She felt saved.

But she was so cold that she found she could hardly call out in reply. "I'm here." There was no way he would hear her. His own voice sounded faint enough.

The lantern light grew nearer and joy of joys, he came to the cottage and found her.

For a moment he stood there and she looked at him. Both of them were too overcome to speak.

Then she was in his arms. Strong, sheltering arms.

"Thank God, Leonie. I was starting to fear the worst."

Leonie could not speak. She clung to him, shivering violently.

"You're freezing." Gabriel pulled off his raincoat and wrapped it around her shoulders while she still held on to him. She could feel the warmth of his chest now, through the fleece he wore underneath.

"Come on, sit down. I've got some hot drink." He manoeuvred her to the slab she had been sitting on and set the storm lantern on the mantel above the ruined fireplace. He brought the flask out of his bag. He poured some out and helped her sip it. Her fingers were initially too cold and stiff to hold the cup.

"I have to send off a flare to let them know I've found you. Keep warm with that. I won't be long."

Gabriel stepped outside again and sent a single emergency flare up. He hoped they would be able to see it back at the school. Then he went back inside.

Leonie, drinking from the cup, looked up at him. "Thank you for coming to find me. I realise how stupid I was. I thought I was going to be here all night."'

114

"The moment I heard you were missing…" Gabriel couldn't continue. He was gazing at her, and the intensity of his blue eyes almost unnerved her. She couldn't be imagining it.

"I thought you must hate me, after what I did the other day. I'm so sorry," Leonie told him.

He was bewildered. "Me hate you? What on earth for? I assaulted you. I can't even begin to apologise for my actions that day. Or for failing to make amends to you since."

"Assault me? I wanted you," Leonie said.

"You asked me to kiss you. You didn't ask me to force myself upon you, or to be so rough with you. I was angry with a lot of things and I lost it, but there's no excuse for what I did."

Leonie was beginning to feel a wonderful warmth in the pit of her stomach. All her fears about him hating her were dissolving. "So you're not mad at me?"

"Of course not! Quite the reverse." Gabriel was astounded that she had thought this, and it made him feel even worse.

"I did want to sleep with you. I know that's very wrong," she said quickly. "But I did. I just got scared because of where we were, and someone finding us."

She had wanted him too? In his frenzy of rage and lust he had barely been aware of her responses. Now, in the dim glow of the storm lantern, he saw her eyes shining at him. Trusting him, desiring him.

"Who was the man?" Gabriel asked. His tone was suddenly stern.

"What?" Leonie was confused.

"Who was the man, you made the confession about?" He was looking down at her, demanding an answer. His hair fell over his forehead, still damp from the rain.

Leonie smiled, realising his misplaced insecurity. She looked up at him. "You."

"You made that confession about me?" There was wonderment on his face. All this time he had imagined another rival, some mystery man.

"Of course it was about you," Leonie said. "Why would you think it was someone else? I was so embarrassed, I assumed you had guessed."

Now that Gabriel thought about it, he wondered why he hadn't. "I suppose I thought that with my being a priest, I wouldn't be an object of interest."

Quite the reverse, Leonie thought. His unavailability had only fuelled his attractiveness.

"Being a priest, do you ever have objects of interest yourself?" she asked.

"What do you think?" He lowered his face to hers.

Father Gabriel's lips were on hers. This time firmly but tenderly, just as Leonie had always imagined.

He cradled the back of her head with his hand as he deepened the kiss. Drawing her lip between his, he tasted her and probed her, his tongue entwining with hers.

Leonie felt her heart flutter in her chest. He wasn't angry with her. He liked her. He wanted her.

She was starting to realise the depth of how she felt about him, and it was even more.

Gabriel broke off. "I want you so badly," he said. "I know it's wrong." He kissed her again, increasing in passion as his hands moved over her back.

How could anything that felt this good be wrong?

Leonie closed her eyes as his lips found her neck. She felt him drawing in her skin, which made her whole body throb. But then he stopped.

"I can't leave a mark on you."

"I wish you would."

Her voice was the sexiest thing Gabriel had ever heard. Had they been in any slightly more comfortable setting he would have lain her down and taken her. Peeled off her clothes, made love to every inch of her body.

It had never felt this way before. Not with Joanne, not with any of the earlier girlfriends he had had. He was more aroused and inflamed just from kissing this girl than from anything he had done with women in the past. Without even making love to her fully.

How he longed to do that. Even as he imagined it, the shadow of the church and his vows fell over the shining scene. He drew away from her.

"You know that once we get back, we have to forget this," he told her.

Leonie looked stricken. "Do we?"

"You're my student, you're years younger than me, and I'm a priest. None of those obstacles are surmountable." Gabriel looked sad as he said this.

Leonie tackled the first one. "In only about half a year I won't be your student any more, and I'm already a legal adult."

"It's still not right."

"If I were thirty, and you were, what?" She didn't actually know how old he was.

"Thirty-seven."

"No one would think anything of that, would they? Or if we were sixty and sixty-seven. Or ninety and ninety-seven," Leonie pointed out.

Gabriel pushed back a strand of hair that still clung to her face, now dried of rain. "But we're not."

"But we could be. We will be one day." Even if we're not together, Leonie thought.

Gabriel had a sudden flash of being with Leonie in ten, twenty and then fifty years' time. What an amazing life that would be, if it were a possibility for him.

But it was not. For there was the third thing, the thing that neither of them mentioned. Because it couldn't be got past. He couldn't think about "if only".

"Please kiss me again. If this one night is all I can ever have with you, I want to remember it," Leonie said.

Gabriel could not resist her or deny her. He brought his lips on hers again, the urgency in him rising. One night, he thought. He'd have to confess and do absolution for it regardless. So why not go for broke? He kissed her eyes, her forehead, her cheeks. He brought his mouth to hers, growing demanding, bruising her lips.

He heard her whimper and it only increased his ardour. He wanted to be a man, a normal man, for just one night. One hour, even.

The raincoat had fallen from Leonie's shoulders so he picked it up and spread it on the floor. Then he laid her on it. He lay over her, wanting her to feel his weight, his power. She had asked for this. Though he wouldn't go all the way, how could he? She was a virgin and it was a step too far.

But he intended to get close.

"Call me by my name, Leonie," he murmured in her ear.

"Gabriel?" It was uncertain on her lips.

"Gabe." He was a different person. He was his past self. Just for this one more, one last time.

"Gabe." She repeated it and he felt himself burn for her.

"I want to take you, Leonie. I want to spread you on this floor, have you naked beneath me. Make you mine. Make you realise what the hell you've done to me."

She shivered at the force in his words. Was he actually going to do that to her?

Gabriel loosened her clothing at the front, unbuttoning her school blouse, cupping his hand inside her bra. He moulded her breast in his hand, bringing his lips down on it. As he drew it firmly in his mouth, his tongue swirling around and tautening it, Leonie felt jolts go from her nipple to between her legs.

His other hand went beneath her skirt, caressing up her thigh. He slipped fingers under the fabric of her underwear, where she was already soaking wet for him. The heat and the wetness nearly drove Gabriel insane. He grazed her nipple with his teeth then brought his mouth back violently on hers, his fingers closing over her breast. He teased it and squeezed it until she gasped, muffled by his embrace.

He needed her to feel his frustration.

Leonie was powerless to resist Gabriel's touch. He was so forceful and assertive, and when he spoke to her she felt her insides melt.

As he lay over her, his body pressing into hers, grinding into her through her clothes, she felt a momentary anxiety. "You're not going to…"

"No. God knows I want to and it's going to take every ounce of self-control to hold back, but I'm not about to take your virginity, Leonie."

Even as he said the words, and she felt her face flush with embarrassment, she realised that she very much did want him to. "I wouldn't mind," she said. Her voice was barely a whisper.

But he could not go that far with her. Even when he slipped a finger inside her and groaned with desire, feeling her slick heat, he managed to resist what every cell of his body craved.

He wanted her helpless. He wanted to command her body so she would remember this always, and the power he could wield over her if he wished. At the back of his mind he felt a twinge of conscience but he angrily shut it off.

"Look at me, Leonie. I want you to come for me, and say my name when you do. I don't want you thinking about anyone else except me, and what I'm doing to you."

Gabriel thrust two fingers inside her now, his thumb rubbing against the front of her. Just where he knew it would bring her over. Instinctively she closed her eyes and moved her head to one side, her breathing growing ragged.

Roughly he forced her face back around to him. "Look at me. Say my name."

"Gabe." Her voice was husky.

"Tell me what you want," he demanded.

"I want you. And I don't want you to stop." Then suddenly Leonie was taken over the edge and she was crying out his name again and again, and writhing beneath his hands. He took possession of her mouth one more, ground his hips against her, and felt his own orgasm rise and pulse through him.

It was like being a schoolboy. He was still fully dressed, and he had lost all control of his body.

Gabriel managed to suppress any remorse directly afterwards. That could come tomorrow. Right now he had switched into another world. A world of darkness and temptation. A world where he desired to possess and control her, even as he sought to

120

revere her. She was the most beautiful and adorable girl he had ever met, and it nearly broke him to realise that one day she would belong to another.

Right now, even his faith, even God, did not seem enough compensation for that.

18

"A hot bath for you immediately, and then bed. I'll have some cocoa sent up." Mother Benedict's tone was brisk when Leonie arrived back at the school with Father Gabriel. "Father, I can't thank you enough for bringing Leonie back safely. I'm sure you need to get back into dry clothes yourself. We'll speak tomorrow."

Gabriel took his leave and Leonie went upstairs, escorted by Matron.

They had sheltered for another hour together, until the storm's raging had ceased. Leonie had felt a growing sense of desolation that this was the first and last time they could ever be together. It felt so right with him.

The things he had done to her body were things that no one else had managed to do. Not that she was super experienced, but still.

He had put his arm around her for most of the trek back, stumbling through the darkness. The rain had fallen to a light drizzle and while it was still windy the storm had played itself out.

The lights of St Winifred's should have been a welcome beacon but instead they seemed to Leonie like the security lights on a prison. Her heart sank as they approached, even though she was in need of warmth and dry.

As they neared, Father Gabriel had dropped his arm. Whatever they had done together, he was her priest and teacher again now. Anything else was off limits.

Soaking in a warm bubble bath, all Leonie could think was how much she wanted his hands on her body again. The rest of the school year was going to be torture.

She was sent to bed straight away in the san, with Matron putting a hot water bottle under the blankets for her. Leonie had protested that she wasn't ill but Matron overruled her. "We don't want you getting a chill and developing pneumonia," she said. "You'll stay in here for the night where I can keep an eye on you."

Leonie drank her cocoa, brushed her teeth, and slipped into bed. As she drew the covers up she thought that maybe it was a better idea, being here. She could be alone with her thoughts. If her dorm-mates had interrogated her about the rescue by Father Gabriel, she might have let something slip.

Despite hoping and imagining she would dream of him all night, she fell into a deep sleep. When she woke, she was alarmed to realise it was already past ten o'clock. It was Sunday, so there were no lessons to miss, but she had missed Mass.

Matron entered. She took Leonie's temperature and declared her fit to get up and rejoin her schoolmates. "There's no fever and you've had a good night's sleep. I imagine Mother Benedict will wish to speak with you later."

The prospect of this left Leonie feeling a sense of dread. What if she were expelled? Not only would her grandmother never forgive her, but she wouldn't get to see Father Gabriel ever again.

The headmistress summoned her just before lunch. Leonie stood before her desk, bracing herself for the worst.

"I'm sure you're well aware that you did an extremely foolish thing yesterday," Mother Benedict began.

She didn't know a fraction of it. God forbid she ever found out the rest. "I know. I'm very sorry. I had no idea the weather could turn like that."

Mother Benedict looked stern. "You must be aware that it is against school rules for any girl to wander off without permission, let alone by herself."

Leonie did her best to look contrite. She didn't really care much for the school rules, she was only obeying to save her skin. She was old enough to go for a walk in the rain if she wanted to.

"I'm very sorry," she repeated.

But the Mother Superior wasn't finished with her. "Not only did you risk your own safety, but you put the safety of another person in jeopardy. Father Gabriel took great personal risk in venturing out to find you. You are very lucky that he did so. Had he not found you, we would likely be having this conversation from a hospital bed. If we were able to have it at all."

"I am very grateful." More than you know, Leonie thought.

"This afternoon I would like you to go and apologise to him, and thank him for his efforts in restoring you to us." Leonie's heart leapt at this, but she kept her eyes down, trying to look demure, as Mother Benedict continued. "I am aware that you have been through an ordeal, which I imagine was very frightening and uncomfortable. That, and the remorse that I hope you feel, should be sufficient punishment."

She was going to get away with this? Leonie had expected to be suspended at the very least. "Thank you. It will."

Mother Benedict dismissed her. "Run along to lunch now. And try to behave with more sense and consideration in future."

Leonie's friends grilled her over lunch. They wanted to know everything that had happened.

"I was terrified for you when the storm broke out," Figgy said. "We should have listened to Harry."

Mai was more interested in finding out about Father Gabriel. "What was he like when he found you? Was he mad?"

Leonie felt her face grow red. "Not really. He was more concerned, and very kind."

"Did he make you pray?" Figgy asked.

"No. We just sat and waited it out," Leonie said.

Figgy was disappointed. "I had a romantic image of him clasping his hands and praying for the storm to be over and your lives to be spared."

Mai had noticed Leonie's reaction. She regarded her with narrow eyes. "So you just sat there, freezing cold and wet? He didn't try and warm you up?"

"Mai!" Figgy objected to the tone in which Mai said this, while Leonie nearly choked on the mouthful of water she had just drunk.

"I only meant offer Leonie a blanket or whatever. But I can see from her face that he did something."

Leonie chewed her lip. She was going to have to reveal a bit. "He did put his arm around me. But only because I was shivering so much."

"One arm or both arms?" Mai asked.

"Does it matter?" Figgy said

Mai grinned. "It matters a lot. One arm is no big deal. Two is an embrace."

Leonie knew her face was on fire. She was supposed to be a competent actress. Why couldn't she better keep her composure? "It was two arms. But only because it was so cold."

She had a feeling that Mai was not entirely satisfied by this answer, but Mai said no more.

After lunch Leonie made her way to the vestry to make her apology to Father Gabriel. She was dying to see him but she didn't think she had ever been so nervous in her life.

She entered. He was standing the other side of the room, in his priestly black. For a while they just stood there, gazing at one another. The vestry seemed to fade away and all she could remember was his lips on hers.

Leonie broke the silence. "I've come to thank you for last night. And to apologise for putting your safety in jeopardy." She used the same phrasing that Mother Benedict had.

"You don't have to thank me. I'm just glad you were okay," Gabriel said.

"I did have to thank you. Mother Benedict said I should. But I wanted to anyway," she said.

Gabriel came over to her and stood in front of her. "I know I owe you an apology for what happened there. But there's no point saying what we both know."

"Do you regret it?" Leonie asked.

"I should. But right now, I don't," Gabriel said. He looked into her eyes. "You know that if circumstances were different, Leonie, I would want to be with you. Even as your teacher, I would have taken that risk. But this" - he touched his collar - "forbids it."

Leonie felt she could hardly bear it. She wanted him so much. "Why did you become a priest?" she asked.

"I believed I had a vocation."

"Only believed? You weren't sure?"

Gabriel sighed. He sat on the edge of a desk. "When you start your training it's a long process. There's a lot of doubt, but it's encouraged. Of course I doubted. But I still chose it. That must mean something, mustn't it?"

He was looking at her now as though he wanted her sanction on his decision. But Leonie couldn't give it. She couldn't see how any God could give human beings the emotions and physical desire they had, and then require them to suppress it. Hardly any other religions or branches of Christianity required their priests to be celibate. If Gabriel had only been born into a different family: Protestant, or even Jewish or Muslim, he could have pursued holy orders and also enjoyed a family life.

The Catholic church was too severe an authority.

"I just wish you hadn't chosen it," she said.

It took the utmost resolve for Gabriel not to express the same wish. "It's the half-term holiday at the end of next week. It will give us both a break and help get things back in perspective. Even if I can't ever pursue a relationship with you, we can still be friends."

Leonie was happy to grasp any crumbs he offered. "You mean that?"

"Of course." He paused for a moment, and lowered his voice. "You know that I'll really miss you, when school is out. Even for a week. I look forward to seeing you in class and in rehearsals. I miss you when you're not there." He knew he shouldn't be saying these things to her but he couldn't help it.

"Will you write to me?" Leonie asked.

"If you give me your address."

He fetched a piece of paper and a pen. Leonie wrote her grandmother's address down. Gabriel folded the piece of paper carefully and put it in his pocket. "We'll get through this," he told her.

Leonie didn't see how. If it had just been a crush or a physical attraction, it would have been easier to get over. "I'll try," she said.

Her assent cut Gabriel to the core. Until she said the words, he hadn't realised how much he didn't want her to give up her feelings for him. He had spent so long brooding over the notion that she liked some other guy, that now he knew it was him, he wanted to hang on to it. Even though he knew how wrong and how hopeless it was.

"I'll see you in class tomorrow, then?" he asked.

She managed a weak smile. "I wouldn't miss it."

19

It should have been a huge relief to escape St Winifred's for a week and enjoy a lot more freedom at her grandmother's house in London. But all Leonie wanted to do was see Gabriel. Even if they couldn't be together, just seeing him around school was better than nothing.

He had acted as normally as possible to her in class and rehearsals. But there were times that they looked at one another, and she knew he was thinking about their time together. That one, stormy, stolen night.

A couple of times Leonie was tempted to wait until after class, stay behind, and just be in his arms. She was sure that if she did so, he wouldn't be able to resist her. Only she knew that he would feel terrible afterwards, so she held back.

One time he asked her to stay back after rehearsals.

"I just wanted you to know that this isn't easy for me. I don't want you to think I've simply cut you off," he said.

"Likewise." Was it ever going to get easier?

"I am very sorry for everything. I had no right to do what I did," he told her. "Not as your teacher, as your priest, as anything."

He had nothing to be sorry for, Leonie thought. "That one time with you was better than never being with you," she told him.

Gabriel gazed at her. His eyes were such an intense blue. "God, Leonie…" He lent towards her.

She had thought he might kiss her again, but they were interrupted.

It was Suki Laverne. "I'm so sorry," she smirked. "I hope I wasn't interrupting any extra rehearsals?" She put a nasty emphasis on these last words. "I forgot my folder."

Gabriel immediately straightened. "Is that it, over there?" He indicated a nearby chair.

It was. Suki took the item in question and flounced out, with an unpleasant smile.

Gabriel stood there awkwardly once she had left. "We'd better go," he said.

Leonie picked up her own things and left him. Tomorrow morning her grandmother's driver would be picking her up, and she wouldn't see him for ten days.

In London, Leonie's grandmother was pleased to hear that she was making progress with her studies and had made suitable-sounding friends. "Would those be the Davenports of Dorset? An old schoolfriend of mine married a cousin of theirs. You must invite Iphigenia to stay."

Leonie had no clue who the Davenports of Dorset were. Figgy had said her family lived in Somerset with a town house in London. She had actually invited Leonie to stay for the holiday, but Leonie had been forced to decline as she knew her grandmother would want her.

Both Figgy and Mai had tried to persuade her to get her grandmother's permission. Mai frequently stayed with Figgy's family for shorter breaks, as it was too far for her to fly back to her parents in Hong Kong. "It will be so much more fun, all three of us. We can always go and visit your grandmother in London, and catch up with Harry."

Harry's family owned a very grand house in central London, as well as a country estate. It was all very Jane Austen, Leonie thought. She half-imagined that Harry's parents drove between the two properties in a horse-drawn carriage.

But there was another reason why Leonie was reluctant to stay with Figgy. Father Gabriel only had her London address. She knew that she was going to be waiting for the mail every morning. She also couldn't risk her grandmother seeing it, in case she opened it. She wasn't sure if her grandmother would snoop or not, but masculine handwriting would definitely arouse her suspicions.

It was already Tuesday, and still no letter. How long did it take to mail a letter in Britain? It wasn't like it was a huge country. By Wednesday Leonie stressed and fidgeted and roused her grandmother's disapproval at breakfast.

"What is the matter? Is something wrong with your food?"

"It's fine, thank you," Leonie said. "I just wondered when the mail might come?"

"It comes at ten o'clock. Are you expecting a letter or parcel?"

"Maybe. A postcard from one of the girls who went overseas," Leonie lied.

Her grandmother looked bemused. "I should hardly think she would have time to write it yet, let alone have the postal service deliver it. You need to learn more patience, Leonie. It is a failing in young people these days, I have often observed."

Leonie mentally rolled her eyes and wished she could roll the clock forward. Part of the stress was preventing her grandmother from getting to the mail first. She tried to bury herself in an essay on The Crucible, but all she could think of was Father Gabriel grabbing her that time in rehearsals. How close they had come to kissing.

And what it felt like when they finally had…

Around half past nine her grandmother put on her hat and coat. "I'm going into town, would you like to accompany me? I need to visit the bank."

Leonie managed to decline gracefully, claiming she wanted to finish off her essay. "I'm nearly done, I'll forget it all if I break the flow."

Impressed by her granddaughter's commitment to her studies, Leonie's grandmother went off on her errands.

Leonie heard her grandmother close the door, and felt huge relief. She couldn't focus on her essay at all, with the clock gradually ticking towards ten. Finally she heard a rattle and light thud and practically fell of her chair racing to the door. There was no one else in the house who could beat her to the door, she was being absurd.

There was a pile of envelopes. Mainly for her grandmother: bills and things. And there, beneath them, was a white envelope with her name and address written in his handwriting.

Leonie simply held it for a while. And then she opened it, and drew out the paper inside.

Dear Leonie,

I've resolved that this is going to be a platonic, friendly piece of correspondence. Even as I write these words, I'm finding it a tough resolution to keep.

The fact is that it has been only two days and I already miss you more than I imagined possible. I never expected to face this kind of challenge in the life I chose. We were warned at the Seminary that the outside world wouldn't simply disappear once we entered orders. Perhaps it was arrogant, but I never thought that I'd find it a problem.

Now, it's the hardest thing in the world.

I remain determined to write to you as a friend. As promised.

I'm writing this letter from my room at St Beuno's in North Wales. It's a Jesuit college and retreat, the place in which Hopkins wrote The Wreck of the Deutschland. It seemed the ideal location to work on my thesis. It's a beautiful part of the country, the mountains of Snowdonia lie to the west, green fields stretching below. To the north, on a clear day one can see across to the coast. Today it's drizzling though not as much as Hopkins' "wiry and white-fiery and whirlwind-swivellèd snow".

It's a good thing that Hopkins didn't write love poetry, or I'd find myself writing many lines of it to you. "Grace you, bride, your bed" is about the closest, but the "lissome scions" would be something of a complication.

It's hard to get much work done around here. I'm frequently distracted. It's not difficult to guess why.

The reality is, my darling, and I'm aware that I shouldn't be calling you that, I can barely sleep for thinking about us. Instead of getting it out of my system, that time we spent together caused nothing but torment. On one hand there's the guilt, on the other hand the longing for a repeat performance.

In another life, this would be easier. We could wait out the school year, do what we wanted. Unfortunately that's not possible.

(The bell that summons guests to supper just went, which means putting the pen down for now)

10pm - apologies for the interruption.

Most meals here are in silence, usually accompanied by some music. The food is good, lots of fresh fruit and vegetables. The silence is supposed to be a liberation, to enable residents to move deeper into prayer and meditation. They don't even have phones here. Yet I struggle to concentrate. We see a retreat guide every day but I can hardly reveal what's on my mind.

It's late now. Bed beckons, naturally my thoughts are turning to you. It's a good thing that London is so far away. If there was the slightest chance of getting you here...

If this is a test from the Almighty, I'm failing abysmally.

Leonie, darling, it's night and the sky is bright with stars outside the window. "The fire-folk sitting in the air". I want you here.

What will happen, who can say. This can't go on, can it?

Well, time to seal this up. The morning post goes out first thing.

All my love, even if that should be friendship.

Gabriel

PS Read A Vision of the Mermaids. In particular lines 20-23. That's what I want to do to you.

Leonie read the letter twice, then a third time. It was more than she could have dreamt of. She went and fetched her copy of Hopkins' poems that she still hadn't returned to Gabriel. He had pretty much told her to keep them.

She found it at the start. It was one of his earliest poems, written when he was only eighteen. The same age she was. Leonie couldn't imagine writing something so brilliant. She counted to the lines in question, but she guessed which ones they were as soon as her eyes fell on them.

Now all things rosy turn'd: the west had grown
To an orb'd rose, which, by hot pantings blown
Apart, betwixt ten thousand petall'd lips
By interchange gasp'd splendour and eclipse

Leonie knew exactly what Gabriel was implying by referencing them. Even as she sat there alone she felt herself blush an even deeper crimson than the sunset Hopkins was describing. She was quite sure that the poet had never meant his verses to be interpreted as erotically as Gabriel was doing.

She wished she could phone him. She wanted to hear his voice. She lay on her bed, reading the letter again and then re-reading the poem.

20

Leonie had started writing a dozen letters and scrumpled them all up when she heard the phone ring. If she had had any realistic hope of it being Father Gabriel, she would have fled down the stairs to answer it. But he didn't have her number or even access to a phone at his retreat.

She had begun yet another attempt at replying to him when her grandmother knocked on the door. "Leonie? There's a telephone call for you. A girl who gave her name as Harriet."

Quickly pushing the latest "Dear Gabriel..." under some books, she followed her grandmother downstairs to the hall and picked up the receiver.

"Hello?" she answered.

"Leonie, it's me, Harry."

"I guessed so. How are you?"

Harry was fine and currently in London. She invited Leonie out shopping, and Leonie was glad to accept. She figured her grandmother would be unlikely to object to her spending the day with an Earl's daughter.

She was right. "How delightful," her grandmother said. "I trust you will be on your very best behaviour." There was a warning in her eye as she said this, and Leonie knew that she was thinking of the trouble that Leonie had got into back home. The reason why she had been sent over here for a year.

"Of course I will," Leonie said. She grabbed her purse and went out of the door. Her grandmother's house was only a few minutes' walk from a London Underground station, which was one of the few advantages of staying there. She could at least get out and about, and her grandmother was happy for her to visit museums and art galleries.

The previous day Leonie was supposed to have visited the National Science Museum, but had instead gone to a matinée in Covent Garden. She knew her grandmother did not greatly approve of the theatre. It was going to be very hard to get her support for going to Juilliard, if she even got accepted.

Harry met her on Oxford Street and they went to a nearby café. Harry usually shopped in Kensington but had thought that Leonie would enjoy more of a tourist trip. "You can get your Christmas presents early," Harry suggested. "I thought you might want to get some souvenirs for your boy back home. If you need me to post them secretly for you, it's no trouble."

"He's not actually in the US," Leonie said, then realised it was probably a mistake to have revealed this.

"Oh? He's in London, is he? If your grandmother's strict and you need me to cover for you so you can meet up with him, you need only ask."

"He's not actually in London," Leonie said. "It's still really up in the air. I'm not sure where we stand."

Harry grinned. "Well the offer's there, wherever he is. I'm guessing's he's not at St Winifred's at least."

Leonie choked on her coffee at this and Harry had to slap her on the back to stop her coughing. When Leonie had recovered, she realised Harry was looking at her searchingly. Harry was frowning.

"He's not at St Winifred's is he? I mean you couldn't possibly have hidden a boy up there. There are only two men in the place. Oh!" Harry stopped, seeing that Leonie had gone bright red.

Leonie tried to make light of it. "I'm never going to make a poker player, am I? Or an actress, with my lack of blush control."

"It's just a crush, right? Lots of girls have crushes on him, he's frightfully good looking," Harry said. She didn't even need to mention his name. They both knew she wasn't talking about Father Stephen. "I mean he doesn't know how you feel, does he?"

"He knows."

"But he hasn't reciprocated, surely?" Light began to dawn. "That night he rescued you from the storm. Did something happen?"

Leonie said nothing. Her face, once again, said it all.

"Oh my God, Leonie. But he's a priest! I mean I'm not personally very religious, but…"

Leonie felt utterly miserable. "I know. I'll get struck down by lightning."

"I didn't mean that," Harry said. "I meant that he must be awfully religious, to have taken orders. So he's stuck, isn't he? You poor thing. And a teacher too. You couldn't have really made it harder for yourselves, could you?"

Leonie toyed with her coffee mug. "You won't tell anyone, will you?"

Harry reassured her. "Of course not. I won't breathe a word, not even to the others. I simply wish I could help you, somehow."

"Do you think it's wrong?" Leonie said.

"Personally, no. You're both legal adults. My grandmother had an affair with her drawing master when she was a girl, it was all very Woman in White. Her parents nearly self-combusted when they found out, and sent her overseas."

"Did they end up together?" Leonie asked.

"Heavens, no. He was an utter drip by all accounts, and she was only sixteen. Barely a month later she fell head over heels in
138

love with a French count, my maternal grandfather. Then she discovered she was pregnant by the art master. Fortunately my grandfather was wild about her and adopted the child. It was terribly romantic," Harry said.

"The baby was your mother?"

"No, my uncle Julian. It all ended very happily, anyway."

Leonie couldn't imagine herself falling in love with anyone else so quickly. She had thought she had been in love before, but none of it remotely compared to how she felt about Father Gabriel.

Leonie finally managed to write a reply to him though she found it difficult. There was so much she wanted to say but didn't dare. She had bought some stamps and was able to mail it quickly in the morning before her grandmother could see.

She knew there wouldn't be time for him to reply to her before school started again. She had read his letter so many times that she knew it by heart.

She tried to enjoy the week. Her grandmother had taken her to the National Portrait Gallery and to lunch at a very expensive and upmarket restaurant. Leonie had done her best to be grateful.

Harry had invited her to a party, which had been fun, even if her grandmother had insisted on a midnight curfew. "I am a legal adult," Leonie had protested.

But her grandmother had put her foot down. "While you are in my care, you will live under my rules," she said.

Gabriel sat at the desk in his room, failing to make any progress on his thesis. He was supposed to pray for three sessions a day but he couldn't focus on that either.

He knew he had stepped over a dangerous line by writing the letter to Leonie. He had genuinely intended to keep it platonic. But the solitude here had made him long for her.

If only he had been sent on the inner city mission as he had wanted, rather than given a teaching job, none of this would ever have happened. Yet even as he considered how much easier his life might have been, he found he could not regret meeting her.

Was it a test? Was the whole point of falling for her, falling into temptation, some kind of trial to prove his commitment to his faith?

He re-read her letter to him.

I think about you every day. I wish I was there with you too. Every night I remember what it felt like being with you in the storm, and I want to be with you again.

I haven't ever felt like this about anyone. I just wish that you were free to do what you want, and I'm sorry if I shouldn't be wishing this.

What had he done? He should never have caused her this confusion, or given her expectations that could never be met. He knew how selfish it was of him.

How weak he had been.

Watch and pray, that ye enter not into temptation: the spirit indeed is willing, but the flesh is weak.

Gabriel had tried turning to his Bible but found no solace there. Lectio Divina, or Divine Reading, was one of the activities encouraged at St Beuno's. It should have brought him into closer communion with God. Read, meditate, pray, contemplate. He hardly got past the first step, and meditation was impossible with all this on his mind.

He had prayed extensively for forgiveness. For strength. For help.

It seemed that none came.

Gabriel travelled back to St Winifred's on Saturday, a day before the students returned. Father Stephen had remained behind in the presbytery, holding the regular services for the nuns who lived at the school all year round.

He had been happy to do this. He knew that his younger colleague needed some time away to resolve whatever it was that weighed on his mind.

Father Stephen was cutting up some vegetables to make an Irish stew for supper when Gabriel arrived. The weather was growing much colder now November was nigh, which called for wintry food.

"Welcome back. How did you find St Beuno's?" he asked as he chopped some carrots.

"Very beautiful. I can see why Hopkins was inspired," Gabriel said.

The older priest transferred the carrot from the chopping board to the pot. "I stayed there myself some years ago. I recall that it rained every single day. They continually suggested that we take walks, but what with the mud and the downpour, I must confess I spent most of my time indoors. I remember it being very green, but that's about it."

"It was very green."

Father Stephen put the lid on the stew pot and adjusted the flame to a lower setting. The he turned his attention more fully to Gabriel, scrutinising him.

"I know you have had things weighing on your mind. I hope the retreat may have brought you some relief regarding that."

Gabriel had hoped this as well, but if anything it had done the opposite. The absence from Leonie had only thrown his thoughts into deeper tumult. "Not exactly."

Father Stephen sat down at the table and indicated for Gabriel to take a seat. "We are not in the Confessional now," he said. "But if I can be of any help or guidance, you have only to confide in me. You are not the first priest to have had doubts or a crisis of faith, or whatever ails you. If I can be of service, I am here."

Gabriel pushed a hand through his hair. He could not tell Father Stephen the whole story, but perhaps confessing the outline would alleviate his turmoil.

"It may be a story you have heard before," he began. "When I committed to my vocation, there was no one and nothing that stood in the way. I freely and willingly dedicated my life to God. Then I met someone. And emotions I believed were long consigned to my former life began to re-emerge."

Father Stephen concealed a small smile. It was indeed a story he was familiar with. Celibacy was not an easy or even natural state for most of the human species.

From nearly the earliest he had known Gabriel, Father Stephen had been aware that the young man was suffering some internal conflict. Thus he now assumed the person Gabriel mentioned was someone he had met well before arriving at St Winifred's. He did not for a moment dream it might be a student at the school.

"Had you had experience with men or women before entering seminary?" he asked. He considered that Gabriel probably had, but there were some very naive young ordinands who entered orders as innocent as lambs. In Father Stephen's view, unorthodox as it perhaps was, it was better for a man to have some worldly experience before committing his life to the church.

"I did, with women. I was even engaged once, but it didn't work out," Gabriel told him.

Father Stephen felt some unease at this. There were those that entered the priesthood in all conscious sincerity, but motivated by

142

heartbreak or disillusionment. These were not healthy reasons to take orders. He remembered the wise words in a movie that was a guilty pleasure of his. "These walls were not built to shut out problems, you have to face them. You have to live the life you were born to live."

"And soon after this engagement was broken, you found yourself drawn to holy orders?" he asked.

Gabriel naturally became defensive at this. "It was sufficiently long afterwards that I had had time to think carefully about my choice. It was a matter I contemplated deeply at all stages of my ordination."

"This might be radical to propose, but is it possible the Lord put this person in your path to show you the error of your choice?" Father Stephen suggested. He saw Gabriel stiffen at this, which told him that he was on the right track. "Let me put it another way. Your choice was right for you and the Church at the time. But an extended service was perhaps not part of the divine plan. The Church does not brand you nor does it chain you, Gabriel. You can at any time leave, freely and gladly."

He stopped, giving Gabriel time to absorb his words.

"There are even those who have left the priesthood to find closer salvation through Jesus Christ," the older priest continued. "I have a book which I should have shared with you earlier. It may give you some insight into your own heart and soul, and the path which lies before you."

"You've read this book? Did it turn you away from your vocation?" Gabriel asked.

Father Stephen set his cup back down on the saucer. "For me it was the reverse. The experiences and analysis in the book reaffirmed that my duties as a priest were the right life for me. But for you that may not be the case."

He stood up again, moving back to the stove to check the simmer level of the stew. "There is no single way to serve the Lord, Gabriel. One does not have to be a priest to live a life in His service."

21

Mother Benedict had a surprise announcement at the first assembly after the half-term vacation.

"As you may know, the actress Anthea Flyte is one of our most renowned old girls. She studied at the Royal Academy of Dramatic Arts after leaving St Winifred's, and went on to have a very successful career on the stage and screen. I am sure we have all enjoyed many of her performances over the years."

Mai nudged Leonie and muttered under her breath. "She's pretty much the only renowned old girl the school has produced. Unless you count missionaries."

Leonie had heard of Anthea Flyte and had seen her in a movie. She was primarily a stage actress.

"Miss Flyte was recently appointed to the board of RADA. She has written to me to announce a new scholarship for a girl from St Winifred's to attend the Academy. Such a girl will, of course, need to win a place there through the usual route. But if there is a successful applicant, she will enjoy free tuition, living accommodation and expenses during her three years in London."

There was a buzz of interest at this news. While many of the girls came from families who could afford to pay for a university degree, to get a scholarship would be hugely prestigious.

To Leonie it would mean the world. She wouldn't need her parents' or her grandmother's approval. She could pursue her chosen career, from an amazing start.

And she would be in the same country as Gabriel. Her dreams of Juilliard had already been overshadowed by the prospect of being an ocean away from him. Even if he continued to reject anything more than friendship, she couldn't bear the thought of being so far from him.

Leonie looked over towards where he was sitting with other staff members. He looked incredibly handsome but she didn't dare to catch his eye. Now that she knew he had feelings for her it was all starting to feel like too much of a risk.

Instead she glanced down at her hymnbook. He was surely going to talk to her and not avoid her. She didn't think she could bear it if he blew cold again.

Outside, many students were talking about the scholarship. Leonie remembered how she had felt when she had seen the exterior of the famous Royal Academy of Dramatic Arts in London. It had only been a short detour from the British Museum on one of her sightseeing trips, and she hadn't been able to resist dropping by. She had simultaneously felt an excitement at seeing it, coupled with a despair that her grandmother would probably reject such a dream outright.

Now there was a chance. A small, shining chance.

Of course it all hung around getting accepted there. The application process involved several rounds of auditions, and there were over a hundred applicants for every place. There was every chance that no one from St Winifred's would be successful.

Leonie saw Suki shoot her a glare. She realised the other girl was as determined as she was to apply for the scholarship. Suki would be no easy competition. The prospect of more than one student from a single school winning a place must be vanishingly small as well.

As they walked to English class, Mai and Figgy were urging Leonie to apply. "You're the most talented actress here, you could easily beat Suki Laverne," Figgy said.

"I'd like to see you get it just so I could see the look on that cow's face," Mai said.

Leonie wondered how many students might apply.

"It's hard to say," Figgy said. "There may be people who weren't considering studying theatre who decide to give it a go. I believe the application process is very tough though. There are endless rounds of auditions. A cousin of mine had a friend who applied, but she didn't get all the way through."

It sounded pretty similar to Juilliard. To get into that school also required various auditions and call-backs. Leonie knew it was going to be a long and difficult path to follow her dream career, but she was determined to do all she could to get there. Nothing felt so right as being on stage, getting inside the skin of a character.

They arrived at the English classroom and took their places, waiting for Father Gabriel to arrive. Harry shot Leonie a glance, guessing what she must be going through. They had spoken briefly about it the previous evening, out of earshot of Figgy and Mai. It wasn't that Leonie didn't trust the other two, it was just such a huge secret that it seemed unwise to let too many people know. Harry had effectively guessed.

There was also something very independent about Harry. She went her own way and did her own thing. She didn't care what other people thought, and didn't judge Leonie for having fallen in love with a priest.

The door opened and the man in question entered. Leonie's stomach turned over. Somehow she got through the lesson on a kind of autopilot.

Afterwards, when the bell went and Father Gabriel dismissed the class, Leonie gathered up her folders, intending to leave with the others.

But he called out to her just before she could exit.

"Leonie Wilson, could you please see me for a moment." His tone was entirely cold and formal.

Was he angry? What had she done?

Feeling her stomach flip with nerves, she stayed behind.

To Leonie's relief, as soon as the last girl was out of the door and safely down the corridor, Father Gabriel's attitude relaxed.

"I've missed you."

It was all she needed to hear. She had been so worried he was going to slam the door shut, figuratively. "I've missed you too."

He looked at her for a while. "I guess you know how I feel about you."

"Do I?" Leonie actually wanted to hear it from him.

He gave a half smile, that was more sad than joyful. "I'm in love with you. But I shouldn't be. The question is what we're going to do about it."

Do about it? Couldn't they just give in to it and be together?

He continued. "So far prayer and trying to convince myself I'll get it out of my system isn't working."

"I don't want you to get it out of your system," Leonie said. She felt annoyed at the idea, and scared.

"What I should do is go very far from here for a very long time, and try to forget you."

This brought tears to Leonie's eyes. "You said we could at least be friends."

Gabriel took her hands. "I know I did, darling. But trying to keep on that side of the line when I see you is almost impossible."

When he called her that it felt as though they were a couple. All the more with him holding her hands.

"What you wrote in your letter, did you really mean it?" Leonie asked.

"Which part?"

"All of it. Being in bed and wanting me with you."

He laughed. "More than you know. I can barely sleep at nights here, thinking of you just a building away and longing for you."

"It's the same for me."

They were both silent for a moment, and then Gabriel swore under his breath. Then his lips were on hers and she was drowning in him. It was like quenching a thirst. Leonie didn't even care at that moment if Mother Benedict walked in, she was so lost in him.

He broke off, and murmured near her ear. "What I want to do is have you in my bed, strip you naked, and make you mine."

Leonie felt dizzy just hearing these words. "Can't we do that? If I managed to get out one night?" It would mean telling the others, but she was sure they would cover for her. Harry would, anyway.

"I couldn't put you at that much risk. Right now if I got discovered and sacked, I almost couldn't care. But we're not risking your future like that."

When he mentioned the future, Leonie remembered the announcement in assembly. "I was thinking of applying for that RADA scholarship. If I managed to stay in London next year, would you still want to see me?"

"Right now if you went back home I would be on the next plane across the Atlantic, the way I'm feeling," Gabriel told her.

"So can't we at least try? Even if we have to be careful for now?"

"Not with this." He indicated his collar.

Fire momentarily flared in Leonie's eyes. "Some days I feel like just ripping it off you."

"The image of you tearing my clothes off doesn't do a lot to help me keep this under control," Gabriel said, smiling.

"Good." Leonie felt defiant. He was giving her such mixed signals. Why did he keep telling her how much he wanted her if he was going to keep insisting it was all impossible? "So it is forever, then?"

"What?"

"This." Leonie ran her finger around the top of his collar. "Can you never leave the priesthood?"

Gabriel looked solemn again. "I don't know. I've been giving it some serious thought. I don't know if this - you and me - is just a temptation along the path."

"You mean you'll eventually get over me?"

"No." He put his hands on either side of her face and looked deep into her eyes. "I don't think I'll ever get over you, Leonie. What I don't know is whether you're a sacrifice I'm supposed to make. Whether my love for you is a burden I'm supposed to bear, as part of my vocation."

Leonie thought this was stupid and unfair. "You mean I'm supposed to just be some kind of test? How is that fair on me? I can't see why a benevolent god would use me like that."

"Leonie." He looked sad now. "I didn't mean this to shake your faith. But you're so young. You'll study, travel, meet people. You'll fall in love again. Probably many times."

As he said this, Leonie rejected it with every fibre of her body. She knew he was wrong. "I won't do. I don't know how I can prove it to you, but I know."

This time she reached up and kissed him, pulling his face down to hers. As the kiss deepened, Gabriel took over and became more forceful, moulding her body to his. He was hungry for her, gripping her, exploring her.

Ending the embrace was a kind of agony but they both had to regain control.

"This is going to be even harder than I imagined," Gabriel said. He pushed his hand through his hair. "For both our sakes I need to develop better self-control. You'd better run along. We'll talk about this again later, when we've both had some more time to think."

22

Gabriel had done nothing but think endlessly about Leonie, that was the problem. He had considered trying to see Leonie covertly.

The problem was doing this while continuing in his role as a priest. As her teacher, the ethical violation was bad enough, though he could cope with it. She was a legal adult, after all.

But as a priest, it was unthinkable. He couldn't carry out his duties and administer to the students' spiritual welfare while he broke his vows in the worst possible way.

Leonie was also significantly younger than he was. In a few months she might not feel the same way, but if he left the priesthood it would be permanent. He had meant what he said: he doubted he would ever get over her. He had the benefit of knowing how she compared to other women, but she didn't have the equivalent experience of men.

Maybe he should just quit anyway. His lack of self-control hardly befitted one who had taken holy orders.

As he walked along, one of his students came up to him. Suki Laverne. He didn't care for her much, there was something sly about her. She was a good actress though.

"Hello Father Gabriel."

"Hello Suki."

She was clutching a bunch of folders. None of the girls seemed to use schoolbags, it mystified Gabriel. They all carried books, folders and pencil cases around loose. Things constantly got dropped.

"I expect you've heard about this scholarship," Suki said.

"I was in assembly when Mother Benedict announced it, yes," Gabriel replied.

"Well…" Suki bit her bottom lip and then ran the tip of her tongue over her top lip. Gabriel had the horrible feeling this was supposed to be alluring. Perhaps another man might have found it so, but Gabriel didn't find her or other school students attractive. Leonie was a complete aberration, which was why he was so disturbed by his feelings for her.

"Well? Can I help in some way?" Even as he said it, he regretted it. He sensed he had fallen into some trap.

Suki's face lit up with a joy mingled with triumph. "I was hoping you would be able to help! I could really use some extra coaching for all the auditions it's going to involve."

They were nearly at the staffroom, which was Gabriel's destination. "I'm not sure that would be considered appropriate. Even if it were, the proper person to help you would be Sister Rosalind, as Head of Drama."

Suki looked pleading. "The thing is, I think it would really help to have a man's perspective as well. I mean Sister Rosalind is great, but she's a nun. I'm not sure she could really help with a scene between a man and a woman, for example."

She was so blatant. Gabriel tried not to let his amusement show. "And you think that I could, despite being a priest?"

"Well, yes. It's different with men, isn't it?"

Gabriel ignored this. He turned to her, just outside the staffroom door. "If Mother Benedict decides that special coaching is warranted for applicants, it will be announced in due course. Whether your acting coach is male or female is completely irrelevant."

He knew his tone was curt but he wanted to brush her off and close this conversation for good. He felt there was a dangerous air about her. If she ever got him into a compromising position, she would manipulate it for all it was worth.

In the staffroom he had a meeting with Sister Rosalind about the production of The Crucible. He didn't bother to mention Suki's request. From his side, rehearsals were going well and the girls were really getting into their roles. They now needed to put some serious work into the set and costumes, which Sister Rosalind was taking charge of.

"I've roped in the Sewing Club to help us out. We'll have a look through any past costumes that may be usable. Then we can take fittings for anything new that's needed," Sister Rosalind said. "I had thought to put the younger female roles in grey and white, but to pick Abigail out in red. This means we can possibly adapt school uniforms to some extent, overlaid with white pinafores and caps. The menfolk in black, and the older female roles either in grey or brown. The aim would be to create a kind of monochrome with Abigail as a symbol of passion and bloodshed."

Gabriel liked the plan. "It sounds great."

"Keeping it simple is paramount, as there's not a great deal of time or resources. Unfortunately I believe most of the costumes in storage tend to be along Tudor lines, due to all the Shakespearean productions the school has done. Nothing that would really work for our era."

"I've assumed a reasonably simple set in terms of the stage directions," Gabriel said. "Just a few benches would be necessary. They're most critical in the courtroom scenes, which take up much of the latter half."

Sister Rosalind agreed. "We might be able to project some backdrops rather than paint everything. Sister Barbara is our technical genius. She managed to rig up quite a beautiful forest setting for last year's production of A Midsummer Night's Dream, which used photographs of the actual woods behind the school. They're wintry now, but that might work better for the darkness of The Crucible. We'll come up with a great set, whatever the case."

Gabriel couldn't think of the woods without thinking of Leonie. He wondered if it would be safe for them to meet there again. There were precious few places where he could risk being alone with her, even for a few moments.

And he wanted much more of her than that.

Leonie was desperate to make Father Gabriel break his resolve. She was past caring whether it was some mortal sin.

She loved him and she wanted to be with him.

Frustratingly there was never any time she got to be alone with him, nor any opportunity to flirt with him. She couldn't dress up in something sexy as she was forced to wear her school uniform every day. Two weeks passed and she felt like she was going out of her mind. She had even thought about climbing out of the window one night and breaking into the presbytery.

Except she had no idea which room was his. Surprising Father Stephen in his bed socks was far too much of a risk.

The only real opportunity to communicate with Gabriel came during rehearsals. Leonie knew that during Abigail's scenes with John Proctor, Gabriel would be thinking of the time they had acted it out. So she went all out, acting as wanton and seductive as possible whenever she had the opportunity.

Fortunately most people just assumed Leonie was throwing herself into the role. Everyone knew she was one of the students planning to apply for the RADA scholarship.

But Leonie saw the look in Gabriel's eye as she said her lines to Mercy, and knew the effect she was having on him.

"That was very well done," he told Leonie and Mercy afterwards, keeping his voice steady. "If you can both sustain that level of intensity on opening night, it's going to be a great performance."

The sewing club girls were busy taking measurements that night. This led to a lot of giggling and sucking in of waists. "If anyone publishes my vital statistics I'll poison their cocoa," Mai threatened.

Leonie was sure she had lost weight due to the awful school food and the endless sports they had to do. She caught Gabriel quickly averting his eyes when a frizzy haired girl ran the measuring tape around Leonie's chest. It was over her school jumper so it was hardly revealing, but Leonie was glad that Gabriel was obviously struggling not to look.

She and Mercy were the last two to be measured as their scene in the first Act had been the final section rehearsed that night. Leonie deliberately lingered, letting Mercy and the sewing girls leave before her. She wanted to give Gabriel a chance to call her back.

He said nothing as she picked up her bag and turned to leave, and she felt her heart sinking and her feet turn to lead. Just as she reached the door, he said her name. "Leonie."

The sound of his voice sent a jolt through her. She turned back to him.

"Come here."

Leonie went up to him.

Gabriel reached out his hands to her and she took them. "I want you," he told her.

She wasn't exactly sure what he meant. "How?"

"With me." His gaze was deadly serious. "It's driving me crazy seeing you and not getting to be alone with you. There's so much I want to say." He pulled her closer to him. "And do."
156

"Did you make a decision?" Leonie asked.

"Partly. I want to spend more time with you. Could you stay with me for a week in the holidays? Postpone your flight home?"

Leonie could hardly believe what he was saying. "Really? Where?"

"An aunt of mine has a holiday cottage in the Cotswolds. She only uses it in the summer. I've got a key to stay there any time," Gabriel told her.

Leonie wasn't exactly sure where the Cotswolds were, or what they were, but had some idea they were near Figgy's part of the country.

An entire week with him. Even as the prospect thrilled her it was also terrifying. What if he regretted it? Or got bored with her? What if they actually did the deed and she wasn't any good at it?

Gabriel saw the doubt in her eyes. "It's okay if you don't want to. We'll work something else out."

"No, I absolutely do want to. I just didn't want you to regret it," she said.

"I'll regret it if I don't do it."

Leonie swallowed. She felt as though they were at a tipping point. On the brink of it all, finally. "You might change your mind by the end of term."

"I won't."

He kissed her then, which she had longed for. Neither of them dared to let it deepen too far in case they lost control.

Then Leonie left. Already the plans for how to do this were ticking through her mind. Hopefully changing the flight wouldn't be too much of an issue. She would have to write to her grandmother and parents as soon as possible. She guessed she could say that one of her dorm mates had made the invitation.

Her grandmother would definitely approve of her spending a week with Figgy or Harry, given their prestigious families. And if her grandmother condoned it, then her parents shouldn't object.

It might also be an idea to ask Harry to cover for her. After all, she had offered to do so before. She didn't seem shocked by the Gabriel-being-a-priest thing either.

Leonie had no idea how she was going to get through the rest of the term.

A whole week with Gabriel. She just had to make sure by the end of it that he would choose her rather than the church. Surely he must be thinking along those lines, to have even made the suggestion?

Leonie walked up the stairs to the dormitory, needing to fetch a book on Goya that she needed for an assignment. The others had gone straight off to the hall for evening prep, which was what they called homework here. It was short for preparation.

She pushed the door open and stopped in shock.

Standing there by Leonie's bed, a triumphant smirk on her face, was Suki Laverne.

In her hand she held the letter that Gabriel had written to Leonie.

23

Leonie froze as the smirk stretched across Suki's face.

"What are you doing here?" Leonie asked. She couldn't take her eyes off the letter that Suki held. Gabriel's letter to her. Signed with his name.

If Suki had read it...

But of course she had. The malicious glee on the girl's face said everything.

"I thought it was time to do a little digging. It was obvious something was going on," Suki said. She tossed her dark hair as she waved the paper.

Obvious? "What do you mean?"

"Yankee girl getting picked for the lead role. All those cosy rehearsals. Him asking you to stay behind after class. And I saw you leaving the vestry. I knew something was up." She dangled the letter. "And now I have proof." She quoted from it: "'Bed beckons, naturally my thoughts are turning to you.' I don't know whether to laugh or throw up. Have you slept with him, then?"

Leonie ignored the question. "You have no right to touch my things." She was furious and terrified.

"Don't I? I wonder what Mother Benedict will say? A student not only having an inappropriate relationship with a teacher, but with a priest as well. So, have you screwed him? Good luck passing off the results of that as an immaculate conception. I doubt anyone would believe the Holy Spirit would impregnate a little slut like you."

"Give it back." Leonie reached for the letter but Suki held it above her head. Her eyes narrowed to a spiteful gleam.

"I hardly think so. It's my duty to take this straight to the head."

With a cold, creeping dread, Leonie knew she had lost. Even if she got the letter back, Suki could still sneak about what she knew. It would be her word against Leonie's, and Suki had all the details in the letter to support her case. Leonie wasn't sure that she could manage to deny things convincingly enough to Mother Benedict even if she tried.

The entire weight of the sky seemed to be falling on her. She felt sick with fear. More for Gabriel than for herself, as he had more to lose.

She resigned herself to her fate. "What do you want?" she asked Suki.

Suki arched her eyebrows, determined to torture Leonie as long as possible. "What makes you think you could have anything that I want?"

"Do you want to play Abigail? Do you want me to quit the role?" Leonie could only imagine what people's reaction would be. Her mind was racing to think of some excuse that she could give.

Suki laughed nastily. "As if some part in a school play would induce me to keep my mouth shut. No, if you want to save your precious little priest, there's something else you're going to have to do."

"What?" How high could Suki's price be?

"Drop out of the RADA scholarship."

Leonie was silent for a while. The scholarship meant everything to her. Freedom and independence. Choosing her own future. Getting to stay in England, and maybe even being with Gabriel.

She played for time. "What makes you think I'd even win it over you? You don't seem to have any regard for my ability."

Suki shrugged. "I don't. But you never know how these things might go. Someone on the judging panel might be as deluded about you as our dear Father Gabriel is. There's no accounting for bad taste."

"If I drop out, will you give me the letter back?" Leonie said.

"Maybe. Not until the applications close though. And I might just hang on to it a little longer, in case I need anything else from you. Some study notes, perhaps. Or an essay or two. We'll see," Suki told her.

Never give into a blackmailer, Leonie thought. They would never stop bleeding you dry. But what choice did she have?

"I'll quit the scholarship process if you give me the letter now."

Suki laughed again. "You're not really in a position to bargain, are you? No, I'll be taking care of this for now." She folded the sheet and put it in her pocket. Leonie could hardly bear to see something so precious as Gabriel's letter in her enemy's hands. But there was nothing she could do.

Suki flounced off in her usual way, buoyant with victory.

Feeling a heavy despair, and wondering how on earth she was going to warn Gabriel, Leonie lay down on her bed. She stared at the ceiling and wished that the whole of St Winifred's would collapse.

Right on top of Suki Laverne.

"Did somebody die?"

Mai was only half joking as she asked this. It was obvious that something was seriously wrong with Leonie. She was lying on her bed, motionless, gazing up at the ceiling with her eyes open, and didn't move or react when the others entered the dorm. She looked absolutely stricken.

Leonie couldn't even respond. She was drowning in the biggest terror and misery she had ever known. She had thought it was bad enough when she had got into her trouble back in the US.

But this was a thousand times worse.

"What is it, Leonie?" Figgy asked. She looked anxious for her friend. "Have you had bad news from home?"

Leonie managed to answer. "It's nothing. I'm okay really."

But she couldn't deceive Harry. "Is it what I think it is?" Harry asked.

"Probably not exactly."

Now both Mai and Figgy were getting curious. "What's going on?"

"It's nothing," Leonie insisted. "Just some personal stuff. Nothing important." Except it was the most important thing in the world.

"If it's something Harry knows, then you can tell us as well," Mai said. She sat on her bed across from Leonie's, cross-legged. "Spill."

Leonie sat up. "You might freak out."

"Nothing freaks me out," Mai said, which was totally untrue.

Leonie took the plunge. She hugged her pillow in front of her. "So it's Father Gabriel."

Mai was nonplussed. "So he gave you detention? He gave you fifty Hail Marys? What?"

"So I kind of have a thing going with him."

Mai's mouth fell open at this and Figgy gaped. She had been tidying up her drawers, folding some clothes away. She was easily the tidiest of all of them, but now she stood there, a pair of grey socks dangling from her hands.

"You mean on his side too?" Figgy asked.

"Yes."

Mai swung around to Harry. "Did you know about this?"

"A little bit, yes," Harry said.

"What exactly do you mean by 'a thing'?" Figgy asked, stuffing the rest of her socks away quickly.

Leonie tried to explain. "I've kind of fallen for him, and he has too. Except he's a priest of course, so it's complicated." She knew this was the understatement of the century. She also knew that Mai in particularly would want every gory detail of how they had got together, and right now Leonie couldn't face talking about that. Not while it was all so threatened. "But that's not the issue right now. The problem is that Suki Laverne found out, and she's blackmailing me."

This part was news to Harry, who looked shocked. "How?"

"My stupid fault. I guess we weren't discreet enough. Like when he asked me to stay back after class and after rehearsals a couple of times," Leonie said.

Mai disagreed. "I didn't notice anything out of the ordinary. Other than you have that poetry book he lent you, which did seem a bit friendly on his part. Did Suki know about that?"

"I don't think so. But he wrote me a letter at half term, and she found it. She went searching through my stuff, and she's taken it."

The others were outraged. "That cow was rummaging about in here?" Mai said. She was indignant. "She had no right to come in here."

Figgy agreed. "It's a matter of honour. Even if things aren't locked, you just don't do that."

Harry was cynical. "You can hardly rely on a girl like that to have any sense of honour. So what did she want? Or more likely, knowing her, what did she want first?"

Leonie told them. They were horrified.

"You can't drop out of the scholarship application. That's totally wrong and unfair," Figgy said. "You've got the best chance of winning it out of anyone here."

Mai's mouth was set in a grim line. "We'll get that letter back. And we'll make her pay."

"It won't make any difference though. She still knows. And if she goes to Mother Benedict with everything, I don't know how convincingly I could deny it," Leonie said.

"Or how convincingly he could," Harry pointed out.

Mai stood up. "Either way, we'll make her pay for this. No one tries that kind of shit and gets away with it. We've got your back, so don't worry."

But Leonie did worry. She had every fear that Suki would get away with it. And where would that leave Gabriel and her?

24

Leonie buried herself in work and rehearsals for the rest of the term. She didn't apply for the scholarship, but most people assumed that this was because she planned to go back to the States. She deliberately mentioned Juilliard a few times as a cover. If anyone had remembered her expressing interest in RADA before, they quickly forgot. At any rate there weren't too many questions.

Gabriel was horrified when she told him what had happened. "You can't do this," he said. "I know how much you wanted that scholarship."

"I've got no choice. We're both dead if she takes that letter to Mother Benedict," Leonie said. She also felt really stupid for keeping it, and not keeping it safe. She should have burnt it, as she supposed. Or at least hidden it safely at her grandmother's house.

"I can only hope she doesn't go poking around the presbytery. I've got your letter there," Gabriel told her.

"Have you?"

"Of course." His blue eyes met hers, and Leonie felt a surge of longing for him. They didn't dare kiss any more as everything seemed so risky.

"I wasn't sure if you would have kept it," she said.

"It's the first and only letter you've ever written to me. Of course I was going to keep it," Gabriel told her.

Leonie felt warm inside. She knew his letter to her by heart, but she still hated that Suki had the actual paper.

Leonie had managed to fix up spending an extra week in England at the start of the Christmas holidays. "Figgy's going to cover for me. So I can spend a whole week with you, if you still want me to. If you don't, I can just stay with Figgy's family for real."

"I'll want every day with you," Gabriel said. "Your parents didn't mind?"

"They were cool. So was my grandmother." If any of them found out the truth it would trigger the next apocalypse, but Leonie didn't want to think about that for now.

They confirmed the arrangements. Gabriel would drive down and Leonie would meet him later by train. Figgy's family would drop her at the station. "Figgy will just tell them I'm taking a train to London to my grandmother's house," Leonie said.

Her friends had all been great, united in their mutual hatred and outrage against Suki Laverne. They had rallied round to help wherever they could.

Sitting around with cups of cocoa and biscuits, they commiserated with Leonie over the situation.

"What really infuriates me is that she doesn't even need the scholarship. Her parents are loaded," Mai said. "She only wants it for the prestige." She pulled her dressing gown more closely around herself. The school heating hadn't been turned up enough to compensate for the falling temperatures. Being from Hong Kong, Mai felt the cold more than any of them.

"As Mother Benedict said, it's not even guaranteed that anyone will get in anyway. Everyone still has to go through the normal audition process," Figgy pointed out.

"If Suki fails that, she'll just buy her way in. Her parents will make a huge donation or whatever. It's a shame, because otherwise we could try and buy her silence. But she has more money than she knows what to do with," Mai said.

166

There was one thing Suki couldn't buy: Gabriel. Leonie knew that Suki had a massive crush on him. She guessed that the blackmail was as much about Suki's jealousy over Gabriel's relationship with Leonie, than over the RADA scholarship. Probably more so.

If Suki wasn't so constantly hateful, Leonie might have felt sorry for her. If Suki felt only a thousandth of what Leonie felt for Gabriel then it must be torture thinking of him with someone else.

Leonie shivered, and not just from cold. Figgy offered her a pair of knitted bedsocks. They had all laughed about Figgy's bedsocks when they had first arrived in the post, a gift from some elderly aunt. Now they were prized possessions.

"We have to get Leonie that letter back," Harry said. She was always the most pragmatic among them. "We just have to figure out where she's hidden it."

Various locations were suggested. In her bedside cabinet seemed too obvious. The lining of her trunk was a possibility.

"She might carry it on herself," Figgy suggested.

"Too risky. If she dropped it, or someone else caught sight of it, it would wreck her plans."

Leonie tried to think of some of the hiding places from adventure stories she had read. The hollowed out handle of a tennis racquet. A bed knob that unscrewed. The lining of a cape. In a box under the floorboards. Underneath the mattress.

Most of these weren't possible: they weren't playing tennis that term, the beds didn't have bedknobs and the floors were covered in lino. They didn't wear lined capes. Putting anything under a mattress was far too risky as Matron turned them over whenever the beds were remade.

For now it was a mystery, but one that they needed to crack.

Were it not for wanting to avoid causing Leonie trouble with her parents, Gabriel would have been tempted to tell Suki to do her worst. As it was he found it to be an increasing ordeal having to teach the girl, knowing how she was plotting against him. So far Suki hadn't dared to blackmail him directly. But he knew it wasn't out of the question that she might suggest he give her a higher grade, or excuse her from an essay.

It infuriated him that a schoolgirl could exert this kind of hold over him, but for Leonie's sake he kept his composure. He remained impassive whenever Suki threw a sly glance his way, or made unpleasant hints. Gabriel reckoned that the girl would eventually be the architect of her own downfall. Suki wasn't as clever as she liked to think she was. She also revelled too openly in her triumph rather than staying judiciously discreet.

Now being early December it was dark and cold, and the wind howled bitterly around the grey stone school buildings at night. Gabriel, alone in his narrow bed in the presbytery, longed for Leonie.

In the front of his mind he had various noble thoughts about what he would do during his week with Leonie. They would talk, and pray, and maintain separate bedrooms.

Deep down he knew the minute he got her there, he wouldn't let her out of bed. It would be all or nothing. He didn't have it in him to resist this anymore.

Suki eventually managed to get some kind of consent from Mother Benedict for extra coaching for the scholarship, so once again she approached Gabriel. "Mother Benedict says it's okay, so can we please go ahead?"

Gabriel had no choice. The last thing he wanted to do was spend any solo time with Suki Laverne, the tormentor of the one he loved, but Suki had forced his hand.

He figured out a way to mitigate it. Another girl going for the scholarship, and in Gabriel's mind a serious contender, was

Mercy Braithwaite. He offered her coaching as well, as a way to counterbalance the sessions with Suki.

Mercy was a pleasure to teach. She was intelligent and had a natural affinity for acting. She also loved Shakespeare, which Suki only displayed a token interest in. Impressed by her, Gabriel also suggested to Sister Rosalind that she give Mercy some extra coaching.

"I'd be happy to, if Mercy wishes," Sister Rosalind said. "It's a shame our American student isn't trying for it, since she's the most talented of the lot. Still, I suppose she prefers to go back home to an American school."

Gabriel said nothing. If Sister Rosalind thought this, so much the better.

He was still running the Poetry Club, which Sister Joan had now entirely handed over to him. She had some other projects she wished to focus on, and thought it was good for the girls to have a change for the term. They were now reading some Keats, and in keeping with the growing winter, Gabriel had chosen The Eve of St Agnes.

Into her dream he melted, as the rose
Blendeth its odour with the violet,
Solution sweet

There was plenty of debate among the girls as to whether this meant that Porphyro had actually seduced Madeline or not.

"It's obvious from the 'throbbing' thing what Keats means," one girl said.

"But that would be rape, if she were asleep," another pointed out.

"She wakes up half way through though. Maybe he hadn't got fully started by that point?"

Gabriel decided it was wiser to steer discussion onto other themes within the poetry. For his part, all he could think about was Leonie lying unclothed in a moonlit bedroom, and what he would be tempted to do to her in such a scenario. It was incredibly hard not to catch her eye when reading certain lines. He hoped that she could guess that he was thinking of her during some of the verses.

But the students were determined to talk more about love and relationships. One girl even dared to ask Gabriel if he had ever dated anyone, before becoming a priest.

This was a subject that Gabriel was reluctant to discuss. He would have preferred to have this conversation with Leonie first. Telling her about Joanne and other things in his past was something he had been planning to do during their week together.

He tried to keep his response general. "It's not uncommon for people to do so, before they decide to take holy orders."

"But did you do so, Father?"

This put Gabriel on the spot. He felt Leonie's eyes on him. He couldn't lie.

"Yes, I did."

He was hit with a volley of questions. "Didn't it work out?" "Did you break her heart when you became a priest?" "Do you ever regret it?"

This at least Gabriel could answer honestly. "It was over long before I took holy orders, and I have never regretted it." He didn't specify whether "it" was the relationship ending or his choosing celibacy. The truth was that he had never regretted breaking up with Joanne, despite the hurt at the time.

But nearly every day he found himself questioning and even regretting his decision to commit his life to the Church. If only he had chosen another way, things would have been far less complicated.

Gabriel took charge. "If that has answered your questions, I suggest we get back to the poem." He knew full well the girls weren't satisfied. Many of them were clearly burning with curiosity. But the finality in his tone told them it would be futile to ask him anything further.

25

Finally the end of term came, and the performance of The Crucible.

The dress rehearsal was a complete disaster. This was a good thing, at least for those who were superstitious. A terrible dress rehearsal was supposed to herald a great first night.

Nerves made people trip over scenery, costumes got mixed up and props were lost. Half the cast managed to forget their lines, and the girls playing Tituba and Sarah Good got a fit of giggles in the prison scene and reduced the entire thing to chaos.

Gabriel and Sister Rosalind could only watch in escalating despair. Neither of them believed in theatre folklore and a "bad dress" suggested an even worse opening to them, not a miraculous turnaround.

Sister Rosalind was pragmatic. "If it goes only half as badly as this, it will look like a comedy, which I dare say many of the parents will prefer anyway."

Gabriel, as the director, was little comforted by this. It would be such a waste of all their hard work if the entire production descended into farce.

Mai and Figgy had been keeping a sharp eye on Suki. Mai, who had a devious mind herself, feared that Suki might try to play some kind of dirty trick. "Itching powder in your costume or glass in your slipper," she suggested to Leonie.

"I'm not wearing slippers."

"In your shoe then. Anyway, I don't trust her," Mai said. "The worse you look, the worse Mercy also looks, and the better Suki appears. I'll bet she's thinking of that."

They were all caught up in a whirl of superstition. Fortunately none of the costumes were blue or involved peacock feathers, two supposed bringers of bad luck. But mirrors, whistling and real money were all outlawed, and there was also a major dilemma over whether having a genuine Bible on stage would be unlucky.

"I know you're not supposed to have an actual holy book," someone insisted. "It needs to be a replica."

"That's absurd. How can a bible bring bad luck?"

"Because it's disrespectful to a holy text to use it as a prop."

In the end the two teachers were dragged into the argument

Nerves were on edge and jitters were high, so Gabriel once again tried to find a solution. "Go and fetch one of the old black hymn books from the vestry. It will look the same from a distance."

"Won't a hymn book be the same thing? It's sort of holy too," the girl managing Props asked.

"A hymn book will be just fine. Go and get it."

It was fetched. Props were supposed to have been sorted out long before the dress rehearsal. Everything should have been ready and perfect, but it felt like nothing was.

As they limped to the end of the final act, Gabriel hoped that at least they could bring down the curtain correctly. This was not to be.

Suki Laverne caused even more havoc by observing another theatrical superstition. She refused to say Elizabeth's last line, the final line of the play.

This was a problem because it was the cue for Lighting to shine artificial sunlight through the window and for the drums to "rattle like bones" for the Grand Finale, according to the stage directions. These things didn't happen, so the Reverend Hale wasn't sure when to start "weeping in frantic prayer" and the curtain was dropped down far too early.

"We'll do that again," Gabriel ordered them. "This time, please say the line."

"I can't do that. It could jinx the whole thing," Suki told him.

Internally rolling his eyes, Gabriel suggested an alternative. "Just say: 'This the final line' in the same tone of voice, and move to the window as you're supposed to."

Suki did this, and the last scene was repeated with slightly more success.

It was hardly ideal. In less than twenty-four hours they would have an audience and only one chance to get it right.

Gabriel was conflicted as to whether to instruct the girls to revise their lines, or tell them to relax. He was pretty sure that they all knew them, and that it was only nerves that had caused minds to go blank. Not all minds: Leonie, Mercy and Suki had all managed to be word perfect.

He spoke fleetingly to Leonie as she left the theatre. "That was great. I know you'll be fine tomorrow."

"Thank you. I hope so." She was moved by expression in Gabriel's eyes. He clearly had faith in her. She was determined to justify it.

The crackle. It was the feeling that Leonie always got before a production, even when she only had a minor role.

It was the hushed darkness behind the curtains off stage. The golden dazzle of the lights illuminating the set. The black void of the audience as one stepped out, with only a few dim, pale faces visible in the front row.

This time, she was one of the stars. Nerves in her stomach combined with adrenalin, and the sudden panic that she would forget every line on stage.

Leonie did what she always did. She quelled any fears by simply casting herself away and becoming the role. She was Abigail. She let the girl of three centuries ago flow into her veins and take her over.

It made her performance electrifying, which lifted the whole cast. Gabriel, barely daring to breathe as he watched her, knew that she was headed for great things. He was sure she could have walked the scholarship if she had felt able to apply. This made him feel even worse for being the reason she had had to withdraw.

He wondered if it was fair to her, getting her to take on even more risk by spending a week with him. Giving her up would be the wisest and most noble thing to do.

But his flesh and his spirt were weak. He had fallen for her, completely. He wanted to be with her.

He watched her, acting as though possessed in the court scene. Whipping up the other girls into hysteria, throwing accusations of witchcraft around. And never naming John Proctor.

What was behind all that? It was so long ago, lost in history now. The full truth could never be known.

Gabriel was so wrapped up in Leonie's performance that he forgot to even notice whether the play ended correctly. He was past caring about Suki Laverne and her stupid last line. Even if she didn't say it, who would notice? The overall play had been so powerful, such an amazing production for a school performance, that the details faded away.

But all the actors excelled that night and the curtain descended to thunderous applause. The cast took several bows, Leonie holding hands with Mercy and the girl who played the Reverend Hale, with Suki on Mercy's other side. They were all beaming with joy and relief, for which Gabriel couldn't blame them. Acting as they had all done took courage and stamina. They were simultaneously elated and exhausted.

As was he.

Afterwards there was a reception. It was more of a formal affair than a regular cast party, since many parents were in attendance and of course all the staff were around. So the girls had to remain on their best behaviour rather than let their hair down.

"That was simply marvellous!" one parent told Gabriel. He had been rapidly surrounded by various mothers and fathers, interested in meeting the young priest who had directed the production. Gabriel thanked the person and cast a glance around for Leonie. He wanted to go and congratulate her but with Suki Laverne lurking around, it seemed too risky.

He saw Leonie standing with a group of girls. He managed to catch her eye and give her a quick smile which she returned. She only had to look at him and his body reacted. Largely because he was thinking about getting her alone for a week. He couldn't wait for the night to be over so they could be together.

Leonie had no one from her family at the reception. It was way too far for her parents to have come, and her grandmother had chosen not to attend. She didn't approve of acting as a school or career pursuit. Although she hadn't expected her grandmother to come, Leonie was still dejected by her absence. It didn't bode well for getting her support to attend drama school.

But more importantly, she would have liked at least some friend or relation there. It was kind of lonely having no one to support her. It made her feel far from home.

Figgy introduced her to her parents, and to her uncle Hugh. He wasn't actually a relation but some kind of godfather or family friend. He was tall, with white hair and white eyebrows, and a pleasant, intelligent demeanour. He asked Leonie where she was from, and what her plans were.

"I'd love to be a professional actress one day," she told him. "I know how hard that will be, but I guess it's my dream."

"If you work hard at anything, you've got the best chance of succeeding," Hugh said, and Figgy's parents agreed.

"We thought you did very well, dear. Some of the scenes were quite hair raising, weren't they?" Figgy's mother said.

As it was already night time and a long drive back to their home in Somerset, Figgy's parents were staying overnight at a hotel in the nearest town. They would then drive back the following morning, which was when the rest of the school went home as well.

One more night. Leonie almost felt she could burst just thinking about how she was going to get through the next twelve hours.

26

Still on a high from the performance and the excitement of getting to go home the next morning, Leonie, Mai and Figgy piled back into the dorm. The found Harry already there. Not part of the cast, she hadn't been able to attend the reception.

"So what did you think?" May asked, bouncing onto her bed. "Wasn't Leonie amazing?"

Harry's face showed a trace of guilt. "I'm really sorry, to all of you, but I had to skip out on it."

"What?!" Mai was horrified and about to be furious with her friend.

But Harry held something up. "This was why."

Leonie, who recognised the item instantly, felt her mouth drop open. "My letter? But where on earth did you get it?"

"That vile little blackmailer's dorm," Harry said. "I figured that this was the one safe chance I would get to retrieve it, with everyone else watching the play." She gave it to Leonie. "I know this might not solve the problem, but at least you've got it back, and she no longer has any actual evidence."

"Where did you find it?" Mai was burning to know.

"In the lining of her trunk. It seemed so obvious that it was actually the last place I looked. I ransacked her drawers, cupboard, under her mattress, everywhere. I even looked in the others' drawers. I knew it had to be there somewhere as she wouldn't risk hiding it anywhere else, or keeping it in her pocket if she had to change for the play," Harry said. "But there it was, finally, in her trunk. Such an obvious hiding place. I'm surprised Matron doesn't routinely check the bottom of every trunk when she makes her inspections. Even in my mother's schooldays they used to hollow out a space and hide cigarettes or even a hip flask of whisky in there."

Leonie was re-reading the letter that she knew by heart. It was so precious to her.

"I didn't read it," Harry assured her. "I did have to unfold it and glance at it, but I didn't see much more than the name."

"It's okay. It's not super explicit or anything," Leonie told her.

Mai was all eagerness to get a look. "Can we read it?"

Leonie guessed so. The others pored over it avidly, with mock swoons at the contents.

"He really is hung up on you, isn't he?" Harry said.

Figgy was thoughtful. "Suki is going to go ballistic when she finds out it's gone. She might go straight to Mother Benedict out of spite."

Harry shrugged. "She might, but she probably would have done so anyway. At least this way Leonie can more easily deny it, and we can back her up. She and Father Gabriel just need to ensure their story is straight. Also Suki won't notice immediately. I folded a blank piece of paper to take its place. She won't think to check it before she goes, it's always such a rush at the end of term, and her trunk was already packed."

"You should have written something on it," Mai said. "I can think of half a dozen things I would have liked to write to that bitch."

"I did consider it," Harry said. "But then I thought it might lend weight to her claim that a letter actually existed. I don't know if she would have even shown it to her cronies. I suspect not, because she's always very sly and smug about stuff, and keeps it close to her chest."

"I can't believe you didn't at least poison her tuck box while you had the chance." This came from Mai.

The recovery of the letter was a high point to an already great evening. Leonie was so wound up with everything that had happened and was hopefully about to happen that she feared she would never sleep.

But the energy of performing and the weeks of stress of over Suki had exhausted her more than she released, and she fell into a deep sleep as soon as her head hit the pillow.

A deep sleep interrupted by wild, wicked dreams of a priest with piercing blue eyes and a body like a god. For some reason Leonie found herself wearing a nun's habit made of transparent black fabric. She couldn't hide her nakedness with it, and Gabriel was looking stern and telling her that she needed to be punished.

"Lie back and be still," he ordered her. "There is only one way you can atone for your wickedness."

"But I've done nothing wrong," Leonie was protesting.

"Then why do you show your nakedness to me? Why do you disgrace your order and your vows?"

Leonie was trying to tell him that she wasn't a nun and she had no idea how she had ended up wearing these robes. She could feel the coldness of the air through the thin fabric, and tried to cover herself but Gabriel pulled her arms away. Then he was lifting up her robes and Leonie was torn between wanting him and struggling against him. "It's wrong, you're a priest," she was telling him.

Just as he was moving closer to her, over her body, his face lowering towards hers, something roused her and she woke. Only to find out that she had kicked her blankets off the bed.

No wonder she had felt so cold in her dream. Shivering, Leonie pulled them back up, and hoped the dream would restart once she fell asleep again. It was only a few hours before she would be with him for real.

Leonie was increasingly nervous as the train approached her destination. The morning had gone to plan so far, with Figgy's parents kindly dropping her off at the station. Figgy's Uncle Hugh hadn't stayed the night. "He had to get back to London last night," Figgy's mother explained.

Leonie was privately disappointed by this. She had enjoyed a long conversation with Hugh, who appeared to be very knowledgeable about the theatre, including in the US. Figgy's parents were more music fans, and conversation focused on a recent concert they had been to, and a charity gala that Figgy's mother was organising in the New Year. Several fairly famous people were attending, even a couple of names that Leonie had heard of.

"It's during term time, I'm afraid, or it would be lovely if you could all come," Figgy's mother told them.

Leonie's own family weren't the kind of people who attended celebrity galas, let alone sat on organising committees. Figgy and Harry in particular were both so well-connected. Neither of them had to worry about their futures very much because their families knew so many people.

It shouldn't matter, Leonie supposed, but she knew that in so many spheres of life, it was all about contacts. Who you knew, and who they knew. This was certainly the case in the acting world. Once again she felt a pang of sadness about having to withdraw from the RADA scholarship.

But as the train rumbled along, past green fields and villages and churches that reminded her of an old movie, her excitement and anticipation at seeing Gabriel grew.

The girls were required to leave school still in uniform, which seemed a completely stupid rule. Leonie had changed into jeans as soon as she got on the train, which wasn't easy as the bathroom cubicles were very small. She wished she had sexier clothes but she supposed if Gabriel had been attracted to her in St Winifred's ugly school uniform, it couldn't be too much of an issue.

The train finally pulled up at her destination and Leonie went to try and haul her trunk out of the luggage car. Fortunately there was a porter who was able to help her. She would eventually be leaving her trunk at her grandmother's as it was too heavy to fly back with. If only it were a suitcase filled with sexy lingerie rather than woollen socks and sensible underwear.

She could always wear no underwear. It might be interesting to find out how Gabriel would react if he discovered this.

There he was, on the station, and her heart stopped. He wore jeans, like the first time she had seen him, and a dark coat since the day was freezing. He didn't look like a priest, just a regular guy.

Not really regular, given how stunningly attractive he was. Leonie saw a couple of women notice him and nudge one another, and felt a mixture of pride and panic at being the one he had come for.

If only they knew that he was a priest. How scandalised they would be.

But there was no one to stop them as Gabriel put his arms around her and brought her lips to his before even speaking to her. His lips were warm despite the cold and his embrace was urgent, quenching a thirst for both of them, while inflaming desire for even more.

He broke off. "I need to get you home," he told her. "I don't think adding a public indecency charge is going to help my resumé." His gaze softened as he looked at her. "I'm so glad you're here. I know this was a huge thing to ask of you."

182

"I'm very glad you asked me," Leonie told him.

Gabriel asked her if she had had any problems getting away. "No issues before you left?"

"If you mean Suki Laverne-shaped, then no. I got your letter back though."

He was surprised. "Did she return it to you?"

"No. Harry managed to sneak into her room during the play," Leonie said. She hoped that Gabriel wouldn't mind too much about her friends knowing, but he seemed fine about it.

He drove them down some country lanes and pulled up at a pub. "We need to get lunch, and I want to talk to you. The way I feel right now I think I'd find it hard to concentrate if we were alone."

Leonie, despite being hungry, was disappointed. She had been looking forward to Gabriel losing his concentration.

It was cool that she could simply walk into a bar here and not have to worry about fake ID. At eighteen, she could legally drink in the UK and Europe. This might be a completely regular date were it not for the fact that the guy she was with was supposed to be celibate. And also her teacher.

The bar menu seemed really English. Shepherd's pie, bangers and mash, fish and chips, Cumberland sausage, toad-in-the-hole, something called a Ploughman's. Leonie had to ask Gabriel what half of the items were. She hoped it would at least be more edible than the stuff served at St Winifred's.

Gabriel ordered fish and chips so Leonie had the same. She had been in England long enough to know that chips were French fries, and crisps were chips. Gabriel didn't drink because he was driving, so Leonie just ordered a coke.

Instead of starting a conversation with her he was gazing at her over the table. "I dreamt about you last night," he told her.

"Did you? I dreamt about you too."

"What happened?"

Leonie felt embarrassed to explain. "I was wearing nun's robes."

"Not like Sister Benedict, I hope?"

She blushed. "They were kind of see through. You weren't very pleased about them."

Gabriel gave her a searing look. "Trust me, if you were wearing anything see-through, I would be more than pleased."

They were interrupted then by the waitress putting their meals on the table, along with cutlery and condiments. Leonie's stomach was such a pit of nerves that she wasn't sure she could manage any of it.

"So what did you dream about me?" she asked.

"Something I've been vowing not to do, and it's going to take all my strength to avoid doing."

He was looking at her so intensely that Leonie felt a throb in her lower belly. Nervously she ran her tongue over her lips, which felt dry.

His gaze narrowed. "Look at me like that and I will lose all resolve and drag you out to the car park. I'm determined we're both going to manage some self-control and actually eat something."

Following his lead, Leonie stabbed a fry - or chip - and managed to swallow it. She took a big gulp of coke. It got easier to eat once she relaxed and the sexual tension wasn't about to boil over. She had no idea how either of them were going to manage when he got her back to the cottage.

There was no way she could resist him. She didn't even want to.

27

Gabriel could tell that Leonie was nervous as they reached the cottage. He didn't want to rush her or push her into anything. Mostly he just wanted to be with her.

He had already brought in plenty of wood from the shed so he set about lighting a fire.

"It will take a while to get some heat going," he told her.

It was a surreal experience. Here he was, in total privacy with the one person he had longed to be with for months, and he even found himself feeling uncertain around her.

The chimney drew well and the wood was dry and ready to burn, so crackling flames didn't take long to flare up. The heat would set in as the embers formed, but it was already making a difference to the room. "Come and stand nearer the fire, you look freezing," Gabriel told Leonie.

She joined him by the fire and held her hands out to feel its heat. She was avoiding looking at him and she didn't know why. It wasn't as though she hadn't been alone with a guy before. Her stomach was a pit of nerves. Even though he had been her teacher and priest at St Winifred's, she had felt on a level with him there.

Now he seemed older, the adult. Leonie cast a glance at Gabriel. At the well-defined angle of his jaw, shadowed by stubble as he hadn't shaved that day. His lips, masculine and firm but sensuous when it counted. His dark brows and the startlingly blue eyes beneath them.

He was so perfect. Educated. Intelligent.

Even without the priest thing, what could he possibly see in her?

"What's wrong, darling?"

When he called her that, Leonie's heart did its usual flip.

"Nothing."

They both knew this wasn't an answer.

"Come here." Gabriel's voice was kind but stern. He took her hands and warmed them in his. "You don't have to do anything you don't want to. If you don't feel comfortable and you want go to home, or you want me to drive you to your friend's house, that's totally okay."

The thought of him driving her away was awful. "That's not it." It was hard to explain.

"Are you having doubts?" he asked.

It was more the opposite. "None. I was more worried that you might have them," Leonie told him.

Gabriel answered her and allayed all her fears by taking her into his arms. She melted against him. He pulled her down onto the sofa and half across him, so he could kiss her more comfortably. "Never," he told her.

They embraced some more and Leonie felt the heat rising. She could feel Gabriel's hardness through his jeans. She had never actually touched him there and she wanted to. So she pressed her hand over it, feeling its shape, and experiencing a pang of alarm over its size. Maybe the material made it seem bigger than it was?

He moved her hand away. "If you want to take things slow, you'll have to stop that."

"I don't want to take things slow."

She saw the heat flicker in his eyes as she said this, and felt glad. She reached up to kiss him and moved her hand back over him, then tried to unbuckle him.

Once again Gabriel caught her hand. "Wait." He wanted to touch her first. He pushed her top up and kissed over her stomach, moving higher as he reached her bra. He freed her breast and his mouth went over it, drawing her in.

Then with a sudden movement he had taken the entire top half of her clothing off and she was lying below him on the sofa, naked from the waist up.

"Now these."

Leonie heard the determination in his voice and didn't resist as Gabriel pulled the rest of her clothing off. He unhooked her underwear and drew it down her legs to the floor, so she was completely bare. Then he gazed at her for a while, and she tried not to feel self-conscious.

"You are so beautiful," he told her. He ran his hands over her body and her skin shivered under his touch. The daylight was already fading and the only light was from the fire, illuminating them both with a gold flicker.

But he still had his clothes on. Leonie wanted to feel his skin against hers, so she reached up and tugged at his top, and he helped remove it. She pulled him down against her, revelling in his warmth and the way his chest felt on hers. He was perfectly muscled, with a dusting of dark hair across his pecs.

They kissed, and she loved the way she was crushed beneath him. He was so much more physically powerful than her, yet still gentle. She loved the smell of his skin, clean and masculine, with a trace of pine from his shower gel.

Gabriel put her hands on his buckle, indicating that she should undo it. Leonie felt nervous about this, as though she didn't have the right to take his clothes off. It was stupid. And it wasn't like she hadn't seen a guy there before. Everything just felt different with him. It was serious, not just playing around.

Once he was naked too he put his lips back on hers and she could feel his hard length against her thigh. She hadn't dared touch it. It felt huge.

As he shifted over her it went between her legs. He wasn't trying to go further, but they were in a dangerous position. She was so wet, and everything could slide so easily…

Gabriel raised himself up and looked at her. "How far do you want this to go, Leonie? Because I can stop, but if we keep going with this, we may end up crossing a line."

Her voice was almost a whisper. "I want you."

"You're absolutely sure?"

"Yes."

Gabriel wanted to make sure that she was really ready, so he spent more time caressing her and teasing her nipples. He ran his hand between her thighs and upwards, stroking along the slick wetness there. Leonie trembled as he brushed past her most sensitive place.

He slipped a finger inside her and curled it up, massaging her tender flesh. She felt even better than he remembered from the night in the storm. Leonie was starting to writhe beneath him, but he didn't want to take her over the edge. Not yet.

He had had the foresight to buy protection. The incongruity of a Catholic priest buying condoms was not lost on him, and he had felt more than a twinge of guilt handing the money over. But he was wearing regular clothes, so the checkout girl had no idea what he was. It felt like being back in his earlier days, before he had ever been ordained. Despite his religion, both he and Joanne had used contraception. After all the sex itself was the great sin; using protection was a minor transgression in comparison.

Looking at Leonie, Gabriel could hardly feel that it was sin at all. It felt like the most natural, healthy thing in the world to want to enter her and make love to her.

She was gazing up at him, her lips parted. Wanting him. Trusting him.

He had a sudden impulse to start this with no barriers, to feel her as intimately as he could. He moved over her, and let himself slip against her opening.

Leonie felt him there. Her whole body ached, like it needed to be filled. But she had a fleeting vision of what St Winifred's uniform would look like with a nine-month bump under it.

"Shouldn't we use something?" she asked.

Gabriel felt a pang of remorse and drew back. "We should. I've got some with me." He reached for the packet.

"Wait." Leonie pulled him back. "Can we start like this, and you put one on later?"

It was exactly what he had had in mind, though he wasn't sure how irresponsible it was of him. "If you're sure." It was going to be the greatest act of self-control ever, to stop half way through, but he cared too much about her to lose control.

"I'm sure." She wanted the ultimate closeness with him, even if only for a few seconds.

Gabriel positioned himself again, and this time nudged forward. Leonie was as ready as she could be for him, but this was her first time. She winced at the slight discomfort as he pushed against her.

Gabriel stopped. "I don't want to hurt you."

"Please don't stop. I want this. I want you."

The words were enough. Slowly but firmly he eased into her, letting her get used to his size. He pressed his whole body down on hers, bringing his mouth over hers to distract her from any pain.

For Leonie any pain was eclipsed by how the rest of her was feeling. It did sting but she could tell he was being as careful as possible. The sensation of fullness was also sending golden jolts of pleasure to other parts of her body. Despite the discomfort she found herself grinding closer to him.

Gabriel withdrew a little and pushed back in, still slowly. He repeated this a couple of times, then stayed still, fully inside her. "I'm going to have to stop this, if we go for any longer it will be dangerous," he told her.

Leonie felt a sense of loss as he withdrew, but he was deft with the condom and returned to her quickly. She gasped as he entered her for a second time. She couldn't feel much difference from before.

"Is it worse for you, like this?" she asked him.

"Nothing is worse with you. Everything about you is perfect, and I love you," he told her. He was moving in and out of her now, building up a pace. Leonie closed her eyes and gloried in every sensation. She found her hips involuntarily rose to match his rhythm.

Gabriel was making love to her. She was no longer a virgin. The man she loved most in the entire world was making her his.

He slid his hand between them, his fingers finding the place that would bring her over with him. He was determined they were going to climax together. He wanted this experience to be as perfect as it could be for her.

When he heard her gasp and her breathing quicken, he knew she was close, and he thrust a little harder and faster. It worked. She started moving around under him and he could feel the ripples going through her, which triggered his own climax. It was far more intense than he had anticipated, it seemed to last for ages.

She was his. He loved her. He wanted her with him, always.

He buried his face in her neck and wondered what the hell he was going to do.

28

"I didn't mean for that to happen so quickly," Gabriel said as they lay together, their bodies warmed by the fire and one another. "It's just that with wanting you for so many months, it was hard to stick to my better intentions."

Leonie was completely happy with what they had done. She could die happy now, she thought. "I'm glad you didn't stick to them," she told him.

"No regrets?"

"No regrets." She felt a little sore physically, but it was absolutely worth it. "I love you. I wanted you to be my first, even if you're going back to the priesthood forever."

Gabriel was silent for a while.

"I'm not going back, Leonie. I'm leaving."

She hardly dared breathe, both thrilled and terrified at the implications of this. "You are?"

"Yes. Though I don't want you to feel pressured by that," he told her. "It would have happened anyway. Meeting you was a kind of catalyst, perhaps. But I've come to realise that if I was meant to remain in the priesthood, to remain single and celibate, I could never have fallen for you as I have. If it was just sexual attraction it would be easy, but it's not."

He looked down at her. "I'm completely in love with you, Leonie. I want to spend every day with you, cherishing you, making love to you. The thought of being apart from you when you fly home is wrenching me. At the same time I don't want to hold you back. You're only eighteen…"

192

"…nearly nineteen," Leonie pointed out.

"Which is hardly any better, is it? You haven't even finished school yet. You haven't started out in life. You'll change, and what you'll want will change."

Leonie didn't know how to convince him, but she knew to the very fibre of her soul that her feelings for him would never alter. "So what do you want? If you're not going to be a priest anymore, what will you do?"

Gabriel sat up and pulled her next to him, cradling her against his chest. "One thing that the past few months has also made me realise is how much I love teaching. Before, I wanted to work in some kind of inner city mission. I'd still like to do that but in a teaching role. Whether that's literature or basic literacy."

"Do you think you could do that in London?" Leonie asked.

"In any big city. But if there's a reason to be in London then I'll try to make that happen." His eyes met hers as he said this.

Leonie didn't really know why she had mentioned London, since thanks to Suki Laverne there was zero chance of her studying in the UK now. London was a super expensive city to live in. She would have to go back to the states and figure out something there.

"So if we were both in London, we could keep seeing one another?" she asked.

"Of course. Even if you're not in London," Gabriel said. "You'll have your pick of colleges, having graduated from both and American and a British high school."

Leonie didn't answer. It was getting uncomfortably close to the thing that she didn't want anyone to know. She was certain that Gabriel wouldn't have gone near her if he knew. He would be disgusted. He would drop her like a stone.

He sensed her mood change. "Are you okay?"

"I'm fine." She tried to make it sound as though she was, to make her voice bright. Where was her acting ability when she needed it? But Gabriel wasn't taken in.

"Something's wrong, isn't it? If you're having regrets it's okay."

"It's not that." She couldn't tell him. He would despise her.

Gabriel tilted her head back to face his. "What is it?" He saw tears in her eyes that she was trying to blink away. "If you're worried about something, please tell me."

"I just didn't do so well at high school, is all." Leonie couldn't bring herself to confess more than this. She felt like she was lying to him by not telling him, but she couldn't face his reaction to her past.

Gabriel was surprised. "You're doing very well in English, I imagine you'll get a top grade if you keep it. It's hard to imagine you not graduating with honours."

Leonie wanted to change the subject so she reached up and got him to kiss her. Gabriel slid her over his lap so she was straddling him.

He ran his hands up and down her body, his thumbs brushing her breasts. Leonie felt totally relaxed being naked with him. It was like being Adam and Eve, sitting there in the firelight. She put her hands against his chest, feeling the hard, sculpted planes of his muscles.

Gabriel was ready for action again within seconds. He took her hand and wrapped it around him. "I want you, but I know it's going to be too soon for you."

"It might not be."

He flicked a finger between her legs, making her writhe and catch her breath. Swirling his thumb around more firmly, he soon had her panting and wanting more. He got her to wrap her arms around him and kiss him while he reached for protection and slipped it on.

"Just take it at your own pace. And if it hurts, then stop. I don't want to wear you out," he told her, a smile crinkling his eyes.

Her arms around his neck, Leonie lowered herself onto him. It did hurt a little but she was determined to do this. He was rock hard which made it easier.

Then they were face to face, inside one another, joined. Looking into one another's eyes. "You feel absolutely incredible," Gabriel told her.

"Do I?"

"More than you can ever know." He started rocking her on top of him with infinite gentleness. In this position he felt so deep inside her.

It was intense. It transcended all Leonie's fears and anxieties, and let her blot the past out. She felt safe with him even as she felt sparks and waves of arousal rippling through her body. Every part of her seemed to be connected. If Gabriel kissed her neck, her breasts ached for his touch. When he slipped a hand between her thighs, stimulating her exactly where she needed it, it sent jolts through her stomach.

"I love you, Leonie." His blue eyes were fixed on hers and it made her feel even more shivery.

"I love you too."

They spent the rest of the day simply being with one another. Gabriel told Leonie about his family and his childhood, and even about Joanne.

Leonie felt insecure at first, hearing about his ex, but Gabriel soon allayed her fears. "It was never with her like it is with you.

It was a relationship that should have ended, we weren't even that compatible. But it can happen like that. You graduate university and you either split up or move in together and get engaged."

"So that's what you chose?"

"Regrettably, yes. Then she met someone else, and I was devastated. But looking back it was more hurt pride than a genuine broken heart. I know that now, being with you."

Leonie was curious to know what Joanne looked like, but obviously couldn't ask without sounding paranoid. "There wasn't anyone else afterwards?"

"No. There was the church, and then you."

Gabriel didn't probe Leonie about her own past, but she felt she should be honest as well about past relationships. "I never felt serious about anyone either. But it was just high school, I guess."

"What about that fellow I saw you with on the first day of school?"

"Who?" Leonie was bewildered. The only man she had been around on that day was her grandmother's chauffeur.

"It looked pretty much like he was going to be sharing your bed," Gabriel said. When Leonie still appeared confused, he added: "He was very hairy. And bear-like in appearance."

Leonie felt her face flame. He meant Buster, her teddy bear. "That was just a thing from home," she mumbled. Poor Buster was at that moment buried at the bottom of her trunk somewhere, cast aside in favour of Gabriel.

Gabriel laughed. "It's alright. I thought it was cute."

Covering her face, Leonie wanted to die of embarrassment. "I was really hoping that you hadn't noticed. Or that you'd forgotten."

"I was never going to forget the moment I first saw you."

She looked up, into his sincere blue eyes. "Really?"

196

"The second I saw you I got my first reminder that there was a world out there. And that celibacy might not always be so easy as it had been up to then." It had hit him like a jolt, seeing her that day. He had felt an instant attraction and connection.

Leonie thought back to when she had first seen him. She mainly remembered the mortification of looking clumsy in front of a totally hot guy. "I remember you seemed kind of annoyed."

"I was, but with myself, and the situation. I hadn't wanted to teach at a school, let alone a private school full of over-privileged girls. And when I found myself attracted to one of them on the very first day, I was particularly irritated." Gabriel's eyes softened as he looked at Leonie, and he stroked her hair. "But it was when I saw you the next day, sitting alone outside, that I completely fell for you. Even though I tried to deny it for ages."

"There were times I thought you hated me, when you ignored me in class," Leonie said.

Gabriel apologised. "I never meant to make you feel bad. I was just trying to keep it all under control, to hold you at arms' length. When you came into the confessional and started talking about some guy you liked, I was beside myself with jealousy."

"Except it was you," Leonie said.

"How was I to know that? I was a priest, remember. Somehow I figured that everyone would just see me as that, rather than as a man."

Now Leonie laughed. "You seriously have no idea, do you? Half the school was crushing on you and probably having totally impure thoughts about you."

"Did you?"

"Maybe." Leonie thought of all the times she had dreamt about him and fantasied about him.

"Tell me some of them." There was heat in his gaze again.

She looked down, not daring to meet his eyes when she spoke. "They were mainly about you disciplining me in the vestry for doing something bad."

"Disciplining you? Would you like that?"

Leonie felt even more embarrassed. "I don't know. It was kind of hot, thinking about you being my teacher."

For Gabriel it was more than hot thinking about Leonie being his student. He was painfully hard again, but aware that three times the first day might be too much for her. "Lie back," he commanded.

Leonie, feeling a shiver of anticipation, obeyed.

When he ran his fingers between her thighs he saw her flinch slightly, and realised he was correct in thinking she needed some recovery time. Instead he put his mouth over her, and teased her gently with his tongue, using it more firmly as he moved over her sensitive spot.

For Leonie it was an addictive bliss. She had been sore, but what he was doing was soothing and also stimulating. He seemed to know exactly what to do and when. She gasped and arched her back, but he gripped her thighs and looked up. "Don't move," he ordered her. "You have to lie completely still as part of your punishment. If you move, it will be worse."

He was only playing but she could hear the authority in his voice, and it was a huge turn on. It was also nearly impossible not to move as he continued going down on her. But every time she did, or shuddered, his hands gripped her even more harshly and he would stop until she lay still again.

When she let out a moan he paused. "Absolute silence," he instructed.

Having to be still and silent just made everything more intense. Leonie felt as strained as a wire about to snap. "Please…" she begged but Gabriel was relentless.

"Don't speak. Don't move. Or you'll be sorry," he warned her.

Finally it was all too much and she cried out, and could not stop her hips from rising and moving around. At this point Gabriel slipped fingers inside her and brought his mouth down as hard as possible on the front of her. Leonie was sobbing as he brought her over, and felt dizzy and faint as the aftershocks rippled through. Every cell of her body was on fire for his touch.

When he finally let her go, he moved back up and looked down at her. His dark hair fell over his forehead and there was a gleam in his eyes. "I like you submitting to me. It makes me feel that you're mine."

29

When Leonie woke the next morning she momentarily forgot where she was. She was lying in a warm, soft bed, far more comfortable than the narrow iron bedsteads and thin mattresses of St Winifred's.

There was something heavy lying across her.

It was an arm. Gabriel's arm.

Leonie had never woken up with a guy before, so this was a first. She lay as still as she could, trying to avoid stirring so she didn't disturb him. She enjoyed the closeness of being with him. She felt safe.

Somehow he sensed she was awake and opened his eyes.

"I've dreamt about this," he told her.

"This?"

"Waking up with you." He rolled over so he was above her, and kissed her. Leonie could feel he was rock hard already. She reached down and caressed him to signal that she wanted him too. She still felt a little bit shy about voicing her desires.

But they didn't need words. Gabriel made love to her gently and tenderly, savouring her body. She was getting used to his size now, and it felt better each time they did it.

They lazed in bed for another hour afterwards as there was no reason to get up. It was Sunday and they had the whole day and the whole coming week entirely to themselves.

"Do you have a double bed in the presbytery?" Leonie asked him.

"No, an exceedingly narrow single bed. Why?"

"I've fantasised about sneaking out of the dorm and joining you. Except I didn't know which window was yours."

Gabriel gave a wicked smile, idly circling her breast with his fingers. "You'd probably give Father Stephen a heart attack if you showed up in his room by accident."

"More likely he'd give me a million Hail Marys," Leonie said.

"My room is the left hand window as you look across from St Winifred's. But for heaven's sake don't try it. The drainpipe would likely come away from the wall and you'd plummet to your death."

Leonie arched her back as his thumb brushed over her nipple. "You could let a rope ladder down."

Gabriel could just imagine explaining to Father Stephen why he had brought back a rope ladder with him. They both knew it was an insane idea, the risk of discovery would be far too high. But it was fun to speculate about.

"I'd have to sneak out before dawn," Leonie said. "What time does Father Stephen get up?"

"Three o'clock if he's at Lauds. Otherwise we're both up by six o'clock, for Prime."

"It might be awkward if he came back from Lauds and found me in the shower," Leonie said.

"Even more so if he found me in there with you. However, he's currently hundreds of miles away, so how about taking a shower with me now?"

As they stood with hot water drumming down, covered with soap and sliding against one another, Gabriel considered how it was the first morning for years that he had risen without praying. Normally he needed prayer both for mental clarity as well as his daily devotions.

But with Leonie, he barely missed it. Being with her made everything feel clear. It felt right.

Shouldn't he be feeling more guilt about this?

They were having breakfast downstairs when the phone rang.

Leonie froze. She knew it was her grandmother or her parents or Mother Benedict, even though there was no rational way that any of them could have the number. She cast a panicked glance at Gabriel.

He picked it up. "Hello?" Then. "Iphigenia. Is everything alright? Of course, here she is." He handed the receiver to Leonie.

Feeling shaky, Leonie took the phone. "What is it? Has someone found out?" She had given Figgy the number of the cottage in case there was an emergency.

"Nothing like that, don't worry! It's something good. Do you have a Telegraph with you? A Sunday Telegraph?"

"A what?" Leonie had no idea what Figgy was talking about.

"It's a newspaper. Go and buy one, there must be a paper shop open somewhere near you. Seriously. I won't spoil it, but turn to page forty-six."

Leonie was impatient. "Tell me! I'm going to panic unless I know."

But Figgy remained as cryptic as the Sphinx. "Go and get a copy. And phone me back when you've read it."

Hanging up, Leonie relayed the instructions to Gabriel. "She wants me to get some newspaper. She wouldn't say why, except it was good news." Maybe St Winifred's had burnt down. Would that be good news or bad news?

202

"I'll clear this up and then we'll drive out and find a copy," Gabriel said.

"Are you sure you don't mind?"

"Not at all. We need some more supplies, anyway."

His emphasis on the word supplies raised Leonie's curiosity. "Supplies?"

"I didn't think we'd get through as many as we have. Given we've got a week together, I'll probably need to buy a crate."

He meant condoms. Leonie felt her face do its normal blush. "You can't buy them all. I should buy some."

"I earn a salary, you don't. I'm the one who needs to protect, so I'll buy them."

Leonie had a brief, forbidden fantasy about Gabriel buying them wearing his priest clothes. She could just imagine the look on the pharmacist's face. She didn't dare to suggest this, as it would probably be disrespectful to his position. But it was very funny to think of, as well as a bit of a turn on.

The Sunday Telegraph was a huge newspaper full of supplementary magazines and pull-out sections. Leonie was glad that Figgy had given her a page number.

She opened it as soon as they got back in the car and began leafing through. "Here it is. Page forty-six." She scanned it. It was the Theatre & Arts section, and at first glance she couldn't see anything of interest.

There was a photograph of some Shakespeare production in London's West End, and a lengthy review. There was a short item on a ballet dancer. Then there was an interview with the director of some new production of an old musical, along with some vintage photographs.

Other than these main articles there was a column, titled "Encore". It had the byline "Hugh Featherstonehaugh". Leonie's eyes flicked down it. It mentioned a couple of plays the columnist had seen, then a brief paragraph of theatrical gossip.

Finally she read the following.

In a rather uncustomary diversion, Encore recently had the pleasure of attending a school production of Miller's The Crucible. The play, featuring an all-female cast, was of a surprisingly high standard, and your correspondent found himself as bewitched as any seventeenth century Puritan. Special mention should be given to the lead, a young actress by the name of Leonie Wilson, who took the role of Abigail. Miss Wilson lit up the stage with an outstanding performance, quite as creditable as any professional actress. Should she harbour ambitions to tread the boards professionally, she is set for a glittering future.

Leonie read it three times, unable to speak. She was shocked and thrilled and confused. How had it happened?

Gabriel, growing worried, leant over to look at the paper. "What is it?"

"There." Leonie pointed to the paragraph.

He read it. "Good lord, that's high praise coming from a critic like that."

"But how did he come to see it?" Leonie asked. Then she read the name again. Hugh Featherstonehaugh. Uncle Hugh. Surely Figgy's uncle couldn't have written it, could he? Wouldn't Figgy have mentioned it if she was inviting some famous theatre critic to their school play?

She shared these thoughts with Gabriel who considered it was possible. "You'll have to call her back and find out. He's a very famous critic here, but as you can see he doesn't have a photograph with his column. So while I recognise the name, I have no idea what he looks like."

Figgy's phone was answered by a very well-spoken male who called her "madam" and said that he would see if "Miss Iphigenia" was available. The Davenports must have a butler or something, because it didn't sound like Figgy's father. And he would hardly refer to his own daughter as "Miss".

"So? Did you see it? What did you think?" Figgy was brimming with excitement when she came to the phone.

"Kind of shocked. How did that happen?" Leonie asked.

"Uncle Hugh. I didn't tell you because I didn't want to make you nervous. But I told him he absolutely had to come up and watch our play, because there was a girl he really had to see. I didn't even tell him which one. But of course he guessed it was you."

Leonie thought how horrific it would be if Uncle Hugh had been impressed with Suki instead, and said so.

"Hardly! I don't think you realise how exceptional you are. I was so cross about her blackmailing you and you missing out on RADA that I had to do something," Figgy told her.

"I wonder if Suki will see it?" Leonie said.

"Everyone will see it. Sister Rosalind always reads the theatre pages. She even cuts reviews out from time to time, and puts them on the Drama noticeboard. She's bound to see it and share it all over the school."

Suki would be furious. As ecstatic as Leonie felt about the review, she felt a creeping fear about how Suki might react. She might be angry and jealous enough to go to Mother Benedict and tell her everything. She didn't say anything to Figgy though, because she didn't want to seem ungrateful for what her friend had done.

"It's really kind of you to have arranged it. And very kind of your uncle."

Figgy was dismissive. "It's not kind of him at all. He'd never put someone's name in his column as a favour. Let alone someone in an amateur production. Even more so to write something like that about them. It's almost unprecedented. You must have seriously impressed him."

"Stop or my head will swell," Leonie warned her.

"You're far too modest. I'm just glad you finally got some recognition."

It would be something to show her parents at least. Unfortunately they wouldn't have heard of Hugh Featherstonehaugh. They didn't know of any US critics let alone British ones. But it would surely impress them a little, to see Leonie's name being printed in a real newspaper?

Gabriel had bought another three copies - "one for me, one for your parents, one for your grandmother" - and said that they should go out to dinner that night to celebrate. "After all, this is your first proper review, and it's amazing."

"It will probably also be my last," Leonie said.

Gabriel was stern when he looked at her. "Don't say that, and never even think like that. If you want to make it in theatre, and you're committed to it, there's every chance it will happen. It's your future, Leonie. Not your parents' nor anyone else's."

He took her in his arms. "And you've got me. If I can do anything to support you, I will. I love you. Whatever happens with us, I want you to succeed and be happy."

30

It was the most wonderful week of Leonie's life. She knew with even greater certainty every day that Gabriel was the one she wanted to be with, forever.

They made love, they talked, they went for walks and visited traditional English pubs. One afternoon Gabriel even dragged her to a museum of Roman remains, and bought her a gold replica coin as a souvenir. "For luck," he told her.

They also worked together: Gabriel marking assignments and working on his thesis, and Leonie doing her vacation homework. It made sense to get it out of the way before Christmas, particularly as she had a personal tutor on hand.

She meant to get it out of the way, anyway. The problem was that when Gabriel came and sat by her she got totally distracted and they ended up doing a different kind of work altogether. And when he was studying, Leonie felt an impulse to see if she could distract him.

She always could. It felt like their bodies were made for one another. Leonie felt as though she had known him for a hundred years, and at the same time she had moments of feeling shivery and nervous around him.

Leonie tried to cook for him but it was a disaster as the kitchen wasn't her area of skill. Gabriel, who was an adept cook, couldn't stop laughing at her efforts.

"I'm good with salad," she protested.

"That's assembling, not cooking," Gabriel said. "How do you plan to get by at college?"

"Salads and take out," Leonie said.

They ended up getting pizza. Leonie was surprised they had pizza restaurants nearby as it seemed so rural. But even the tiny picture-postcard villages, built golden Cotswold stone, had plenty of modern conveniences.

"This would be a nice place to live," Leonie said.

"I've always thought so. It would be a good place to raise children, with all the outdoor space," Gabriel said.

He was presumably talking in the abstract, since he must have given up on that idea when entering the priesthood. But it still gave Leonie a weird feeling in her stomach. She didn't want to have children for years and years, but if she ever did, she couldn't help imagining a little boy with Gabriel's blue eyes.

She changed the subject, not wanting to sound like a crazy woman. "How did you learn to cook?" He had cooked for her with spectacular success.

Gabriel didn't want to mention that Joanne had hated cooking, so he had taken on those duties. "Just a knack, and plenty of practice. At seminary we had all our meals prepared, but at St Winifred's Father Stephen and I take turns."

Leonie felt oddly envious of Father Stephen, getting to spend every evening with Gabriel.

On the Thursday there was another call from Figgy.

"I hate to interrupt the two of you, but is there the faintest chance you could come up to London for the day? It's Uncle Hugh. He's keen to meet you again, for some reason."

"For some reason?"

"He wasn't very forthcoming. He made it sound very casual, but I can tell that it's not. He wouldn't ask me to arrange it without some reason," Figgy told her.

Leonie was reluctant to give up any of her time with Gabriel, but the Uncle Hugh thing sounded potentially important. Gabriel thought so too. "I have no more idea than you or Figgy what it could be about, but it doesn't sound like the sort of invitation you pass up on."

He was happy to come up to London for the day as well, since he could use the opportunity to visit the British Library. It was agreed with Figgy that the two of them would catch the train the next morning.

"It's going to be very strange seeing you with Father Gabriel," Figgy said.

"He'll just be wearing normal clothes," Leonie told her. "He won't be dressed for mass."

"But I'll still have to call him Father, surely? I can't call him Mr Brydon, can I? It seems so weird."

"If he's wearing jeans and you call him Father, people are going to think he's your dad," Leonie said. "And that would be super weird."

They decided that Figgy should just avoid calling him anything.

"Does he want to come to lunch too? I'm sure he would be welcome," Figgy said.

Leonie was struck with how awkward it would be, introducing Gabriel as her what? "Boyfriend" seemed presumptuous and "date" sounded way too casual. "English teacher" and "former priest" were clearly completely out of the question. There was also the chilling possibility that Figgy's Uncle Hugh might recognise him, from the reception after the play.

Fortunately Leonie knew that Gabriel wanted to get down to his research, so she was able to decline for him. But thinking about the awkwardness of it all made her worried for the future. How could they go from what they had been, to something normal? And did Gabriel even want that?

It would be just Leonie's luck if she bumped into her grandmother in London. The restaurant they were going to was in the West End, not far from Covent Garden underground station.

Figgy met her at Paddington Station, having also caught a train up from the country. Leonie was very grateful to see her. She felt unaccountably nervous about the whole trip. She wasn't sure why, but somehow it all felt significant.

Figgy managed to greet Gabriel without too much embarrassment and he left for the British Museum, kissing Leonie goodbye.

"I can hardly believe I just saw that. How on earth will I look at him normally again in class?" Figgy said. The she looked anxious. "You are alright, aren't you? I mean it is working out okay? Going for a weekend with a boy - a man - is quite a big step."

Leonie assured her that she was fine. "It's just easy with him. I feel happy around him, and he's really amazing to me."

Satisfied for now, Figgy hailed a cab. Leonie had expected they would go by the tube and it felt kind of luxurious taking a black London taxi. It was also a much better way to see the sights than stuck in a tunnel, though Leonie supposed a London bus would have offered the same advantage.

The restaurant, according to Figgy, was "teeming with theatre people. But don't stare," she warned.

Of course once she said this, Leonie found herself dying to spot some famous faces. Uncle Hugh was already there, seated at

210

a table with another man. This man had steel grey hair and a creased, intelligent face. Both men rose as Leonie and Figgy approached, and Hugh introduced his friend as Jack Edwards.

The usual polite greetings were made and inquiries about their journey. This was interrupted by a row breaking out between the maître d' and an angry-looking young man. He looked very much the worse for wear even though it was only midday. "Don't you know who I am?" he was yelling.

"Do you have a booking, sir?"

"I don't need a damn booking, I just want a damn table."

He was eventually ushered out. The restaurant, which had frozen into silence as diners watched with bated breath, relaxed into the clink of cutlery and chatter once more.

"Who was that?" Figgy asked.

Jack Edwards spoke. "Just an actor who is going to wreck his career if he doesn't sort out his drinking problem."

The incident helped break the ice, and Leonie found herself enjoying the occasion. The food was great, there was a wonderful buzz in the atmosphere, and she was genuinely glad to see Uncle Hugh again.

"It was very kind of you to write such a favourable review," she told him.

Hugh broke off a piece of bread roll and buttered it. "It wasn't kindness at all. I meant every word." They got onto the subject of Boston, Leonie's home town, and how she had found the transition to St Winifred's.

Leonie ended up telling them about her various disasters, such as flashing her gym knickers and twisting her ankle, getting lost in a storm, as well as various cultural misunderstandings. She was a natural storyteller but something seemed to inspire her that day. She had the men roaring with laughter several times.

"Dear God, it sounds worse than St Trinian's," Jack said.

"The uniforms aren't quite as fetching, are they?" Leonie said to Figgy.

"Not quite, no."

They were onto the dessert course before Hugh got down to business. "St Winifred's school antics have nearly distracted me from my purpose in inviting you here. As you realise, I was surprised and extremely impressed by your performance in The Crucible. It was far beyond anything I would expect to see in a school production, and impressive even for a professional production. I happened to mention it to Jack here, and he was interested in meeting you."

Jack took over. "This is a bit out of the blue, I'm sure, but my company is producing a film that starts shooting next spring, and we're still looking to cast a couple of the roles. We have a few possibilities in mind, but nothing set in stone. I know it's short notice, but if you're available next week, I'd like you to take a screen test."

Having spent the first half of the meal barely able to stop talking, Leonie was now struck dumb. Figgy had to kick her under the table.

"Are you serious?" she asked. "I'm not actually an actress yet. I don't really have any experience other than school productions."

"From what Hugh tells me, you are certainly already an actress. I assume you don't have an agent, though? How old are you?"

"Eighteen."

Jack's face relaxed. "That's perfect, then. We can try you next week, and take it from there."

"Perfect?" Leonie was confused.

"You're not a minor. We don't need parental consent or a guardian or anything," Jack explained.

Leonie's mind was whirling. She was supposed to fly out on Sunday night. She had already postponed it once, could she do so again? Would her parents be furious?

"Can you tell me a bit about it, the script, I mean?" she asked.

It was a contemporary crime thriller being shot largely in Eastern Europe. There were drugs, a smuggling plot, political corruption. Two of the characters were a pair of English girls on a backpacking trip who got caught up in it all. Jack had Leonie in mind for one of these roles.

"Would I need to do an English accent?" Leonie asked, hoping she wasn't jumping the gun by her question.

"Not necessarily. There's no reason one of them couldn't be American, it wouldn't be much of a stretch. Can you do an English accent?"

Leonie gave a perfect imitation of Figgy's cut glass British tones. "I can certainly try, thanks to hearing little else over the past three months."

This caused more laughter, including from an embarrassed looking Figgy. "I'm sure I don't really sound like that," she said. "I had no idea you could mimic voices."

"I can't do them all, only some," Leonie said, lapsing back into her Boston accent.

She would definitely try to change her flight. Even if it meant losing the ticket and borrowing money to get a new one, she absolutely had to do this. Even if the chance of getting the role was slim.

She was dying to tell Gabriel. If nothing else, it meant she could spend a precious few more days with him.

31

As Leonie had feared, her parents were upset when she rang them to say that she wanted to postpone her flight.

"You've already delayed your return by a week. I can't think what's keeping you over there. It had better not be a repeat of trouble, young lady."

Her father sounded stern, her mother anxious when he passed the receiver to her. "Will you even be here for Christmas? You already missed Thanksgiving, honey, we've been looking forward to seeing you."

Leonie bit the bullet. "I didn't want to say anything unless nothing came of it, but I've been offered a screen-test."

"A what? Is this some kind of joke? She says she's been offered a screen test, Brian. What? You speak to her, then."

Leonie's father got back on the line. "What do you mean by a screen test? Who have you been speaking with? You know there are people that prey on vulnerable young women with this kind of offer."

A few thousand miles away, Leonie mentally rolled her eyes. "It's not fake or anything, it's genuine. The producer is a friend of Figgy's family. Please don't be worried, it's all fine. I really want to do this."

Her father was unyielding. "We've had this conversation before. You've already messed up one year of high school, that's the whole reason you're over there. A second chance to do it right, thanks to your grandmother's generosity. Not to go messing around with this dumb acting stuff. You need to get your

214

head down and study and focus on getting into a college for a proper career."

Leonie had heard it all before. "I know. It's just another few days. Please."

"We'll be having a serious talk about all of this once you get back. If this school is allowing you to mess around..."

"It's not. It's really disciplined and I have been taking my studies seriously, I promise."

Her parents weren't convinced, but short of getting on a plane themselves and physically dragging her back, there wasn't a lot they could do. Leonie knew she would have to brace herself for a huge row when she did get home.

She had gone back to Figgy's London house to make the call. Fortunately it was only a few hours' time difference, so it was already mid-morning in Boston by the time they finished lunch in the UK.

Figgy had been over the moon with excitement as they walked back together through Covent Garden. "If Jack Edwards is involved, it won't be some small time production. I've never met him before personally, but Uncle Hugh has mentioned him. He's definitely a big shot."

If only her parents had heard of him. Hanging up the phone, Leonie put her head in her hands, wishing they could understand and be happy for her. Instead of always insisting that acting was a risky waste of time.

"Are you okay?" Figgy came into the room where Leonie was sitting. "How were your parents?"

"Not great. Pretty furious and worried. I told them he was the real deal. Not some sleazy guy shooting adult movies, which is what my dad seemed to assume."

Figgy laughed. "I can only imagine how Jack Edwards would react, to be accused of that. He's pretty famous. Over here anyway."

"My parents aren't the kind of people who notice the names of producers and directors. Unless it's someone like Walt Disney or Spielberg. They only remember the names of the actors in a movie," Leonie said.

"I think most people are like that, myself included," Figgy admitted. "So what are you and Father Gabriel up to tonight? Are you catching the train back?"

Leonie blushed. "We're actually getting a hotel room. Gabriel thought it would be fun to spend a night in London, and go out on the town."

"You could have stayed with us! You didn't need to run to the expense of a hotel," Figgy said.

"That's really kind, but I can't imagine how I would explain him to your parents. Presumably they saw him at St Winifred's in his usual priest clothes. Bringing him along would be even more awkward than Look Who's Coming to Dinner."

Figgy's parents would hardly put their daughter's friend in the same bedroom as the school priest. It would be scandalous. And Leonie had every intention of getting up to plenty of scandalous activity with Gabriel that night.

She was nervous about telling Gabriel of the screen test, based on her parents' reaction. But he couldn't have been happier about it or more supportive. She met him outside the British Library and when she told him, his face lit up. "That's brilliant news! People wait years for a chance like that. Just let me know if I can do anything to help. You're obviously welcome to stay with me as long as you like."

Even without the screen test it would be worth staying for three more nights with him.

"Mr Edwards gave me a script. You could help me run lines. I have no idea what scene they're going to want me to try." Having never done anything like this before, Leonie had no idea what was involved. She had already leafed through the script. Her character - she was already thinking of it as "hers", which was probably tempting fate - would be an absolutely amazing role if she got it.

"Anything you like. I admit my intentions are partly self-interested. If you get this role, you'll be staying in London or at least Europe, which is closer than the US."

They were walking along a darkened London street, past squares of houses with shadowy gardens barely illuminated by streetlights. As her own euphoria subsided, Leonie was starting to think about all the complications it represented.

Gabriel sensed she was worried, and asked what the problem was.

"I'm just worried how I'll manage it all, with school and exams and everything," Leonie said.

Gabriel stopped her and stood in front of her. "If you get a role in a film like this, you could quit school, surely? Just defer a year and go to college in the following autumn, if you wanted to. There's nothing stopping you, is there?"

Only there was. Leonie took a deep breath. She was going to have to tell him the truth, and she dreaded losing his good opinion of her.

"I have to tell you something. There's something about me you need to know."

The seriousness in Leonie's tone surprised Gabriel, but he wasn't concerned it could be anything that bad. After spending the past few days with her, he felt as though he knew her pretty well. There were times that he couldn't imagine not knowing her.

"You look worried. Whatever it is can't be that bad." He brushed her hair behind her ear, tilting her face towards his. "It's freezing cold out here. Do you want to head back to the hotel, or go to a bar?"

Leonie wasn't sure. It might make it worse if there were other people around. "Can we just sit over there?" She indicated a park bench that was shielded from a nearby streetlight by a tree. Even though it was bare of leaves in winter, it still created a dark and shady space.

They sat down, Gabriel wrapping his arm around Leonie to keep her warm. He looked at her, waiting for when she was ready.

"It's about high school. I never actually finished. I dropped out. Actually, I got kicked out." Leonie couldn't bring herself to look at Gabriel as she said this. She stared down at her hands instead.

Gabriel was surprised but let her continue.

"I got mixed up in some trouble. I know you're going to hate me when I tell you, and that I should have told you before. I'm just so ashamed about it all, I feel so stupid."

Gabriel turned Leonie to face him. "Whatever is in the past is over and done. In the time I've known you I can tell you are a good person. You're intelligent, hard working, talented. And I love you. Nothing can change that."

Leonie's eyes filled with tears. "It's really bad. You won't think the same when you know."

"You don't have to tell me anything. If you just want to tell someone, you can always go to confessional with Father Stephen," Gabriel told her.

Leonie could just imagine that. Telling Father Stephen, and then being asked "is there anything else you wish to confess?" and having to admit to a string of mortal sins with his colleague.

She decided just to get it out and over with. "When I was in my senior year I did the usual stupid thing of getting mixed up with the wrong crowd. There was this boy, and well, you know. I was dumb. They were all into drugs and some of them were older. The boy I was with already had a criminal record. Then the police raided a party and he got caught with more stuff, so he got me to say it was mine. So I got arrested and charged instead."

Gabriel stroked Leonie's hair to let her know that it was okay. "So what happened?"

"Eventually they dropped the charges. I think they figured out it wasn't mine. But I got some kind of caution and it's on my record. Then of course I got kicked out of school and my parents were furious. Then my grandmother offered to send me to a strict school to complete high school, and cut me off from the people I was hanging out with."

"That must have been very hard."

Leonie felt tears running down her face. "It was awful. I felt like I wrecked my whole future. A high school dropout. I didn't realise how important it all was, getting the right grades and actually graduating, until I'd lost the opportunity. I didn't want to come to St Winifred's, I was so homesick. But then I met you, and there was the play, and now this. I can't bear to lose it all again."

Gabriel kissed her. "You don't have to lose any of it. None of it makes any difference to me. All you did was cover for someone you liked."

"Someone I thought I liked. The moment I took the rap he dropped me like a stone. And I found out he was seeing some other girl behind my back." Leonie still felt stupid and humiliated about it all. It had all been for nothing. At the time she had felt completely heartbroken as well. But looking back, she wondered what she had ever seen in him. Compared to Gabriel, and how amazing he was, and how she felt about him, the other boy seemed like nothing.

Then she panicked, because Gabriel was looking serious and even sad. She had blown it. "You are disappointed in me, aren't you?"

"Not at all. It's not that." He struggled to find the right words to say without scaring her. "I just wish we had met a couple of years later. The way I feel about you..."

Leonie's heart jolted. He was looking at her so intensely. "Why? What's wrong with now?"

Gabriel managed to continue. "The way I feel about you is pretty much it. You're the one for me. If you were a few years older, and had graduated and were setting out on what you wanted to do, we might be having a different conversation. But you're eighteen, and it's way too early for that."

Now her stomach was flipping knots. "What do you mean?" she asked, having a pretty good idea what he meant.

"I mean that I'd want to ask you to share my life permanently. But there's no way I'm burdening you with that kind of a request or a promise at this time of your life."

"What if I wanted the same?" Leonie couldn't imagine not wanting to be with Gabriel forever.

He held her hands, warming them. "We've both got a lot of things to sort out. I have to figure out leaving the priesthood and what I'm going to do with my career. You have this incredible opportunity. Even if you don't get it, though I think you will, it will only be the start of things."

"So you're saying you don't want to be with me? That we have to break up because I'm too young?"

"God no!" Gabriel kicked himself for not expressing it more clearly. "I want to be with you. We might not have had a formal conversation about this, but I have every intention of continuing
220

to see you and be with you. We can't go back to St Winifred's hand-in-hand, but we'll work it out. I just don't want you to ever feel trapped if you decide that this isn't right for you. People change a lot through college and in their twenties."

Leonie barely heard the last part because she was imagining the looks on people's faces if she and Gabriel returned to school together holding hands. She briefly imagined Mother Benedict's reaction if she asked to share a dorm with the school priest, or move into the presbytery with him. Mother Benedict and Father Stephen would probably implode.

This caused her to laugh, and Gabriel asked why, so she told him.

He closed his eyes. "Don't put ideas into my head. Do you have any idea what it's going to be like for me, lying there at night listening to Father Stephen snoring through the wall, and thinking about you just metres away?"

"It won't be any easier for me, seeing you and having to pretend you're just my teacher," Leonie said.

"And no more cartwheels, or whatever you were doing that day. It's going to be hard enough just seeing you around, without you flashing your underwear at me."

"Those awful grey things?" Leonie said, referring to the huge gym knickers. "You can't possibly have found those attractive."

"I find everything about you attractive. You could wear a sack and I'd be struggling to keep my head clear," Gabriel said.

Leonie was secretly delighted by this. Knowing she could have an effect on Gabriel even in her school uniform suggested all sorts of wicked possibilities next term.

She also felt like a huge burden had been lifted. Her past and her guilt about screwing up school and upsetting her parents had been a constant shadow. Being a high school drop-out had made her feel like the biggest loser.

Having someone like Gabriel not even seem to mind, and still be in love with her regardless, was finally letting her forgive herself. It felt like a second chance.

"Let's go to the hotel," she said.

"You don't want to get some food first?"

"Couldn't we just get room service?" It might be a waste of a night out in London, but wasting the chance of being alone with Gabriel seemed worse. She wanted him badly. Which meant getting to their hotel as quickly as possible, before she got them both arrested for public indecency.

32

Leonie put everything she had into the screen test. It felt like a second chance, after losing out on the opportunity to try for the RADA scholarship. Her parents' lack of support only motivated her to try even harder.

She read the script and loved the role. The character Gemma was immediately real to her. One moment Leonie was imagining her, looking upon her from a distance. The next she was inside Gemma's skin, looking at the world through her eyes.

Not having many clothes in England helped, as she didn't have to agonise over what to wear. All she had were jeans and a few tops to choose between. She kept her makeup simple - if they used proper lights it would drown it out anyway - and just brushed her hair and tied it loosely back. It was probably how Gemma would have worn hers, backpacking and staying at cheap hostels.

As nervous as Leonie was when arriving at the studio, it became easy once she stepped in front of the cameras. She didn't have to be herself any longer. There were three people observing her, a woman and two men, though Jack Edwards wasn't among them. Leonie guessed he would review the tapes later. If they were considered good enough to be worth his while, anyway.

There were lights and they were switched on, and she felt illuminated from the inside. As though she were drawing energy from them. As with theatre, their dazzle created a kind of veil between Leonie and those observing her, which helped her inhabit her own world.

The scene she was asked to do was when Gemma, separated from her friend, was being interrogated by police in an Eastern European country. One of the men fed her the police officer's lines in a flat voice.

Leonie played it bravely, with Gemma showing resilience and even defiance. "I can't tell you anything because I don't know anything."

When she had finished, the people thanked her. "Could you try it again, but make her more vulnerable?" the woman asked. "I like what you did with it, but we had imagined the character as more scared, more out of her depth."

Leonie wasn't sure she agreed with this characterisation, but did it anyway. Gemma became wide eyed and scared. Her voice wobbled and faltered as she gave her responses to the police officer.

Afterwards the three of them exchanged words, the woman frowning. Then she turned back to Leonie. "It's funny, that's how we'd always envisaged the role, but it seemed to work better the way you did it the first time. Could you please try one more time from the top, the way you did it originally?"

Leonie did so, but with a change. Bravery became bravado, with defiance a mask for fear. She was both scared and brave. As she spoke Gemma's lines, the character finally clicked for her.

When she finished she hardly dared look at the three people behind the table. There was no way they would give her a fourth attempt. If they hadn't liked it, then that was that.

But there was surprise on the woman's face as she shook Leonie's hand and thanked her for coming. "That was quite something. It's certainly given us some new ideas about how it could look." She gave nothing further away about whether they were impressed or not.

Leonie thanked her and the two men. Feeling in a complete blur, she hurried out.

Gabriel was waiting for her and she was so glad he was there. Having been on a kind of high while she was reading the lines, all the energy had ebbed out of her. She felt flat and the world seemed monochrome. She also felt fiercely protective of Gemma in the same way she had done about Abigail.

If she didn't get the part that would be one thing, but it would be hard to ever watch someone else playing it a different way.

Most people would have asked how it went, how did it go. But Gabriel merely said: "I bet you blew them away" and kissed her. And colour started to seep back into the world as his lips were on hers. Whatever happened, she had him.

Even though she had to fly home the next day and not see him for nearly three weeks. It was going to be the longest three weeks of her life. She would also be waiting anxiously to hear about the role. If she didn't get it, she would also feel that she had let Figgy's Uncle Hugh down. Somehow that was worst of all, given the faith he had shown in her.

All in all, Christmas was going to be torment.

After five of the longest days ever, a priority airmail arrived for Leonie. She seized it as soon as she saw it on the dinner table, prompting her parents to ask who it was from.

"Just a friend from school," Leonie said.

Her mother peered over at it. "It looks like male handwriting. Who is 'G Brydon', I don't remember you mentioning such a person."

Gabriel had fortunately only put his initial on the sender-address.

Leonie lied. "It's Ginny. She's one of the girls in my math class. She's very studious, her handwriting is always quite small."

There was no one called Ginny in the whole of St Winifred's, but there was also no way for her parents to check.

Seeing her family and friends again had at least been some distraction during the Gabriel drought. Leonie wanted to phone him but making a long distance call was complicated, as was receiving a call from a male English voice. Her parents would instantly be suspicious about how she could have met a man, being at an all girls' boarding school.

But she had his letter now. She prayed that it didn't contain something awful such as Gabriel deciding to stay in the priesthood. Then she felt awful for praying for something so unholy.

"Aren't you going to open it?" her sister Deborah said, always curious.

"Later. Ginny will only be excited about some math problem or other. She's kind of weird," Leonie said.

Deborah poured herself some more milk. "Your voice has gotten all English since you've been over there," she said. "Like the Queen."

Leonie didn't want to get into a discussion about her accent. She wanted to escape them all and read Gabriel's letter. "I'm going out," she announced.

"Where to? And who with?" Her parents were still suspicious of everything she did, given what had happened last year.

"Just the mall. To buy your Christmas presents. And no, you can't come," she told Deborah. "Otherwise it will ruin the surprise, won't it?" She stuffed the envelope in her pocket and hurried out of the house. Normally in this cold weather she would drive to the mall but today she wanted the exercise. Once she was out of sight of the house she opened it and read it while she walked.

Darling Leonie,

It's only a few hours since your flight left, but with the Christmas post delays this will probably take forever to get to you.

The week we've just spent together was the best week of my life. It's going to be very difficult to be around you at St Winifred's next term, trying to act like nothing happened.

If I have to play the role of your severe English teacher again in class, know that I'll be thinking something very different. Being with you has only increased my desire for you. It won't be easy to conceal it. God knows it was hard enough last term.

So you had better behave and act accordingly student-like yourself. No trying to wind me up in the middle of Shakespeare. Otherwise you can definitely expect some discipline. Even if I have to wait until Easter to administer it...

What's going through my head right now is completely unprintable so I'll leave it to your imagination.

I am completely in love with you, Leonie, in a way that I never imagined possible. We both face some huge changes over the next year so I'm not going to put any pressure on you. But you know what I want, longer term.

If you can spend another week with me at Easter (or the entire holiday), that would be great. We can stay at the cottage again or go somewhere else, anything you like. I just want to be with you.

All my love,

Gabriel

PS Whatever happens with the screen test, you have a very bright future ahead of you. I'm not saying that because I'm in love with you. It's simply true. You are exceptionally talented.

Leonie's heart flipped at the letter, even as she felt frustrated over the distance and how far away Easter was. She had no plans to make it easy for him next term. She planned to absolutely torment him, at least when Suki Laverne wasn't in range.

Because there was no way she could go nearly three months without even kissing him.

The lead up to Christmas dragged, which made Leonie feel guilty since the rest of her family were always so excited about it. She just couldn't get into the gold and glitter herself this year. It felt hollow.

She caught up with some old friends but she felt like she had moved on. Most of them were back from their first semester at college but they seemed younger than Leonie remembered. Even though she was the one still at high school, she felt like she had grown up ten years in the past few months.

It wasn't just falling in love with Gabriel that had changed her. It was the whole experience of travelling and living abroad, being cast in the play, going up to London for a screen test. Being taken out to lunch by a famous theatre critic and film director, and being served wine like it was no big deal.

Whereas here, alcohol was once more illegal. She was a kid again, back in her parents' home. She felt caught between two worlds and it was hard to relate.

On Christmas Eve a parcel came, airmail. From Gabriel. Leonie was both thrilled and troubled as she hadn't sent him anything. She didn't even have an address for him.

Inside the mail packet was a gift-wrapped box. Dying to open it but not wanting to jinx Christmas or invoke some kind of festive curse, she put it under the tree.

"Who's that from?" Deborah asked.

"Just one of my roommates," Leonie said. It wasn't even a lie. She had been Gabriel's roommate, kind of, for a week.

Now she was as excited for the big day as everyone else.

When it finally came to opening it, she had to act all cool about it, pretending it was just like any other present. She unwrapped it to find a red jewellery box, marked Garrard in silver lettering, which made a lovely creak as she opened it. Inside was a beautiful citrine and silver pendant; the gem a sparkling pale yellow.

Leonie adored citrines as they went with her colouring. She had worn citrine earrings when they had gone up to London. Gabriel must have noticed and chosen the matching pendant. She was dying to thank him, and tried sending him a silent, psychic message of gratitude.

"That looks very lovely," her mother said. "And expensive. Which one of your friends was that from?"

"The one I stayed with," Leonie said.

"It was very generous of her. I guess many of these girls are very wealthy. Your grandmother did say it was a very exclusive school."

Leonie, thinking of her own reaction when she had first seen the names and titles of her dorm mates, couldn't disagree.

"Be sure to write and thank her," her mother said. "You'll have to take some American souvenirs back for them all."

Leonie could just imagine presenting them all with plastic Statues of Liberty and Stars and Stripes paperweights to decorate the dorm. Let alone giving Gabriel something like that. What on earth was she going to get him?

33

There were several shocks in store for Leonie when she went back to St Winifred's the following term. England was even more cold, dark and miserable than before, and she had a knot in her stomach as her grandmother's chauffeur once more drove her up through the remote countryside.

She was dying to see Gabriel but was also terrified of how it would be between them. Whether he might have had regrets and changed his mind. Or whether it would be agony having to act like student and teacher again. Or worse, student and priest.

They had managed to phone one another a couple of times, and it had been amazing hearing his voice. The problem was that there was always someone around in Leonie's house over Christmas, with the weather being so cold. If her sister and father were out taking the dog for a walk, her mother and brother would be in the kitchen, in earshot of the phone. When her mother was out, her father was always pottering about the house fixing something and constantly going through the hall. So Leonie couldn't have the kind of intimate conversations that she wanted to.

Gabriel had decided the safest thing to do would be to act normally as though nothing was going on. "For your sake more than mine. I couldn't care less what happens to me, but I know you would be in horrible trouble with your grandmother."

He would discuss the process of giving up his vocation with Father Stephen, and figure out what he would do next. It was unlikely the school would retain him as a teacher if he had left holy orders. But he was reluctant to quit mid-year and leave the

A-level students in the lurch. Getting another teacher might disrupt their progress.

Leonie understood all of this, but it was still hard. Having been so close and gone about so openly together, going back to pretending as though nothing was happening was going to be tough.

Despite preparing herself, the first shock was seeing Gabriel back in his priest's robes. Leonie caught sight of him across the front yard as her car pulled up in the driveway. He looked incredibly handsome and incredibly forbidden. After being with him in regular clothes for over a week, it felt like a reversal. It also made Leonie realise the enormity of what he was giving up to be with her.

Should she let him do it? What would everyone else think if they knew? Most would be horrified, she imagined, and some envious. Like Suki Laverne.

She passed him as she was carrying her things into school, and he greeted her. "Leonie. Good to see you back. I hope you had a good holiday?"

His voice was so ordinary and teacher-like that Leonie's heart sank. He must have decided it was over.

Then he lowered his voice. "I've missed you. Nothing's changed. Just be patient."

Suddenly the world was full of sunshine again, despite the grey misery of the day. "I will."

But then came the second shock. It shouldn't have been a shock really, since Leonie knew something was coming. But when she entered her dorm - the first of the four of them to arrive - and began stashing her clothes away, Suki Laverne entered.

"Hello Leonie. Did you have an enjoyable Christmas?" Suki's voice dripped with venom.

Leonie gritted her teeth. "Great, thank you. And you?"

"So so. Unfortunately I was rather busy, and didn't get the chance to do my English assignment. I'm sure you'd only be too happy to lend me yours, wouldn't you?"

"We can hardly turn in the same assignment, can we?" Leonie pointed out.

Suki smiled, her eyes glinting. "Of course not. So you'll have to come up with another one for yourself. I trust the one you've done is peachy perfect enough for me to get an A? I can't imagine you've done anything less than wonderful for Father Gabriel, have you?" She put a nasty emphasis on "Father", twirling a strand of her dark hair as she spoke. "Or perhaps you were planning to get an A another way…?"

Leonie had to bite her tongue and not react. "I can lend you my assignment if you think it will help you. Was there anything else?"

Suki paused for a moment, tilting her head onto one side as though thinking. "Not today. But I expect there will be soon." She waited while Leonie went through her folders to give her the assignment.

Leonie suddenly remembered the letter. Had Suki not realised that it had been retrieved? She decided to bluff it out. "What about my letter? You said you would return it if you did what I wanted."

Suki smirked. "You haven't finished doing everything that I want, yet. But don't worry. It's safely tucked away." She left with a triumphant look on her face.

So Suki hadn't discovered the replacement with the blank slip of paper. That was something, at least. Leonie was glad that Harry had had the foresight to leave the envelope in place and put a blank page inside it. Likely if Suki had checked, she had only looked to see that the envelope was there.

Gabriel was going to know about the assignment though. Leonie had worked on it while she had been with him, and while he hadn't done it for her, he had suggested some angles. He would surely recognise them once they appeared in Suki's handwriting. And now Leonie was going to have to cobble something together at the last minute that was going to look weirdly rushed and low-effort.

She should tell him, she supposed. But she figured he was probably already going through enough stress and didn't want to add to his woes. He'd be telling Father Stephen of his decision to leave the priesthood soon, which Leonie suspected would be a very difficult conversation.

But there was another shock to come. In some ways, the biggest of all.

It happened later that evening, when the four of them were in the dorm catching up on holiday news. The other three were avid to know what was happening with Leonie's love life. They all knew about the screen test, but no one asked very much about it because Leonie was currently in limbo. She hadn't heard anything back, good or bad. Figgy had kindly suggested that it might be "slow over Christmas" but Leonie was increasingly fearing that no news meant bad news.

Leonie tried to tell herself that it was still a great compliment to have even been asked to audition. But after the high she had been on, and all the excitement, it all felt like a lead balloon.

Instead, she focused her thoughts on Gabriel. Surviving the rest of the year having to suppress their relationship and deal with Suki's blackmail wasn't going to be an easy ride. But it would be worth it. It had to be.

"So how was it back home for Christmas?" Mai asked. "Did you get snow? Did you get any cool presents? Did Somebody send you anything?"

234

Leonie brought the precious box out to show off the pendant. "He sent me this. It was a total surprise. It's to match my citrine earrings, I just wish I could wear it every day." She brought out the earrings as well to show the others.

"It's really beautiful," Figgy said. "It is quite a good match, isn't it? The citrines are a shade lighter, but only when you put them side by side."

"Citrines vary in colour a lot," Leonie said. "I guess that's why the pendant is darker."

Figgy was holding the pendant. "Of course. But this isn't a citrine, is it?"

Leonie frowned. "I think so. I mean it could be glass, not that I would really care if it was as it's so pretty. But citrine's not super expensive, and it seems like a really fine necklace."

Figgy now looked embarrassed, and exchanged a glance with Harry. "I'm not sure that Garrard does citrines."

Picking up the box and reading the logo again, Leonie was surprised. "I don't see why not. Even the box looks pretty high quality."

"Yes, but that's what I mean." Figgy was getting flustered, and Harry interrupted.

"Garrard is a very exclusive jewellery brand. It's almost certainly a diamond."

A diamond? "It can't be. That would cost a fortune, surely?"

"I don't know about a fortune, but Garrard wouldn't do plate or paste," Figgy said. "My father bought my mother some earrings from there for her fortieth birthday, and they had to be insured."

The citrine and silver pendant that Leonie had loved now felt like an alien bauble. Something way out of her league that she surely didn't deserve. "What am I going to do? I mean if it is what you say. I had no idea it could be super valuable."

"Either wear it under your clothes, all the time," Harry said. "Or give it to Mother Benedict to put in the school safe. Just lie and say your grandmother gave it to you and you brought it with you by accident. That's probably the safest option, as someone is bound to see it otherwise. And if it got broken or lost or stolen, it would be a huge shame."

It would be devastating. Leonie put the pendant carefully back in its box. She was going to have to talk to Gabriel about it. How on earth could he have afforded it on a priest's salary? It must have been his entire savings.

Getting a private talk with him was much harder. They no longer had rehearsals, so she couldn't arrive early or stay late. Staying after English class seemed like too much risk. If Suki had become suspicious enough to snoop, others might do so as well.

What to do? In the end she decided it would have to be the vestry. The chances of someone dropping by there were much lower than anywhere else. Then by chance, Mother Benedict passed Leonie and Mai in the courtyard one day, and sent them on an errand to fetch some prayer books.

Mai saw the advantage even before Leonie could ask her. "How about I hang out in the chapel while you catch five minutes with Father Gorgeous? You must be dying to speak with him. If Father Stephen stops by, I'll distract him. Asking him something about Thomas Aquinas always sets him off for hours."

Leonie was hugely grateful. "Would you? I'd owe you big time if you could do that."

"It's no problem. But if I do get stuck with a forty minute theology lecture, I get to copy your Shakespeare notes."

It was a deal. The two of them made their way to the chapel, knowing that Father Gabriel worked in the vestry at this time. So

Mai hung around the prayer book shelves while Leonie slipped into the vestry.

Gabriel's face lit up but he also looked concerned when he saw her. "Is everything okay?"

"I know we agreed to keep our distance, but I had to speak with you." This was really awkward. "It's about the pendant you gave me. I really loved it, I mean I still love it, but I didn't realise it was maybe very expensive. Like a diamond or something."

"It is a diamond. A 'golden diamond', they call them. I got that colour because of your earrings. Would you prefer a white one?"

Leonie was horrified. "God no. It's perfect. But I can't accept something so valuable..." she trailed off. She didn't want to insult him by suggesting he was too poor because of being on a priest's salary.

But Gabriel had laughter in his eyes. "It wasn't the Crown Jewels, Leonie. And if you're worried about my financial status..." He became serious again. "I didn't really want to bring this up, because it has always been more of a burden than anything. But there's a family trust. Not just mine, my sister and brother are also beneficiaries. It's why money doesn't mean a great deal to me, or to any of us."

Leonie knew that both Gabriel's siblings worked for charitable organisations. His sister worked for an educational NGO and Gabriel had described his brother as a "suit-wearing eco-warrior". She didn't know much about trusts, except that they were things rich people had. She had thought that most people with trusts would spend their lives on yachts drinking champagne, but maybe some took a completely opposite route.

"I didn't realise." She was at a bit of a loss for words.

"Don't worry about it. I'm just happy you liked it. Also I really didn't plan on having this conversation now, but if you do want to study and your family aren't on board, I can give you the money." Gabriel saw Leonie about to object but forestalled her. "It can just be a loan if you want. The point is that there's money available. If being with me causes you such problems with your family that they withdraw your college money, it's the least I can do."

It was way too much to take in. "I don't know what to say. It's really generous of you, but I have to do this my own way." Leonie would manage it somehow. She absolutely could not take money from Gabriel. If RADA was not possible and Juilliard was out, she would get a job waitressing and take acting classes at night school. She had fought her parents for so long about being an actress that it had become her battle, and her battle alone.

"Whatever you want. It's a decision for the future anyway, not now." Gabriel looked her in the eyes, his gaze intense. "Just remember that I love you. Whatever happens, I'm here for you."

34

Gabriel knew that something was up as soon as he read Suki Laverne's essay. There were several ideas in it that he remembered discussing with Leonie, and he didn't think that Suki had the ability to have come up with them herself.

It could be coincidence. Except for the fact that Leonie's essay was both rushed, and contained none of them.

He was certain that Suki had somehow taken Leonie's work, but he knew his hands were tied when it came to dealing with the girl. He could face the fallout himself but he wasn't going to put Leonie through it. He felt a white fury that Leonie was suffering at the hands of her classmate, and that if he tried to help her, it would only make it worse.

Six more months. Somehow they must both survive it.

He couldn't in all conscience not award Suki's essay an A. He also couldn't give Leonie's effort anything more than a B. It wasn't part of their coursework so it wouldn't affect their overall exam results, but it was still unfair.

Gabriel had also been steeling himself for a serious discussion with Father Stephen. He knew he needed to break the news that he would be leaving the church, and the longer he left it the harder it would be.

That evening, as they ate a lamb curry that Father Stephen had cooked, Gabriel broached the subject.

"I have given a lot of thought to your advice, and my own situation over the past weeks. It has brought me to a decision, though not an easy one."

Father Stephen set down his glass. "I feared it would be a difficult decision for you, whichever way it went."

"I have decided to leave the church. Or my vocation, at least."

It was out. Gabriel was anticipating shock and condemnation. But Father Stephen only gave a kind, if sad, smile.

"I thought it would be such. I have prayed for you, my son, and I will continue to do so. I know that you face a difficult journey."

"You think I am making a mistake?" Gabriel was concerned. "That I should pray more, for a different outcome?" He had no intention of doing this.

Father Stephen raised a hand. "No, no, you misunderstand. Neither choice was wrong. Leaving the priesthood does not mean leaving God or the church. It simply means that your devotion will follow a different path, and that you may have more earthly love ahead of you than solely spiritual love." He piled up some more rice and meat on his fork.

This brought Gabriel onto an even more delicate issue. "Can I continue in my duties, having made this decision? I had thought to wait until the end of the school year, so that I could at least fulfil my tasks here."

"I see no problem with that. It is not as though a formal divorce takes place. After all, we have lay ministry. Have you considered that as a possible alternative?"

Gabriel had not. "It's something to consider."

"Well then, think upon that, and by all means continue as you are until the end of the year. I have no objections to you continuing with your offices, though if there are some you wish to decline then I am happy to cover those duties."

"Thank you." Gabriel had already decided that it would no longer be appropriate for him to hear Confession. Having sinned so mortally himself, he could hardly order others to atone for their trespasses.

"And of course this need not affect your teaching work," Father Stephen continued. He got up and began clearing the table, carrying the plates to the sink. "You will be missed, Gabriel. But I suspect there is someone out there who is looking to a new and happy future as a result of your decision."

Literally out there. Right outside. Gabriel thought of Leonie just across the courtyard in the main school building, and wondered how horrified Father Stephen would be if he knew the full truth. He felt some considerable guilt that he was withholding this from his colleague. But it would only put Father Stephen in a very difficult position if he did learn of it, and bring embarrassment and scandal to the school.

Later, lying in bed, Gabriel thought of Leonie again. Not that she was ever far from his mind or his heart. He had vowed to at least remain celibate over the coming term, which meant not even indulging in fantasies about her. But conjuring up the image of her in his mind left him so aroused that he struggled to sleep.

It wasn't just about missing her physically. Gabriel also longed to be with her. To hear her laugh, and talk with her, and simply spend time in her company. English lessons were a form of exquisite torture for him. He got to see her, but there was a wall between them.

At Easter he fully planned to tear it down. He needed her. He needed to be one flesh with her.

Leonie found it no easier than Gabriel to be apart from him. When he had made love to her it had awoken her in a way she couldn't switch off.

She had always figured it was pretty easy to control her libido. But she found herself wanting him so much that she could barely concentrate in class. She couldn't stop thinking about how his lips felt on hers, or the scent of his body as he arched over her and filled her.

Sharing a dorm with three other people didn't help either. Leonie had such erotic dreams about him that she was fearful she must be moaning or talking in her sleep. It would be super embarrassing if she woke up the others.

She was heading back with Figgy from the library one day, having just completed another double assignment due to Suki's blackmail, when a girl came up to them, out of breath. "There's a phone call for you in Mother Benedict's office," she told Figgy.

Figgy was anxious. "I hope it's nothing serious."

"I'm sure it won't be," Leonie said. "I can walk there with you and wait outside if you like."

Figgy thanked her, and the two of them hurried to the headmistress's study. Leonie sat on the wooden bench outside, crossing her fingers that nothing was wrong with Figgy's family. It was unusual to get a call from your parents during term time, and it often meant something awful like a grandmother dying.

But Figgy emerged looking puzzled. "It's my mother. She actually wants to speak to you."

Now Leonie was the confused one. She went to pick up the phone. Mother Benedict had a small antechamber by her office, and retired here to give privacy to anyone using the phone. There were two other phones the students could use to phone home, but these made outgoing calls only.

"Hello?" Leonie said, picking up the receiver.

"Leonie, dear, it's Figgy's mother. I'm sorry if I've called an awkward time, but the film people are trying to get in touch with you. I wasn't sure if I should give them the school number, so I've taken down their details for you."

Leonie felt her heart beat faster. Grabbing a pen and a scrap of paper from Mother Benedict's desk, she carefully wrote the number down. Would they ring with bad news? Was it just to let her down gently?

She wasn't sure if it was appropriate to use Mother Benedict's phone to call them, and she was too nervous to do so straight away. So she thanked Figgy's mother and went back outside.

Figgy was burning with curiosity. "What did she want? She didn't tell me."

"It's Jack Edwards' company. I'm supposed to call them."

Figgy gasped. "You must have got the part! Oh my goodness, this is so exciting."

Leonie was also feeling a surge of excitement but wasn't going to get her hopes up. It could just be a rejection. Particularly as there was a kind of family connection, perhaps they felt they needed to do her the courtesy of letting her know by phone.

"When should I call them, do you think?" she asked Figgy.

"Now, of course!" Figgy practically dragged her to the communal phones and got her to dial the number. Leonie's palms were actually damp and her head buzzing as she waited for someone to answer.

"Radiant Productions, how may I help?"

"My name is Leonie Wilson. I was given a message to call Pauline Bishop."

"I can put you through now."

More ringing tones, this time internal. Another woman answered. "Hello?"

"It's Leonie Wilson."

"Ah, Leonie, thank you for calling us back. I'm sorry we haven't been in touch again sooner, there were some issues here and then of course Christmas. Anyway I wanted to give you the shooting dates and confirm everything. Or would it be best to do that through your agent?"

"My agent?" Leonie felt faint. "Do you mean that you want me for the role?"

Pauline sounded surprised. "Yes, of course. Hasn't someone already contacted you?"

"No, I hadn't heard anything." Leonie's head was spinning. It felt like she was in a dream.

"Oh for goodness sake. I am sorry, it's usually chaos here but not quite that disorganised. Yes, I believe they were very impressed by your screen test. Now, what's the name of your agent? Or the agency you're with?"

Leonie wasn't sure what to say for a few moments. "I don't actually have one."

"A manager, or anyone?" Pauline again sounded surprised.

"No. I haven't acted professionally before."

"You'll probably want to get one. You'll need someone to check over the contract for you. I'll have a word with Jack and we'll see what we can sort out. Now, just to give you some of the details..."

Pauline started listing various dates and locations, while Leonie struggled to take it all in. She had spent so long preparing for disappointment as the days and weeks went past that she almost feared it was some huge joke. She even felt an odd numbness.

Next to her, Figgy had practically been jumping up and down with excitement. "So you did get it? I knew you would. Oh, how exciting, you're going to be a film star!"

"I think that's a long way off," Leonie said. "But yes, they want me."

Suddenly all the excitement and adrenalin burst through. The two of them started freaking out, jumping and hugging in the corridor. Leonie was saying "Oh my God! Oh my God!" a thousand times over like a madwoman and Figgy was repeating "I just can't believe it! I absolutely just can't believe it!"

Eventually they managed to calm down enough to walk back to the dorm. As they climbed the stairs, reality started to sink in just a little. "It all kicks off toward the end of February," Leonie said. "That's still in term time. They'll never let me take that much time off. What am I going to do?"

Figgy had no answers. "You can work something out. Maybe you could commute back to London on weekends. There was a girl here who was a brilliant ballerina, and she did that for special lessons. She went to the Royal School of Ballet after leaving St Winifred's."

"But most of the shooting is overseas. It would never work, even Mother Benedict agreed. Even if I could fly back," Leonie said.

"We'll talk it over. There must be a solution, you can't miss out on an opportunity like this. You simply can't."

Leonie thought of Gabriel. He was the one person whose advice she wanted on this. How could she arrange to see him?

35

As luck would have it, Leonie managed to speak with Gabriel outside the dining hall. Keeping her expression neutral so as not to arouse any suspicions, she told him the amazing news.

"The film people rang. They want me for the role."

Gabriel found it hard to suppress his surprise and delight. "That's brilliant. But you don't look as happy as I imagined you would. What's wrong?"

"Shooting starts in term time. What am I going to do about school?"

"What do you want to do about school?"

Leonie had no idea. She told him the locations they would be filming in. "I can hardly commute, can I?"

"I suppose not."

Before Gabriel could continue they were interrupted by another of the nuns approaching. "I'd better go," Leonie said.

"You look glum, Leonie. Anything the matter?" It was Sister Rosalind. "Afternoon, Father," she greeted Gabriel.

Father. If she only knew, Leonie thought. "Just a difficult decision I have to make. About school and stuff."

Sister Rosalind looked inquiringly from Leonie to Gabriel. "I always find Mother Benedict very wise whenever I have a conundrum. I should go and have a chat with her, if something is troubling you."

Never in a million years would Leonie have thought of going to the stern nun. But now she found herself thinking that it was probably the most appropriate thing to do. Mother Benedict was going to have to be told.

"I guess so."

She went, reluctantly leaving Gabriel with Sister Rosalind.

"She's a very bright girl," Sister Rosalind said. "Very talented. I was disappointed she didn't apply for the RADA scholarship. I expect she would have been in with a good chance. She wants to be an actress, doesn't she?"

"I believe so."

"Let us hope she realises her dream. It's a tough career path to follow." Sister Rosalind went on her way, leaving Gabriel alone. He strolled back to the vestry, feeling a secret joy in his heart. If Leonie accepted the film contract she wouldn't have to go back to America. He hated the thought of having an ocean between them. Being with her had changed his entire life.

He wondered how his family were going to react to him leaving the priesthood. His mother had never been entirely comfortable with his decision to enter holy orders. She had never said why, but Gabriel knew she was not fully in accord with his choice.

His father would accept the news with equanimity. He had always been content for his children to pursue whatever careers they chose. If he had been disappointed that Gabriel hadn't followed his footsteps in business, he had never revealed it.

Gabriel knew just two things. He wanted to do some kind of humanitarian work, and he wanted to be with Leonie. Whether those things were ultimately to be, he would have to wait and see. Their current forced separation was an ordeal. But it was probably a good test of how they truly felt about one another.

Leonie found Mother Benedict in her office, fortunately not occupied with anyone else.

"I wondered if I might have a word with you, Reverend Mother?" Leonie asked, hovering in the doorway.

"By all means. Come in."

Leonie entered and sat down on the chair in front of the headmistress's large desk. She came straight to the point. "You remember the phone call that Figgy - Iphigenia - got earlier? It was actually for me. I've been offered a role in a movie."

Mother Benedict was taken aback. "Goodness me. How did this all come about?"

"I had a screen test over the holidays. I wasn't really expecting it to come to anything, but now it has."

"I see. And when does the filming for this movie take place?" the nun asked.

Leonie shifted in her chair. "That's the problem. It's later this term. And I know it's going to massively interfere with my schoolwork, and exams. But if I turn it down, I'm worried it might be my only chance."

Mother Benedict smiled, rather sadly. "My child, do you seek permission or approval?"

The question startled Leonie. She hadn't really considered either. She was seeking someone to tell her what decision she should make. "I'm not sure. I know my parents will freak. And my grandmother."

Mother Benedict was silent for a while. "Leonie, you are eighteen. Nearly nineteen, I believe. You have the full right to make decisions about your own future. What do you want to do?"

This was easy. "I want to make the movie. But I don't know if it's the right thing to do, giving up school. Especially since what happened last year." Leonie knew that Mother Benedict had access to her academic record, if not the reasons as to why she had failed to graduate high school.

"Education isn't supposed to be a punishment, Leonie. Nor is there only one way to get an education. What subjects are you taking, remind me?"

"English, Maths and History of Art," Leonie told her.

"Ah yes. Since none of those require practical assignments, such as laboratory work, I see no reason why you couldn't continue through correspondence, if you wish. But if you plan to start your career now, there is no rush. You could just as easily go to university or college later on. Many students here take a gap year as it is," Mother Benedict said.

"So you don't think it's wrong, if I quit school?"

"Morally I see nothing wrong. I assume that this is a reputable production, and not something that you would be ashamed to have your parents see? Practically speaking it does not seem an unwise move, given you wish to pursue a career in acting. I understand that your family may not share this view, but that is something for you to deal with, if you wish to become an independent adult."

Leonie felt very alone. Suddenly realising she could exactly as she liked, legally, with no one to stop her was kind of alarming. "What would you do?" she asked Mother Benedict.

The nun gave a dry chuckle. "I hardly think I'm likely to be cast in the next Gone With the Wind, do you?"

Leonie privately thought The Sound of Music would be a better choice. Quite a good choice, if Mother Benedict could sing. "But if you were? I mean if you were me?"

"When I was your age I was fiercely rebellious. I had no intention of following the path my parents wanted for me. So I ran away from home," Mother Benedict told her.

Such a thing was very hard to imagine. "So what happened?"

"This happened." The nun gestured with her hands. "And I have never regretted it, even though it caused my parents pain for some time. And for me too, on account of them."

"You ran away to become a nun?"

"To enter a convent, yes. I had a vocation and it was stronger than any other calling. In time my family understood, as best they could. As I am sure yours will, if you continue to live a good life and give them reason to make them proud of you."

One week later it was all signed and sealed. Figgy's parents had put Leonie in touch with their lawyer, who had checked over the contract for her. Everything seemed fine, so Leonie had signed.

Her grandmother's reaction had been apocalyptic, so the plan was for Leonie to stay at Figgy's house until she had the means to rent her own place. Leonie was excited about it all, but felt torn about being away from Gabriel. Even though she couldn't be with him at school, she liked seeing him. She was terrified he might forget her once she had gone.

"It's incredibly kind of your parents," she said to Figgy as she packed her belongings.

"Nonsense. They're delighted to have you stay. If you get famous, my mother will probably rope you into all sorts of charity things," Figgy warned her.

"I think that's a very long way off, if ever. It might be a total disaster and I'm a washed up school drop out by the summer."

Figgy thought this very unlikely. "And if you are, you can just get a job in London and do acting classes at night. There's always a way."

Her trunk half-packed, Leonie walked out with Figgy towards the dining hall for supper. No one else knew that she was leaving except for her dorm mates.

Lo and behold, there was Suki Laverne with her usual nasty look on her face.

"Hello Leonie. I hope you haven't made plans this weekend, because I need a couple more essays from you." She smirked, tossing her hair.

"I'm afraid that won't be possible," Leonie told her.

Suki's eyes narrowed. "Won't it? You know what the consequences are otherwise."

"I guess I'll just have to face them, then."

"You'll be expelled. And your precious priest will be kicked out as well," Suzi threatened.

Leonie smiled, using the same fake sweetness that Suki often affected. "I'm leaving anyway, you'll be happy to know."

"Leaving? So they kicked you out already?"

"No. I've been offered a part in a new Jack Edwards film, so I have to finish school early." Leonie was sure that Suki would have heard of Jack Edwards.

She was proven right as Suki's mouth dropped open.

"You're lying. As if someone like you would get that."

Figgy interjected nervously. "It is actually true. Leonie had the screen test when she was staying with me before Christmas."

Suki was defiant. "I don't believe it. You've been expelled and this is some stupid attempt at a cover up."

Leonie shrugged. "Believe it or don't believe it. I won't be here after tomorrow, so you can do your own essays from now on."

Fury blazed in the other girl's eyes. "I can still go to Mother Benedict and tell her about you and the priest."

"Do as you like. You don't have any evidence. They'll just think you're acting out of some weird jealous fit. After all, I won't be here, will I? So it's not as if anything can be going on."

Suki gave a triumphant sneer. "You forgot about the letter."

"What letter?" Leonie smiled sweetly again.

"You know what letter. In his handwriting, addressed to you. All that poetry and shit."

Leonie turned to go. "I think you must be imagining things." She hurried off with Figgy as the bell had already gone.

Figgy was out of breath when they finally reached the hall. "Suki will be furious when she finds out you got the letter back."

"What can she do? I won't be here, and I doubt she'll dare to cross Gabriel. Especially with no proof. Besides, she needs his reference for her RADA application," Leonie said.

The two girls braced themselves against the fumes of boiled cabbage and went in to supper. Leonie felt as though a very heavy weight had been lifted from her shoulders. If nothing else, no more school meant no more Suki Laverne. And that was a huge reason to celebrate.

36

On the way back from lunch, Leonie passed Mother Benedict and Father Stephen in the entrance hall. Father Stephen carried a small bag with him and was wearing a coat as if going out.

"I hope the convention goes well Father, and we'll see you later tomorrow," the headmistress was saying.

"Thank you. I should be back well before evening." The priest nodded to Leonie and her dorm mates, and went out into the driveway.

"Is Father Stephen going away?" Mai asked.

"Just for the night. He's attending a meeting of Catholic school ministers, which has a very early start tomorrow. Father Gabriel remains here in his place," Mother Benedict said, and returned to her own office.

Leonie thought the obvious. But she wouldn't have dared to act on it if Mai hadn't nudged her.

"So, Father Gorgeous is all alone tonight, is he?" Mai was grinning. "Maybe it's time you paid a midnight visit to his bedroom."

Figgy was very shocked. "Mai! As if that would be appropriate in any way."

Mai shrugged. "I don't see why not. After all, Leonie leaves tomorrow. So long as she's not parading around the presbytery in her knickers by the time Father Stephen gets back, I don't see the harm."

Leonie said nothing. The image that Mai was putting in her mind was hugely tempting.

Harry was practical as ever. "You'd have to get out pretty carefully. It can be done by the drainpipe, but it depends how good you are at gym. And in the pitch dark, of course."

"Or she could just slip out of the front door," Mai said.

"The bolt is very heavy and noisy. And there's bound to be some sister doing Vigils or whatever in the middle of the night, who walks past and hears," Harry said.

Mai was undeterred. "We could make a rope from knotted sheets. And then stuff Leonie's bed with clothes so it looked like she was still there, in case Matron came round."

Leonie was quite amazed at her friends trying to arrange this incredibly risky and doubtless sinful escapade for her. It was all starting to sound very Girls' Adventure Story. "I don't think he - Father Gabriel - would approve," she said as they climbed the stairs to Pentecost dorm.

"Good God, don't tell him!" Harry said. "Just slip in there and surprise him. After all you may not see him for weeks. Months, even. I think you're entitled to one last, illicit tryst."

"Make sure he has a good memory of what he's going to be missing," Mai added.

Figgy was still looking very uncomfortable. "It's not that I have anything against you two," she said to Leonie, "but it does seem terribly risky, for both of you."

"They're both consenting adults, what's the worst that can happen?" Mai asked.

There was silence for a few moments. The worst that could happen would be a scandal of apocalyptic and far reaching impact, if it ever got out. A schoolgirl and a Catholic priest. Leonie could only imagine what the newspaper headlines would be.

254

Harry had a strangely yearning look in her eyes. "I almost wish it would get out, if only to enjoy the fireworks. What an absolutely spectacular outrage it would cause. But seriously, it won't get out. They'd hush it all up, particularly as you're leaving."

"Do you really think I should do this?" Leonie asked.

"Only if you want to. But he's absolutely gorgeous and crazy about you. I wouldn't hesitate, in your shoes."

It was a tantalising idea. Leonie longed to be with Gabriel. But the practicalities were daunting. "What would I wear?" She could hardly imagine showing up for a liaison in her school winter pyjamas and dressing gown. At the cottage she had avoided wearing anything in bed, but it was warm there. Tiptoeing across the courtyard in sub-zero temperatures would require more than a t-shirt.

Harry didn't see an issue. "The man is a Catholic priest, for heaven's sake. You could turn up in Mother Benedict's bedsocks and wimple and he wouldn't notice, compared to having you there in his bedroom."

"He might even be turned on. Maybe you should borrow a habit with nothing under it and go and flash him," Mai suggested, an evil grin on her face.

"Not unless she's playing the lead role in Carry On Nun," Harry said. "He'd more likely burst out laughing. You'll have to put a coat on. The night air will be freezing."

They had reached the dorm, where Leonie threw herself down on her bed. "I'm not going to really do this, though, am I?"

"You'll regret it if you don't," Harry said.

Would she? The thought of being Gabriel's bed - in his arms - was beyond amazing to Leonie. But did she dare?

Even though it was her last night at school, Leonie still felt terrified sneaking out of the dorm that night. She had decided to accept Harry's challenge and try the drainpipe.

This turned out to be easier than she had anticipated, as there were various ledges and other footholds as well. She was glad she had worn her dressing gown, however unalluring it might be. January was definitely not the warmest of months in England.

It was only when she crossed the courtyard, sticking to the shadows and hoping desperately that none of the nuns were looking out of their windows, that she realised the presbytery door might be locked. Damn. Amid all their plans, no one had stopped to consider this. The chapel was open at all hours, allowing for prayers throughout the night.

The presbytery might be a different matter. Leonie would have uttered a silent prayer, except there couldn't be anything much more sacrilegious than praying for access to seduce a Catholic priest.

She would just have to hope. And worst case scenario, throw gravel at the window. At least she now knew which window belonged to Gabriel.

Her hands were so cold after the icy metal of the drainpipe that she had to rub some warmth back into them to even try the handle. When she did, and it turned, she felt almost weak with relief. Leonie quickly slipped inside, trying to get her eyes to become accustomed to the dark. She didn't dare switch a light on.

She crept up the stairs, trying not to make them creak. At the top was a small landing with three doors. One was ajar, and a shaft of light from a window revealed it to be the bathroom. Then she had to take a guess which of the other two was Gabriel's door. Figuring out three dimensional spaces wasn't her skill, but she decided his was more likely to be the door on the right. Should she knock or just open it? It was past midnight so he'd almost certainly be asleep. If she slipped in and he woke to see her there, it might freak him out.

Leonie tapped the door and waited. Nothing. She tapped a little more loudly. "Gabriel. It's me, Leonie."

There was movement inside. "What?" He sounded sleepy and confused.

She pushed the door open to find Gabriel sitting up in bed, his eyes widening with shock as he looked at her. The moon shone through the window as the curtains weren't drawn.

Leonie felt lost for words. "I just wanted to say goodbye before I left."

"I don't know whether I should be hoping that this is a dream or not. What on earth are you doing here?" Gabriel didn't seem angry, just bewildered. "How did you get here?"

"I climbed down the drainpipe. Your door wasn't locked."

Gabriel swore. "For heaven's sake, Leonie. You might have fallen and been seriously injured."

"I wasn't though. It wasn't even that hard. Harry showed me how."

He groaned. "Don't tell me all your friends are in on this?"

"Kind of. They've stuffed my bed with blankets in case Matron does a midnight inspection."

Gabriel was silent for a moment, then started laughing. "You'd better come over here, you look freezing."

Leonie, who had been standing tentatively in the doorway, went over to the bed. The room was very spartan. There was a cross above the bed which gave her a rather guilty feeling. A very guilty feeling, in fact.

He pulled her into the bed with him. "Since you're here..." Then he rolled so he was over her, and brought his mouth down on hers. Just being kissed by him was amazing. Having to pretend he was only her teacher for the past few weeks had been a kind of starvation.

His lips were warm and firm, and his embrace insistent as he explored her.

Despite the several layers of clothes between them, Leonie could feel him pressed hard against her thigh. She shifted, wishing she could get rid of all the fabric that was in the way.

Gabriel slipped a hand under her pyjama top and enclosed it over her breast. Feeling his thumb swirl around and brush her nipple made Leonie gasp. She reached for him, trying to loosen his clothing.

He paused. "Leonie, it might be wiser if we kept some layers between us."

"Why?"

"Because if I get you naked against me, I'm going to struggle to keep this within limits."

Leonie didn't understand. "Don't you want me anymore?"

Gabriel buried his face in her neck. "More than ever. But I don't have any condoms."

"Didn't you have any left from before?" He had bought loads of packets. Surely he couldn't have used them all up?

"Yes, but I could hardly bring them here, to school, could I?"

The image of Gabriel rocking up to St Winifred's with a suitcase full of contraceptives suddenly came into Leonie's head. She started giggling. "I don't suppose Father Stephen keeps any in his bedside drawer?"

"I highly doubt it. God, Leonie, you're going to get us struck by lightning at this rate."

Leonie started pulling off her clothes. "I'm hot. I'm going to take these off even if you're not. It's dark, so it's not like you'll see much."

Gabriel switched on the bedside lamp.

Leonie looked at him defiantly, and saw the heat grow in his eyes as she continued to slip out of her things, casting them on the floor. She sat up in bed naked before him. The bedroom was not very heated and she could feel her nipples hardening in the cool atmosphere.

"Hell." Gabriel ripped off his own top and crushed her against him. "This is insanely risky, just you being here." He kissed down her throat and over her chest, drawing her left breast into his mouth while his hand caressed the other. He slipped fingers between her legs, flicking them over the point where he knew she would lose control.

Leonie fought against it, wriggling away from his touch. "I don't want it to be just me. I want you, fully," she said.

"It's too risky."

"Can't you just pull out?" She was determined to get him to make love to her.

His voice was thick with desire. "Not with any certainty, given how you're making me feel."

"I'll be in London later tomorrow. I'll get Plan B."

"It's still ridiculously irresponsible."

Leonie tried another tactic, the same that Harry had used on her. "How much will you regret it if you don't do it? When you're lying here tomorrow night, thinking about what we could have done?" She reached for him, running her fingers around him, and he flinched and gasped.

"I'll feel a lot less worried."

"Well, don't worry. I'm not going to trap you. I have this movie to make, remember?" She knew she was winning.

"I didn't mean that. One day it might even be nice…" Gabriel didn't finish the sentence.

"Nice what?"

He looked her directly in the eyes, his gaze more intense than she had ever seen. "One day it might be nice to get you pregnant for real."

They were both silent. Leonie could hardly believe he had said it, and it made her entire body throb for him.

"You want children one day?"

"With you, maybe," Gabriel said. "But it's years too early to even think about that. Or have this conversation."

He wanted to be with her in the future. He wanted to have a baby with her! Half of Leonie was terrified, and the other half wanted to dance and sing.

Instead she pulled him back down, to kiss her again.

Now the words were said, Gabriel felt as turned on as he had ever been. She was right, if he held back he would spend the rest of the term kicking himself. He was close to exploding as it was. "This won't last very long," he warned her.

"We've got all night. I recall you recover pretty quickly," Leonie said, with a wicked smile.

Gabriel pushed her back down on the bed. He got rid of the rest of his clothing, and moved over her. She was so perfect. Beautiful, intelligent, talented, and his. All his.

Covering her mouth with his, he entered her. It felt better than he ever remembered. He lay on top of her for a few seconds not daring to move. One more movement and he would lose it. His ego wanted him to last at least a bit longer.

But Leonie had other ideas. The feeling of him inside her: the man she loved, the man she wanted to spend the rest of her life making love with, was too much for her to lie still. She started moving against him, wanting to feel him drive into her.

"I'm not going to be able to control - " Gabriel began, then caught his breath. He grabbed her against him, hard, and thrust into her violently. Two, three, four, and it was enough. It seemed to last forever. "I love you, I love you so much."

Just as he was coming down from it, he moved his hand between them and applied pressure where he knew she needed it. Leonie, who was half there, was brought straight over. The ripples that ran through her as she moaned his name extended the sensation for Gabriel. It had simply never been like this before. Never this intense.

"I love you. God, Leonie, how I love you."

Gabriel held her afterwards, and they fell asleep in one another's arms. They ended up making love several times in the night. Gabriel finally had to wake an exhausted Leonie just before dawn so she could sneak back to her dorm without being caught.

"I'll write to you and phone you whenever I can," he promised her. "And I'll see you at Easter."

Leaving him felt like a physical pain. But Leonie knew they were meant to be together. Somehow, they would work it out.

37

One year later

"This may be the end of an era," Gabriel said. He was fastening the tiny hooks on the back of Leonie's dress, a 1930s style floor-length sheath of amber-gold satin.

Leonie looked in the mirror. The studio had sent a hair and make-up artist around earlier, and every part of her now looked immaculate. Even her fingernails.

It was her first premiere, the limo would be there soon, and her stomach was dizzy with nerves. "Why the end?" she asked.

"After tonight, if the movie is a hit, people will know your name. It will change things."

Gabriel was beyond gorgeous in a beautifully cut jacket that showed off his broad shoulders and athletic build. Black tie suited him perfectly. He looked like a model.

The whole premiere thing was kind of weird, Leonie thought. It felt like returning to something she had finished ages ago. She had already shot another movie the summer after the first film, and was about to start shooting a third. No one knew who she was except for people in the film world, but word was getting around. Leonie had signed with a wonderful agent, and was in growing demand. Some really cool scripts were getting sent her way.

While she was working on the second movie, the first had started post production, and finally the publicity tour and premiere got underway. Leonie wasn't needed as much as the other actress for this, since she wasn't a star yet. The media was more interested in established names. There had been some interviews though, and seeing her words and face in print had been a very strange experience.

Leonie had also become firm friends with her co-star, and had learnt a lot from her. They had shared a flat in London for a couple of months, but the other girl had then moved to LA. Which might be a move that Leonie needed to make in future. This was also stressing her out a bit, even though it was exciting.

Gabriel had finished up at St Winifred's at the end of the summer, and quietly left the priesthood. He had been working for a local government project with disadvantaged youth in London. It was only a six month contract, but he was hopeful of finding another similar position.

"If there are pictures of us in the papers, and someone at St Winifred's sees…" Leonie wasn't sure how she felt about the nuns finding out. They had been very kind to her. She didn't want them feeling upset or scandalised.

"They have no reason to believe anything happened while you were at school. After all, you left months before I did. If they guess that I left the priesthood because of you, then so be it. I did do, after all," Gabriel said.

Leonie supposed that Suki Laverne might spill dirt to a tabloid newspaper. She had been absolutely furious about Leonie escaping St Winifred's to actually star in a film. But Suki had been forced to button her lip as she had had no proof. She also didn't want to alienate Gabriel, her English teacher. She had still held some deluded hope that with Leonie gone, she might be in with a chance with him herself.

Of course she wasn't. And even worse for Suki was losing the RADA scholarship. To some people's surprise, though not Leonie's or Gabriel's, Mercy won it. Suki hadn't even won a regular place, and was taking a gap year while she reapplied.

"I wish my parents could have been here. I think they nearly did come, but my dad is being so damn stubborn," Leonie said.

"It's a long way for them to fly. I'm sure they'd come to the US premiere. They are proud of you, deep down."

It didn't feel like it. Leonie's parents and grandmother had been apocalyptic when she quit St Winifred's. Even a really kind letter from Figgy's mother hadn't improved things very much. "You must be so very proud of your daughter. It's such a wonderful opportunity, and we're delighted to have her stay with us in London for as long as she needs," she had written.

But even Leonie's grandmother, with her snobbery, hadn't thawed. "I wash my hands of you. I gave you an opportunity to make good your education, and you threw it back in my face," she had said. She didn't even know about Gabriel yet. Leonie could only imagine her grandmother's horror at finding out her granddaughter had seduced a priest into giving up his vocation.

Leonie's sister and brother had been excited at least. Deborah wanted constant updates, as well as a signed photo of the hot young actor in Leonie's second film. Leonie had initially been embarrassed to ask him, but he had only been flattered by the fact that her sister wanted his autograph.

Deborah had been desperate to fly over to London for the premiere of the first movie, but her parents had forbidden it. Even though Leonie had offered to send her the air fare.

"They hate what I'm doing. They still don't get that it could be a career for me," Leonie said.

"It is already a career for you. You were born to do this. Once they see your movie, or at least some reviews, they'll start to get it," Gabriel told her.

At least she had managed to get invitations for her friends. The three of them were all coming and Leonie would see them later that evening.

Harry was studying history at a university called Loughborough and had been selected for the England Women's lacrosse team. Figgy had deferred her university place, at Edinburgh, for a year. She had been working on a sustainability project overseas. Mai had defied her parents' wishes for her to do medicine, and was enrolled at business school. They were all happy and well, dating various guys, though nothing serious.

Not like Leonie and Gabriel, who were rock solid. Leonie missed him terribly whenever she was filming, which always seemed to be miles away from where he was. But a phone call, hearing his voice, having him fly out to make her a surprise visit: somehow they had made it work. And now here they were, in London at an amazing five star hotel where the studio was putting her up, about to walk down the red carpet together.

Leonie fastened her earrings, and then clasped Gabriel's diamond pendant around her neck. She wasn't quite at the level of success and fame of having major jewellery brands loan her gems for the occasion. But she would have rejected them anyway. She wanted to wear Gabriel's gift that night. It was the most precious thing she owned, in every sense.

She looked at her fingers, wondering which of her rings to wear. She had one that sort of matched the necklace but it was a bit of a hippy design. She wasn't sure if it would work with the dress. Then another ring she had was more elegant, but the stone was the wrong colour.

Leonie decided that she was being ridiculous, as who was going to look at her fingers anyway? She was about to pick out the elegant ring when Gabriel stopped her.

"I think this would go better," he said, handing her a small velvet box.

Surprised, Leonie opened it. Inside was a huge, sparkling solitaire surrounded by smaller, amber coloured stones that perfectly matched her pendant. It was absolutely stunning.

"Where did you get this?" she asked, not knowing what else to say. "It's beautiful."

Dark blue eyes looked into hers, their expression holding a question and an intensity that Leonie hadn't seen before. "It was my great-aunt's. I had it reset with the stones to match your other jewellery."

"But it must be worth a fortune! I can't accept it. What if I lose it?"

Gabriel half smiled. "I think we've had this conversation before." He took the box from her and drew out the ring. Taking her hand, he slid it on her finger, while Leonie stood there, frozen.

Surely he didn't mean…?

He saw her bewilderment as she gazed at her hand. He tilted her face up to his. "Yes, Leonie, I want to marry you. But this doesn't have to be an engagement ring just yet. I don't want to mess with your head by proposing to you on your big night, and stressing you out even more. Just consider this a symbol of my love, which happens to go very well with your gown."

Leonie looked back down at the ring. "It wouldn't stress me out," she murmured, more to herself because she didn't quite dare to say it loud enough for Gabriel to hear.

"What?"

She summoned her courage. "I said it wouldn't stress me out."

Gabriel was silent for a while. Then he dropped to his knee. "Leonie Wilson, I love you. Will you marry me?"

The room spun.

Gabriel wanted to marry her. He was actually asking her to marry him. Leonie could hardly take in the other things he was saying.

"I know I should have probably done this at the top of the Eiffel Tower, or on a bed of rose petals with an orchestra playing. I can still do that if you want. If you don't feel ready to say yes,

266

then it's okay. I've waited a lifetime to find you, I can wait a few more months or years."

"It's yes." Once again Leonie spoke so quietly that Gabriel didn't seem to hear and kept talking.

"I know you're not even twenty yet. I was going to wait until your birthday. Or your twenty-first even. But I want you to know how I feel, and that I'll be here for you always. If you want me."

"It's a yes." Leonie spoke more loudly, startling the man kneeling before her.

"What?"

"I said yes."

The joy on his face said it all. "You're sure? Because we don't have to rush this," Gabriel said.

Leonie was completely sure. She had been in love with him for a year and a half now, with her feelings only growing stronger every day. "I want to spend the rest of my life with you."

He answered her with his lips on hers. Not caring that it would be smudging the lip gloss carefully applied by the make-up artist, Leonie lost herself in Gabriel's embrace. His, always.

38

Four years later

It was always sunny in California. Yet despite the luxury and the glamour that surrounded her, Leonie was conscious that there was another world out there. A world Gabriel worked in, where people's lives were much harder and more troubled.

It kept Leonie grounded. It even gave her a reason to work, because she committed some of her income to the charitable foundation that Gabriel and his sister had set up.

The past few years had been a whirl. Leonie had never worked so hard or partied so hard. Partying was work, in Hollywood. There were always people to meet, or movies to market. Someone or something demanding her time and presence.

Now she sat by the pool, enjoying a rare moment of peace. She wondered if she should take a dip or wait for Gabriel to arrive home. He had been out meeting with philanthropists who wanted to be involved in his organisation.

For Leonie, the current time was a brief respite between movies. She had just wrapped filming for a romantic drama the previous week, and next month she started shooting a major action thriller.

Everything had happened so fast that she had barely had time to reflect or even appreciate much of it. First class travel, five star hotels, luxury limousines, assistants attending to her every need: it was all a strange kind of glitzy blur. She had now reached a stage where she could probably take some time out without it hurting her career. But there was always one more great script.

She leafed through the pages of the action movie she had signed up for. The character, Juliana, had intrigued her. She could have been written like any cookie-cutter, skimpy-clothed, babe-with-gun action chicks. But Juliana had backstory, well developed relationships and credible scenes. She even got a happy ending if, not one that movie goers might expect.

And then there was the thing that particularly intrigued Leonie. The one aspect that had made her sign, even though she was longing for a break.

She heard a car pull up and finally Gabriel appeared by the poolside. He bent to kiss her. "You look beautiful but tired," he told her. "I'll cook."

They could have afforded any number of staff, but they both preferred to keep things simple and low-key. They had some domestic help during the day but Leonie wanted her evenings totally private and intimate with Gabriel. She looked at her finger, where a softly gleaming gold band sat next to her beautiful engagement ring.

"You've never regretted any of this, have you?" she asked him, suddenly anxious. "When you're with Father O'Malley, you don't wonder what might have been?" Father O'Malley was a priest whom Gabriel worked with on some of the foundation's projects. He ran an inner city mission for homeless kids in Los Angeles.

Gabriel laughed and kissed her. "Not for one second. Meeting you was meant to happen. I fell in love with you pretty much from the first moment I saw you, and I love you more every day." Sitting down on a deckchair beside her, he eyed the film script. "But you are sure about this? I don't want you getting exhaustion."

"Absolutely sure. I'll take a long break afterwards, I promise. We'll go back to England and visit your family. Or fly them over here."

Leonie's own family had finally come around to her choice of career. Shortly after her first film was released, setting one of that year's box office records, her parents started getting reporters knocking on their own door. Magazines and TV stations wanted to do stories on Leonie's childhood, her family, her background. It had made Leonie's parents finally realise that their daughter had made her own future.

They had actually apologised, though relations had been awkward for a while. Similarly, while Leonie didn't get an apology from her grandmother for the hurtful things she had said, her grandmother had turned out to be grudgingly proud of her. Even though she had nearly fainted from shock when she discovered her granddaughter was engaged to a former priest. But Gabriel's charm won her around, and she had attended their wedding in the South of France.

A destination wedding had simply made sense. Back home in Boston they would have been hounded by media. By the time Leonie and Gabriel had got married, on her twenty-second birthday, she had easily earned enough money to fly everyone over. Another movie actor had loaned them a beautiful and secluded villa near Cannes, and it had been an absolutely amazing week.

Figgy had recently become engaged and was getting married the following year, with Leonie as a bridesmaid. Mai was single but having a ball of a time in New York. Harry, now in the British Olympic squad, was dating a fellow Olympian.

"We're so lucky, aren't we?" Leonie said, looking at the brilliant bougainvillea tumbling down the villa wall. "Sometimes life feels like a fairy-tale." She still felt so crazily in love with Gabriel even after all this time. She still marvelled every day that such a gorgeous, intelligent and compassionate man wanted to be with her.

"You work incredibly hard for it. It's not just luck," Gabriel told her. He remembered how Leonie had fainted with exhaustion when she'd got sick during a particularly demanding shoot. He kept a vigilant eye on her now. She was his wife, and he had committed to protect her. This sometimes meant protecting her from her own crazy work ethic.

"I know. But so many people would kill for the chance to do this work. I do feel fortunate," Leonie said. "I should have asked you about your meeting. How did it go?"

"Great. Far better than I expected. They want to do something global, not just in the US," Gabriel said.

Leonie knew how much this had meant to him. "That's brilliant! We should celebrate."

Gabriel ran his eyes over the slender curves that he never got tired of. "I know how I'd like to celebrate."

Leonie looked up at him from under her eyelashes. "Does it involve me removing this?" She hooked her thumbs under her bikini, teasing him.

"Yes. But not here." Despite the high walls, Gabriel was always conscious of paparazzi or even prying neighbours. Intimate photos of Leonie would be splashed everywhere if someone managed to take them.

Gabriel led her to the bedroom, where he made slow and tender love to her. He could never get enough of her. For his part, he remained amazed that such an incredible girl had chosen to be his wife.

"So this latest script," Leonie said, as they lay next to one another afterwards. "Did you read it?"

"I glanced through it. Should I read it?"

"I think you should."

She handed him a copy of it. The one by the pool was a spare, in case it fell in the water and got wet. After a previous disaster Leonie had always had at least three duplicates made.

Gabriel started reading it while Leonie fixed them both a drink. People often found it absurd that Gabriel didn't work in movies as well. He easily had the looks, and was frequently approached by agents. But it just wasn't his passion.

"Oh, I forgot to tell you. I heard from Mercy. She got part in a new BBC costume drama," Leonie said.

"That's great to hear. We'll have to get my parents to tape it and send it over."

Mercy had experienced a tougher climb than Leonie. After graduating from RADA, she had mainly managed to get theatre work. She loved Shakespeare, but the pay wasn't always great and she had a lot of "resting" periods. Leonie had tried to persuade her to come to Hollywood so she could introduce her to agents and producers. But Mercy always ended up getting another role just as she planned to fly out. This TV series would be a major breakthrough for her.

There had been no such success for Suki Laverne. No one had heard anything about her in years.

Leonie checked and replied to a few emails while Gabriel continued with the script. He was intrigued. "It's not the outright glamour part I thought it would be. Like a Bond girl or Lara Croft, or whatever."

"It's not, is it? That's why I liked it."

"I guess they'll make you some kind of prosthetic." Gabriel was still turning the pages.

Leonie smiled mischievously. "About that..."

"About what?"

"The prosthetic. I may supply my own."

Now he was confused. "Your own? Why would you do that?"

"Because I'm kind of making one. We're making one, I should say."

Gabriel frowned. "We're making a prosthetic?"

Leonie took his hand and put it on her stomach. "Right there. Juliana's not going to need a rubber belly, when she has the real deal."

He was silent for a moment. "Do you mean…? But how?"

"Remember when I got sick that time? Well, stupid me, I forgot it messes up the pill if it happens too soon after taking it."

Gabriel was struggling to take in the revelation. "You're having our baby?"

"So it seems."

There was such shock, wonder and joy on his face that it brought tears to Leonie's eyes.

"My darling." He embraced her, now fearful of how he was touching her. Suddenly she seemed like a fragile piece of china. "Are you okay? Do you need me to do anything?"

Leonie laughed. "You already did it. And I'm more than okay." She had never been happier in her life.

"I can't believe you're having our child." Gabriel had wanted to start a family for a while, but hadn't liked to pressure Leonie by saying anything. Now he found himself absurdly turned on by the thought of her pregnant with his baby. "There's a lot of action in this movie. Are you sure it will be safe?"

"It will have to be. They'll get a stunt double for much of it, so I guess she'll wear a prosthetic."

Gabriel was caressing Leonie's stomach, aching to make love to her again. "I suppose I'll have to be careful now." He was briefly worried he had been too vigorous before, and said so.

Leonie dismissed his concerns. "I'm having a baby, I'm not an invalid. I'm perfectly robust and able to perform all my marital duties. Should you require any."

Gabriel did require some. "They're only duties to you?" He was teasing her.

"Very pleasurable duties."

The gleam in Leonie's eye drove Gabriel wild. At the same time, as he stroked the slight new curve by her waistline, he felt strangely lighter. It was as though a weight he hadn't known he was carrying had been lifted from his shoulders.

They had created a life.

If he had chosen a different path, if he had stayed within the priesthood, that life would never have been. And Gabriel knew, deep in his soul and in his heart, that it was meant to be.

It was the final vindication of the choice he had made. Any lingering guilt could evaporate. They were blessed, and his choice to leave the church for her was blessed.

He was made to be with her, and she with him, eternally.

God with honour hang your head,
Groom, and grace you, bride, your bed
With lissome scions, sweet scions,
Out of hallowed bodies bred.

Each be other's comfort kind:
Déep, déeper than divined,
Divine charity, dear charity,
Fast you ever, fast bind.

Then let the March tread our ears:
I to him turn with tears
Who to wedlock, his wonder wedlock,
Déals tríumph and immortal years.

"At The Wedding March" by Gerard Manly Hopkins

About Noël Cades

Noël Cades is a British writer who currently lives in Sydney, Australia. A fan of romance, particularly historic, some of Noël's favourite authors include Jilly Cooper, Georgette Heyer, Elizabeth Rolls, Anne Mather, Sara Seale and Victoria Holt.

Noël is always delighted to hear from other fans, readers and writers of romance.

You can contact Noël at noelcades@gmail.com

Noël's website is at **www.noelcades.com**

Visit Noël's blog to sign up for exclusive news and the chance to receive new free book giveaways.

More hot, forbidden romances by Noël Cades available in paperback:

The Substitute Bride

When the Marquis of Westford offers to marry disgraced Elizabeth Cosgrove to save her family's honour, little does he realise that she has swapped places with her younger cousin Lily.

His Model Student

When Sera's new art teacher mistakes her for a model and demands that she strip naked, sparks start to fly. Will Mr Marek be able to keep his student at arm's length after seeing everything she has to offer?

Tempting Her Teacher

Catholic school teacher Carl Spencer faces a crisis of faith when he falls for his student Juliet, how can he resist the temptation to be with her? But while he struggles to resist his growing attraction, she's starting to realise that it's become more than just a game for her.

Summer's Edge

When sports coach Stewart Walker finds out the girl he kissed is a student at his school he's furious and determined to keep away. But 18-year-old Alice has fallen hard and won't give up.

Man of the Match

Broken-hearted student Cara has no idea that the handsome stranger who seduced her on holiday is England cricket captain Matt Curran. Shocking twists and sexy action in the glamorous world of international cricket.

Excerpts from *Summer's Edge* by Noël Cades

Alice remained silent throughout this. She was still feeling disappointed and uncertain. She tried to tell herself it was for the best. Really, she should be grateful that he had just decided to move past it.

But she still felt embarrassed. She picked at the grass next to her, pulling off a small flower, avoiding looking at the play.

Then a shadow fell over them. She looked up.

It was Mr Walker.

"I want a word with you. In the pavilion, now," he ordered her. His eyes pierced into hers and he looked furious.

Numb, she obeyed, walking ahead of him.

Inside it was empty and he closed the door behind them and turned to her.

"What the fuck do you think you're playing at?"

He was absolutely incensed. He stood there, suddenly the adult, the authority, not just some guy she had kissed in a pub.

Someone she had compromised. Alice couldn't think of anything to say.

She stood there in front of him. His scent of faint cologne and sun-warmed skin was disturbingly familiar to her, mingling with the dusty wood and sports equipment smell of the pavilion.

"Did you know who I was?" he asked.

"Yes." There didn't seem to be any point in lying.

He glared at her and she looked back at him. His eyes pierced into her, their light grey-blue contrasting with his tanned complexion. He was one of the most devastatingly attractive men she had ever seen. All the more so now as his anger turned his face into carved steel.

As terrified and awkward as Alice felt, she also felt slightly defiant. After all she hadn't done anything wrong or illegal.

278

Then suddenly he grasped her by the shoulders and brought his mouth down on hers, hard. Surprised, she initially squirmed to escape his grasp then yielded as her forced his tongue into her mouth. His lips were bruising hers, he was almost biting her yet she wanted more.

Her hands, which had pushed against his chest to try and get away, went round his neck and she arched against him.

He was trying to hurt her, devour her. Punish her. All at once. But he wanted her too. She could taste his need, raw and urgent. Feel the hotness of his breath as he nearly suffocated her with his kiss.

His mouth left hers and moved to her neck, half embracing, half biting it. She tasted blood on her lip where he had crushed it with his own. He was gripping her hard and she clung to him. She didn't even care that he was hurting her.

He could have ripped all her clothes off right there and forced himself upon her. She had never wanted anyone so much.

Then just as suddenly he thrust her away from him. He swore under his breath as he tried to recover himself.

"Is that what you wanted?"

"No... yes... I mean..." Alice had no idea what to say. She was shaken and half in misery, half in ecstasy.

His face was like granite, its angles unyielding.

"Get out and don't come back here again. Stay out of my way," he said.

* * *

Alice tried to enjoy herself at the barbecue but she couldn't relax with Mr Walker just metres away, deliberately avoiding her. She had no appetite but knew she needed to eat something to avoid getting completely drunk on an empty stomach.

Graeme was good company and buoyed up by misery, alcohol and perhaps a desire to make a point to Mr Walker she flirted with him a bit. He was the kind of guy you could flirt with without it meaning much. Besides she knew he preferred Jules. She also noticed that Mr Walker's gaze was frequently on her and he didn't look happy about her flirting with Graeme. Or she hoped that was why he looked annoyed.

As the beer went down the revelry increased and someone accidentally knocked a glass full of beer over Alice. It went all over her top.

Feeling as though nothing much more could go wrong with the day she found her way to the kitchen and tried to sponge out the worst at the sink. If the beer dried on it, it would smell awful and probably stain the fabric. Hopefully even though she was getting her top even more wet it would dry quickly in the sun.

As she was finishing getting the worst off someone else came into the kitchen. She knew even before she turned that it was Mr Walker. He looked angry.

"Did you come here deliberately?" he asked.

She faced him. "I came here with Becky. I didn't know you'd be here. Or care," she added.

"What have you done to your shirt?"

"Someone spilt beer on it. I was washing it off."

"You can't go back out like that. You look like a wet t-shirt competition," he told her.

Alice looked down and went red. The wet fabric had gone transparent and soaked through her bra too.

Without a word Mr Walker pulled off his own shirt and handed it to her. He wore nothing under it. Alice was transfixed by his physique. His arms rippled with muscle and his flat, hard chest was tanned a deep gold. He was far fitter than she expected a cricketer to be, really powerful looking.

"Put this on."

The shirt was white cotton and warm from his body. She held it. It smelt of him. She wanted to envelop herself in it but she didn't follow his order.

"You want me to walk out of here wearing your shirt with you following me, topless?" she asked him.

He was silent for a moment, glaring at her. She was right, it would have exactly the opposite effect he intended. The situation was bad enough as it was.

280

"I don't want them gawping at you."

Alice's stomach gave a secret flip. Possessive and protective. He clearly didn't feel as neutrally towards her as he wanted to.

"The sun will dry it. I'll cross my arms." As she said this, she deliberately left her arms uncrossed and put her shoulders back slightly.

It had the desired effect. He was momentarily transfixed.

"Jesus Christ."

Alice took charge of the situation. "You should put this back on." Instead of just handing it to him she went to put it over his head meaning her arms were raised and her body was nearly against his. He was still for a second before taking a step backwards. A muscle clenched in his jaw.

"Just give me the shirt." She did so and he put it back on.

Then they both stood there. The tension was unbearable. She knew he wanted her and was fighting against it with every fibre of his being.

She broke the ice. "I am sorry you know. We were all just having fun the other night and I just didn't think about the implications."

"You were just messing around with me because I'm employed at your school?"

"God no, that wasn't why." Alice couldn't believe he thought this. Surely he'd realised how much she also wanted him to kiss her that night?

"So even if I hadn't been, you would have still put on your little act?" he asked.

What act? "I wasn't acting, I genuinely..."

"You wanted it too?"

"Yes." It was barely a whisper.

For a moment she thought he was going to kiss her again. He was wavering. Then he stood straighter. "I'm way too old for you, Alice, and I work at your school. Get back outside."

To find out what happens between Alice and Mr Walker, get Noël Cades' thrilling taboo student-teacher romance, Summer's Edge.

www.ingramcontent.com/pod-product-compliance
Lightning Source LLC
Chambersburg PA
CBHW022002010726
47494CB00003B/851